SHAMBLEAU
and Others

SHAMBLEAU
and Others

by

C. L. Moore

GNOME PRESS, Inc.
Publishers New York

PRINTED BY H. WOLFF
MANUFACTURED IN THE U.S.A.

Contents

Black God's Kiss

THEY brought in Joiry's tall commander, struggling between two men-at-arms who tightly gripped the ropes which bound their captive's mailed arms. They picked their way between mounds of dead as they crossed the great hall toward the dais where the conqueror sat, and twice they slipped a little in the blood that spattered the flags. When they came to a halt before the mailed figure on the dais, Joiry's commander was breathing hard, and the voice that echoed hollowly under the helmet's confines was hoarse with fury and despair.

Guillaume the conqueror leaned on his mighty sword, hands crossed on its hilt, grinning down from his height upon the furious captive before him. He was a big man, Guillaume, and he looked bigger still in his spattered armor. There was blood on his hard, scarred face, and he was grinning a white grin that split his short, curly beard glitteringly. Very splendid and very dangerous he looked, leaning on his great sword and smiling down upon fallen Joiry's lord, struggling between the stolid men-at-arms.

"Unshell me this lobster," said Guillaume in his deep, lazy voice. "We'll see what sort of face the fellow has who gave us such a battle. Off with his helmet, you."

But a third man had to come up and slash the straps which held the iron helmet on, for the struggles of Joiry's commander were too fierce, even with bound arms, for either of the guards to release their hold. There was a moment of sharp struggle; then the straps parted and the helmet rolled loudly across the flagstones.

Guillaume's white teeth clicked on a startled oath. He stared.

7

Joiry's lady glared back at him from between her captors, wild red hair tousled, wild lion-yellow eyes ablaze.

"God curse you!" snarled the lady of Joiry between clenched teeth. "God blast your black heart!"

Guillaume scarcely heard her. He was still staring, as most men stared when they first set eyes upon Jirel of Joiry. She was tall as most men, and as savage as the wildest of them, and the fall of Joiry was bitter enough to break her heart as she stood snarling curses up at her tall conqueror. The face above her mail might not have been fair in a woman's head-dress, but in the steel setting of her armor it had a biting, sword-edge beauty as keen as the flash of blades. The red hair was short upon her high, defiant head, and the yellow blaze of her eyes held fury as a crucible holds fire.

Guillaume's stare melted into a slow smile. A little light kindled behind his eyes as he swept the long, strong lines of her with a practised gaze. The smile broadened, and suddenly he burst into full-throated laughter, a deep bull bellow of amusement and delight.

"By the Nails!" he roared. "Here's welcome for the warrior! And what forfeit d'ye offer, pretty one, for your life?"

She blazed a curse at him.

"So? Naughty words for a mouth so fair, my lady. Well, we'll not deny you put up a gallant battle. No man could have done better, and many have done worse. But against Guillaume—" He inflated his splendid chest and grinned down at her from the depths of his jutting beard. "Come to me, pretty one," he commanded. "I'll wager your mouth is sweeter than your words."

Jirel drove a spurred heel into the shin of one guard and twisted from his grip as he howled, bringing up an iron knee into the abdomen of the other. She had writhed from their grip and made three long strides toward the door before Guillaume caught her. She felt his arms closing about her from behind, and lashed out with both spiked heels in a futile assault upon his leg armor, twisting like a maniac, fighting with her knees and spurs, straining hopelessly at the ropes which bound her arms. Guillaume laughed and whirled her round, grinning down into the blaze of her yellow eyes. Then deliberately he

set a fist under her chin and tilted her mouth up to his. There
was a cessation of her hoarse curses.

"By Heaven, that's like kissing a sword-blade," said Guillaume, lifting his lips at last.

Jirel choked something that was mercifully muffled as she
darted her head sidewise, like a serpent striking, and sank her
teeth into his neck. She missed the jugular by a fraction of an
inch.

Guillaume said nothing, then. He sought her head with a
steady hand, found it despite her wild writhing, sank iron
fingers deep into the hinges of her jaw, forcing her teeth relentlessly apart. When he had her free he glared down into the
yellow hell of her eyes for an instant. The blaze of them was
hot enough to scorch his scarred face. He grinned and lifted
his ungauntleted hand, and with one heavy blow in the face
he knocked her half-way across the room. She lay still upon the
flags.

2

Jirel opened her yellow eyes upon darkness. She lay quiet for
a while, collecting her scattered thoughts. By degrees it came
back to her, and she muffled upon her arm a sound that was
half curse and half sob. Joiry had fallen. For a time she lay
rigid in the dark, forcing herself to the realization.

The sound of feet shifting on stone near by brought her out
of that particular misery. She sat up cautiously, feeling about
her to determine in what part of Joiry its liege lady was im-
prisoned. She knew that the sound she had heard must be a
sentry, and by the dank smell of the darkness that she was
underground. In one of the little dungeon cells, of course.
With careful quietness she got to her feet, muttering a curse as
her head reeled for an instant and then began to throb. In the
utter dark she felt around the cell. Presently she came to a little
wooden stool in a corner, and was satisfied. She gripped one
leg of it with firm fingers and made her soundless way around
the wall until she had located the door.

The sentry remembered, afterward, that he had heard the
wildest shriek for help which had ever rung in his ears, and
he remembered unbolting the door. Afterward, until they

found him lying inside the locked cell with a cracked skull, he remembered nothing.

Jirel crept up the dark stairs of the north turret, murder in her heart. Many little hatreds she had known in her life, but no such blaze as this. Before her eyes in the night she could see Guillaume's scornful, scarred face laughing, the little jutting beard split with the whiteness of his mirth. Upon her mouth she felt the remembered weight of his, about her the strength of his arms. And such a blast of hot fury came over her that she reeled a little and clutched at the wall for support. She went on in a haze of red anger, and something like madness burning in her brain as a resolve slowly took shape out of the chaos of her hate. When that thought came to her she paused again, mid-step upon the stairs, and was conscious of a little coldness blowing over her. Then it was gone, and she shivered a little, shook her shoulders and grinned wolfishly, and went on.

By the stars she could see through the arrow-slits in the wall it must be near to midnight. She went softly on the stairs, and she encountered no one. Her little tower room at the top was empty. Even the straw pallet where the serving-wench slept had not been used that night. Jirel got herself out of her armor alone, somehow, after much striving and twisting. Her doeskin shirt was stiff with sweat and stained with blood. She tossed it disdainfully into a corner. The fury in her eyes had cooled now to a contained and secret flame. She smiled to herself as she slipped a fresh shirt of doeskin over her tousled red head and donned a brief tunic of link-mail. On her legs she buckled the greaves of some forgotten legionary, relic of the not long past days when Rome still ruled the world. She thrust a dagger through her belt and took her own long two-handed sword bare-bladed in her grip. Then she went down the stairs again.

She knew there must have been revelry and feasting in the great hall that night, and by the silence hanging so heavily now she was sure that most of her enemies lay still in drunken slumber, and she experienced a swift regret for the gallons of her good French wine so wasted. And the thought flashed through her head that a determined woman with a sharp sword might work some little damage among the drunken sleepers before she was overpowered. But she put that idea by, for Guillaume would have posted sentries to spare, and she must not give up her secret freedom so fruitlessly.

Down the dark stairs she went, and crossed one corner of the vast central hall whose darkness she was sure hid wine-deadened sleepers, and so into the lesser dimness of the rough little chapel that Joiry boasted. She had been sure she would find Father Gervase there, and she was not mistaken. He rose from his knees before the altar, dark in his robe, the starlight through the narrow window shining upon his tonsure.

"My daughter!" he whispered. "My daughter! How have you escaped? Shall I find you a mount? If you can pass the sentries you should be in your cousin's castle by daybreak."

She hushed him with a lifted hand.

"No," she said. "It is not outside I go this night. I have a more perilous journey even than that to make. Shrive me, father."

He stared at her.

"What is it?"

She dropped to her knees before him and gripped the rough cloth of his habit with urgent fingers.

"Shrive me, I say! I go down into hell tonight to pray the devil for a weapon, and it may be I shall not return."

Gervase bent and gripped her shoulders with hands that shook.

"Look at me!" he demanded. "Do you know what you're saying? You go—"

"Down!" She said it firmly. "Only you and I know that passage, father—and not even we can be sure of what lies beyond. But to gain a weapon against that man I would venture into perils even worse than that."

"If I thought you meant it," he whispered, "I would waken Guillaume now and give you into his arms. It would be a kinder fate, my daughter."

"It's that I would walk through hell to escape," she whispered back fiercely. "Can't you see? Oh, God knows I'm not innocent of the ways of light loving—but to be any man's fancy, for a night or two, before he snaps my neck or sells me into slavery—and above all, if that man were Guillaume! Can't you understand?"

"That would be shame enough," nodded Gervase. "But think, Jirel! For that shame there is atonement and absolution, and for that death the gates of heaven open wide. But this other—Jirel, Jirel, never through all eternity may you come out, body or soul, if you venture—down!"

She shrugged.

"To wreak my vengeance upon Guillaume I would go if I knew I should burn in hell for ever."

"But Jirel, I do not think you understand. This is a worse fate than the deepest depths of hell-fire. This is—this is beyond all the bounds of the hells we know. And I think Satan's hottest flames were the breath of paradise, compared to what may befall there."

"I know. Do you think I'd venture down if I could not be sure? Where else would I find such a weapon as I need, save outside God's dominion?"

"Jirel, you shall not!"

"Gervase, I go! Will you shrive me?" The hot yellow eyes blazed into his, lambent in the starlight.

After a moment he dropped his head. "You are my lady. I will give you God's blessing, but it will not avail you—there."

3

She went down into the dungeons again. She went down a long way through utter dark, over stones that were oozy and odorous with moisture, through blackness that had never known the light of day. She might have been a little afraid at other times, but that steady flame of hatred burning behind her eyes was a torch to light the way, and she could not wipe from her memory the feel of Guillaume's arms about her, the scornful press of his lips on her mouth. She whimpered a little, low in her throat, and a hot gust of hate went over her.

In the solid blackness she came at length to a wall, and she set herself to pulling the loose stones from this with her free hand, for she would not lay down the sword. They had never been laid in mortar, and they came out easily. When the way was clear she stepped through and found her feet upon a downward-sloping ramp of smooth stone. She cleared the rubble away from the hole in the wall, and enlarged it enough for a quick passage; for when she came back this way—if she did— it might well be that she would come very fast.

At the bottom of the slope she dropped to her knees on the cold floor and felt about. Her fingers traced the outline of a circle, the veriest crack in the stone. She felt until she found the ring in its center. That ring was of the coldest metal she had ever known, and the smoothest. She could put no name to it. The daylight had never shone upon such metal.

She tugged. The stone was reluctant, and at last she took her sword in her teeth and put both hands to the lifting. Even then it taxed the limit of her strength, and she was strong as many men. But at last it rose, with the strangest sighing sound, and a little prickle of goose-flesh rippled over her.

Now she took the sword back into her hand and knelt on the rim of the invisible blackness below. She had gone this path once before and once only, and never thought to find any necessity in life strong enough to drive her down again. The way was the strangest she had ever known. There was, she thought, no such passage in all the world save here. It had not been built for human feet to travel. It had not been built for feet at all. It was a narrow, polished shaft that cork-screwed round and round. A snake might have slipped in it and gone shooting down, round and round in dizzy circles—but no snake on earth was big enough to fill that shaft. No human travelers had worn the sides of the spiral so smooth, and she did not care to speculate on what creatures had polished it so, through what ages of passage.

She might never have made that first trip down, nor anyone after her, had not some unknown human hacked the notches which made it possible to descend slowly; that is, she thought it must have been a human. At any rate, the notches were roughly shaped for hands and feet, and spaced not too far apart; but who and when and how she could not even guess. As to the beings who made the shaft, in long-forgotten ages— well, there were devils on earth before man, and the world was very old.

She turned on her face and slid feet-first into the curving

tunnel. That first time she and Gervase had gone down in
sweating terror of what lay below, and with devils tugging at
their heels. Now she slid easily, not bothering to find toe-
holds, but slipping swiftly round and round the long spirals
with only her hands to break the speed when she went too fast.
Round and round she went, round and round.

It was a long way down. Before she had gone very far the
curious dizziness she had known before came over her again, a
dizziness not entirely induced by the spirals she whirled
around, but a deeper, atomic unsteadiness as if not only she
but also the substances around her were shifting. There was
something queer about the angles of those curves. She was no
scholar in geometry or aught else, but she felt intuitively that
the bend and slant of the way she went were somehow outside
any other angles or bends she had ever known. They led into
the unknown and the dark, but it seemed to her obscurely that
they led into deeper darkness and mystery than the merely
physical, as if, though she could not put it clearly even into
thoughts, the peculiar and exact lines of the tunnel had been
carefully angled to lead through poly-dimensional space as
well as through the underground—perhaps through time, too.
She did not know she was thinking such things; but all about
her was a blurred dizziness as she shot down and round, and
she knew that the way she went took her on a stranger journey
than any other way she had ever traveled.

Down, and down. She was sliding fast, but she knew how
long it would be. On that first trip they had taken alarm as
the passage spiraled so endlessly and with thoughts of the long
climb back had tried to stop before it was too late. They had
found it impossible. Once embarked, there was no halting. She
had tried, and such waves of sick blurring had come over her
that she came near to unconsciousness. It was as if she had tried
to halt some inexorable process of nature, half finished. They
could only go on. The very atoms of their bodies shrieked in
rebellion against a reversal of the change.

And the way up, when they returned, had not been difficult.
They had had visions of a back-breaking climb up interminable curves, but again the uncanny difference of those angles
from those they knew was manifested. In a queer way they

seemed to defy gravity, or perhaps led through some way outside the power of it. They had been sick and dizzy on the return, as on the way down, but through the clouds of that
confusion it had seemed to them that they slipped as easily
up the shaft as they had gone down; or perhaps that, once in
the tunnel, there was neither up nor down.

The passage leveled gradually. This was the worst part for
a human to travel, though it must have eased the speed of
whatever beings the shaft was made for. It was too narrow for
her to turn in, and she had to lever herself face down and feet
first, along the horizontal smoothness of the floor, pushing
with her hands. She was glad when her questing heels met
open space and she slid from the mouth of the shaft and stood
upright in the dark.

Here she paused to collect herself. Yes, this was the beginning of the long passage she and Father Gervase had traveled
on that long-ago journey of exploration. By the veriest accident
they had found the place, and only the veriest bravado had
brought them thus far. He had gone on a greater distance than
she—she was younger then, and more amenable to authority
—and had come back whitefaced in the torchlight and hurried
her up the shaft again.

She went on carefully, feeling her way, remembering what
she herself had seen in the darkness a little farther on, wondering in spite of herself, and with a tiny catch at her heart,
what it was that had sent Father Gervase so hastily back. She
had never been entirely satisfied with his explanations. It had
been about here—or was it a little farther on? The stillness
was like a roaring in her ears.

Then ahead of her the darkness moved. It was just that—
a vast, imponderable shifting of the solid dark. Jesu! This was
new! She gripped the cross at her throat with one hand and
her sword-hilt with the other. Then it was upon her, striking
like a hurricane, whirling her against the walls and shrieking
in her ears like a thousand wind-devils—a wild cyclone of the
dark that buffeted her mercilessly and tore at her flying hair
and raved in her ears with the myriad voices of all lost things
crying in the night. The voices were piteous in their terror and

loneliness. Tears came to her eyes even as she shivered with
nameless dread, for the whirlwind was alive with a dreadful
instinct, an animate thing sweeping through the dark of the
underground; an unholy thing that made her flesh crawl even
though it touched her to the heart with its pitiful little lost
voices wailing in the wind where no wind could possibly be.

And then it was gone. In that one flash of an instant it vanished, leaving no whisper to commemorate its passage. Only in
the heart of it could one hear the sad little voices wailing or
the wild shriek of the wind. She found herself standing
stunned, her sword yet gripped futilely in one hand and the
tears running down her face. Poor little lost voices, wailing.
She wiped the tears away with a shaking hand and set her teeth
hard against the weakness of reaction that flooded her. Yet it
was a good five minutes before she could force herself on.
After a few steps her knees ceased to tremble.

The floor was dry and smooth underfoot. It sloped a little
downward, and she wondered into what unplumbed deeps she
had descended by now. The silence had fallen heavily again,
and she found herself straining for some other sound than the
soft padding of her own boots. Then her foot slipped in sudden wetness. She bent, exploring fingers outstretched, feeling
without reason that the wetness would be red if she could see
it. But her fingers traced the imense outline of a footprint—
splayed and three-toed like a frog's, but of monster size. It was
a fresh footprint. She had a vivid flash of memory—that thing
she had glimpsed in the torchlight on the other trip down. But
she had had light then, and now she was blind in the dark, the
creature's natural habitat. . . .

For a moment she was not Jirel of Joiry, vengeful fury on
the trail of a devilish weapon, but a frightened woman alone
in the unholy dark. That memory had been so vivid. . . .
Then she saw Guillaume's scornful, laughing face again, the
little beard dark along the line of his jaw, the strong teeth
white with his laughter; and something hot and sustaining
swept over her like a thin flame, and she was Joiry again,
vengeful and resolute. She went on more slowly, her sword
swinging in a semicircle before every third step, that she might
not be surprised too suddenly by some nightmare monster

clasping her in smothering arms. But the flesh crept upon her
unprotected back.

The smooth passage went on and on. She could feel the cold
walls on either hand, and her upswung sword grazed the roof.
It was like crawling through some worm's tunnel, blindly
under the weight of countless tons of earth. She felt the pressure of it above and about her, overwhelming, and found
herself praying that the end of this tunnel-crawling might
come soon, whatever the end might bring.

But when it came it was a stranger thing than she had ever
dreamed. Abruptly she felt the immense, imponderable oppression cease. No longer was she conscious of the tons of
earth pressing about her. The walls had fallen away and her
feet struck a sudden rubble instead of the smooth floor. But
the darkness that had bandaged her eyes was changed too,
indescribably. It was no longer darkness, but void; not an ab-
sence of light, but simple nothingness. Abysses opened around
her, yet she could see nothing. She only knew that she stood
at the threshold of some immense space, and sensed nameless
things about her, and battled vainly against that nothingness
which was all her straining eyes could see. And at her throat
something constricted painfully.

She lifted her hand and found the chain of her crucifix taut
and vibrant around her neck. At that she smiled a little grimly,
for she began to understand. The crucifix. She found her hand
shaking despite herself, but she unfastened the chain and
dropped the cross to the ground. Then she gasped.

All about her, as suddenly as the awakening from a dream,
the nothingness had opened out into undreamed-of distances.
She stood high on a hilltop under a sky spangled with strange
stars. Below she caught glimpses of misty plains and valleys
with mountain peaks rising far away. And at her feet a ravening circle of small, slavering, blind things leaped with clashing
teeth.

They were obscene and hard to distinguish against the darkness of the hillside, and the noise they made was revolting.
Her sword swung up of itself, almost, and slashed furiously
at the little dark horrors leaping up around her legs. They

died squashily, splattering her bare thighs with unpleasantness,
and after a few had gone silent under the blade the rest fled
into the dark with quick, frightened pantings, their feet making a queer splashing noise on the stones.

Jirel gathered a handful of the coarse grass which grew
there and wiped her legs of the obscene splatters, looking
about with quickened breath upon this land so unholy that
one who bore a cross might not even see it. Here, if anywhere,
one might find a weapon such as she sought. Behind her in the
hillside was the low tunnel opening from which she had
emerged. Overhead the strange stars shone. She did not recognize a single constellation, and if the brighter sparks were
planets they were strange ones, tinged with violet and green and
yellow. One was vividly crimson, like a point of fire. Far out
over the rolling land below she could discern a mighty column
of light. It did not blaze, nor illuminate the dark about. It
cast no shadows. It simply was a great pillar of luminance
towering high in the night. It seemed artificial—perhaps man-
made, though she scarcely dared hope for men here.

She had half expected, despite her brave words, to come out
upon the storied and familiar red-hot pave of hell, and this
pleasant, starlit land surprised her and made her more wary.
The things that built the tunnel could not have been human.
She had no right to expect men here. She was a little stunned
by finding open sky so far underground, though she was intel-
ligent enough to realize that however she had come, she was
not underground now. No cavity in the earth could contain
this starry sky. She came of a credulous age, and she accepted
her surroundings without too much questioning, though she
was a little disappointed, if the truth were known, in the
pleasantness of the mistily starlit place. The fiery streets of hell
would have been a likelier locality in which to find a weapon
against Guillaume.

When she had cleansed her sword on the grass and wiped
her legs clean, she turned slowly down the hill. The distant
column beckoned her, and after a moment of indecision she
turned toward it. She had no time to waste, and this was the
likeliest place to find what she sought.

The coarse grass brushed her legs and whispered round her

feet. She stumbled now and then on the rubble, for the hill was steep, but she reached the bottom without mishap, and struck out across the meadows toward that blaze of far-away brilliance. It seemed to her that she walked more lightly, somehow. The grass scarcely bent underfoot, and she found she could take long sailing strides like one who runs with wings on his heels. It felt like a dream. The gravity pull of the place must have been less than she was accustomed to, but she only knew that she was skimming over the ground with amazing speed.

Traveling so, she passed through the meadows over the strange, coarse grass, over a brook or two that spoke endlessly to itself in a curious language that was almost speech, certainly not the usual gurgle of earth's running water. Once she ran into a blotch of darkness, like some pocket of void in the air, and struggled through gasping and blinking outraged eyes. She was beginning to realize that the land was not so innocently normal as it looked.

On and on she went, at that surprising speed, while the meadows skimmed past beneath her flying feet and gradually the light drew nearer. She saw now that it was a round tower of sheeted luminance, as if walls of solid flame rose up from the ground. Yet it seemed to be steady, nor did it cast any illumination upon the sky.

Before much time had elapsed, with her dream-like speed she had almost reached her goal. The ground was becoming marshy underfoot, and presently the smell of swamps rose in her nostrils and she saw that between her and the light stretched a belt of unstable ground tufted with black reedy grass. Here and there she could see dim white blotches moving. They might be beasts, or only wisps of mist. The starlight was not very illuminating.

She began to pick her way carefully across the black, quaking morasses. Where the tufts of grass rose she found firmer ground, and she leaped from clump to clump with that amazing lightness, so that her feet barely touched the black ooze. Here and there slow bubbles rose through the mud and broke thickly. She did not like the place.

Half-way across, she saw one of the white blotches approach-

ing her with slow, erratic movements. It bumped along unevenly, and at first she thought it might be inanimate, its
approach was so indirect and purposeless. Then it blundered
nearer, with that queer bumpy gait, making sucking noises in
the ooze and splashing as it came. In the starlight she saw
suddenly what it was, and for an instant her heart paused and
sickness rose overwhelmingly in her throat. It was a woman—
a beautiful woman whose white bare body had the curves and
loveliness of some marble statue. She was crouching like a frog,
and as Jirel watched in stupefaction she straightened her legs
abruptly and leaped as a frog leaps, only more clumsily, falling
forward into the ooze a little distance beyond the watching
woman. She did not seem to see Jirel. The mud-spattered face
was blank. She blundered on through the mud in awkward
leaps. Jirel watched until the woman was no more than a
white wandering blur in the dark, and above the shock of that
sight pity was rising, and uncomprehending resentment against
whatever had brought so lovely a creature into this—into
blundering in frog leaps aimlessly through the mud, with
empty mind and blind, staring eyes. For the second time that
night she knew the sting of unaccustomed tears as she went on.

The sight, though, had given her reassurance. The human
form was not unknown here. There might be leathery devils
with hoofs and horns, such as she still half expected, but she
would not be alone in her humanity; though if all the rest
were as piteously mindless as the one she had seen—she did
not follow that thought. It was too unpleasant. She was glad
when the marsh was past and she need not see any longer the
awkward white shapes bumping along through the dark.

She struck out across the narrow space which lay between
her and the tower. She saw now that it was a building, and that
the light composed it. She could not understand that, but she
saw it. Walls and columns outlined the tower, solid sheets of
light with definite boundaries, not radiant. As she came nearer
she saw that it was in motion, apparently spurting up from
some source underground as if the light illuminated sheets of
water rushing upward under great pressure. Yet she felt intuitively that it was not water, but incarnate light.

She came forward hesitantly, gripping her sword. The area
around the tremendous pillar was paved with something black
and smooth that did not reflect the light. Out of it sprang the
uprushing walls of brilliance with their sharply defined edges.
The magnitude of the thing dwarfed her to infinitesimal size.
She stared upward with undazzled eyes, trying to understand.
If there could be such a thing as solid, non-radiating light, this
was it.

4

She was very near under the mighty tower before she could
see the details of the building clearly. They were strange to her
—great pillars and arches around the base, and one stupendous
portal, all molded out of the rushing, prisoned light. She
turned toward the opening after a moment, for the light had a
tangible look. She did not believe she could have walked
through it even had she dared.

When that tremendous portal arched over her she peered
in, affrighted by the very size of the place. She thought she
could hear the hiss and spurt of the light surging upward. She
was looking into a mighty globe inside, a hall shaped like
the interior of a bubble, though the curve was so vast she was
scarcely aware of it. And in the very center of the globe floated
a light. Jirel blinked. A light, dwelling in a bubble of light.
It glowed there in midair with a pale, steady flame that was
somehow alive and animate, and brighter than the serene
illumination of the building, for it hurt her eyes to look at it
directly.

She stood on the threshold and stared, not quite daring to
venture in. And as she hesitated a change came over the light.
A flash of rose tinged its pallor. The rose deepened and darkened until it took on the color of blood. And the shape under-
went strange changes. It lengthened, drew itself out narrowly,
split at the bottom into two branches, put out two tendrils
from the top. The blood-red paled again, and the light somehow lost its brilliance, receded into the depths of the thing
that was forming. Jirel clutched her sword and forgot to
breathe, watching. The light was taking on the shape of a
human being—of a woman—of a tall woman in mail, her red

hair tousled and her eyes staring straight into the duplicate eyes at the portal. . . .

"Welcome," said the Jirel suspended in the center of the globe, her voice deep and resonant and clear in spite of the distance between them. Jirel at the door held her breath, wondering and afraid. This was herself, in every detail, a mirrored Jirel—that was it, a Jirel mirrored upon a surface which blazed and smoldered with barely repressed light, so that the eyes gleamed with it and the whole figure seemed to hold its shape by an effort, only by that effort restraining itself from resolving into pure, formless light again. But the voice was not her own. It shook and resounded with a knowledge as alien as the light-built walls. It mocked her. It said,

"Welcome! Enter into the portals, woman!"

She looked up warily at the rushing walls about her. Instinctively she drew back.

"Enter, enter!" urged that mocking voice from her own mirrored lips. And there was a note in it she did not like.

"Enter!" cried the voice again, this time a command.

Jirel's eyes narrowed. Something intuitive warned her back, and yet—she drew the dagger she had thrust in her belt and with a quick motion she tossed it into the great globe-shaped hall. It struck the floor without a sound, and a brilliant light flared up around it, so brilliant she could not look upon what was happening; but it seemed to her that the knife expanded, grew large and nebulous and ringed with dazzling light. In less time than it takes to tell, it had faded out of sight as if the very atoms which composed it had flown apart and dispersed in the golden glow of that mighty bubble. The dazzle faded with the knife, leaving Jirel staring dazedly at a bare floor.

That other Jirel laughed, a rich, resonant laugh of scorn and malice.

"Stay out, then," said the voice. "You've more intelligence than I thought. Well, what would you here?"

Jirel found her voice with an effort.

"I seek a weapon," she said, "a weapon against a man I so hate that upon earth there is none terrible enough for my need."

"You so hate him, eh?" mused the voice.

"With all my heart!"

"With all your heart!" echoed the voice, and there was an undernote of laughter in it that she did not understand. The echoes of that mirth ran round and round the great globe. Jirel felt her cheeks burn with resentment against some implication in the derision which she could not put a name to. When the echoes of the laugh had faded the voice said indifferently,

"Give the man what you find at the black temple in the lake. I make you a gift of it."

The lips that were Jirel's twisted into a laugh of purest mockery; then all about that figure so perfectly her own the light flared out. She saw the outlines melting fluidly as she turned her dazzled eyes away. Before the echoes of that derision had died, a blinding, formless light burned once more in the midst of the bubble.

Jirel turned and stumbled away under the mighty column of the tower, a hand to her dazzled eyes. Not until she had reached the edge of the black, unreflecting circle that paved the ground around the pillar did she realize that she knew no way of finding the lake where her weapon lay. And not until then did she remember how fatal it is said to be to accept a gift from a demon. Buy it, or earn it, but never accept the gift. Well—she shrugged and stepped out upon the grass. She must surely be damned by now, for having ventured down of her own will into this curious place for such a purpose as hers. The soul can be lost but once.

She turned her face up to the strange stars and wondered in what direction her course lay. The sky looked blankly down upon her with its myriad meaningless eyes. A star fell as she watched, and in her superstitious soul she took it for an omen, and set off boldly over the dark meadows in the direction where the bright streak had faded. No swamps guarded the way here, and she was soon skimming along over the grass with that strange, dancing gait that the lightness of the place allowed her. And as she went she was remembering, as from long ago in some other far world, a man's arrogant mirth and the press of his mouth on hers. Hatred bubbled up hotly within

her and broke from her lips in a little savage laugh of anticipation. What dreadful thing awaited her in the temple in the
lake, what punishment from hell to be loosed by her own
hands upon Guillaume? And though her soul was the price it
cost her, she would count it a fair bargain if she could drive
the laughter from his mouth and bring terror into the eyes that
mocked her.

Thoughts like these kept her company for a long way upon
her journey. She did not think to be lonely or afraid in the
uncanny darkness across which no shadows fell from that
mighty column behind her. The unchanging meadows flew
past underfoot, lightly as meadows in a dream. It might almost
have been that the earth moved instead of herself, so effort-
lessly did she go. She was sure now that she was heading in the
right direction, for two more stars had fallen in the same arc
across the sky.

The meadows were not untenanted. Sometimes she felt presences near her in the dark, and once she ran full-tilt into a nest
of little yapping horrors like those on the hill-top. They lunged
up about her with clicking teeth, mad with a blind ferocity,
and she swung her sword in frantic circles, sickened by the
noise of them lunging splashily through the grass and splattering her sword with their deaths. She beat them off and went
on, fighting her own sickness, for she had never known anything quite so nauseating as these little monstrosities.

She crossed a brook that talked to itself in the darkness with
that queer murmuring which came so near to speech, and a
few strides beyond it she paused suddenly, feeling the ground
tremble with the rolling thunder of hoofbeats approaching.
She stood still, searching the dark anxiously, and presently the
earth-shaking beat grew louder and she saw a white blur flung
wide across the dimness to her left, and the sound of hoofs
deepened and grew. Then out of the night swept a herd of
snow-white horses. Magnificently they ran, manes tossing, tails
streaming, feet pounding a rhythmic, heart-stirring roll along
the ground. She caught her breath at the beauty of their motion. They swept by a little distance away, tossing their heads,
spurning the ground with scornful feet.

But as they came abreast of her she saw one blunder a little

and stumble against the next, and that one shook his head be-
wilderedly; and suddenly she realized that they were blind—
all running so splendidly in a deeper dark than even she
groped through. And she saw too their coats were roughened
with sweat, and foam dripped from their lips, and their nostrils
were flaring pools of scarlet. Now and again one stumbled
from pure exhaustion. Yet they ran, frantically, blindly
through the dark, driven by something outside their comprehension.

As the last one of all swept by her, sweat-crusted and staggering, she saw him toss his head high, spattering foam, and
whinny shrilly to the stars. And it seemed to her that the sound
was strangely articulate. Almost she heard the echoes of a name
—"Julienne! Julienne!"—in that high, despairing sound. And
the incongruity of it, the bitter despair, clutched at her heart
so sharply that for the third time that night she knew the sting
of tears.

The dreadful humanity of that cry echoed in her ears as
the thunder died away. She went on, blinking back the tears
for that beautiful blind creature, staggering with exhaustion,
calling a girl's name hopelessly from a beast's throat into the
blank darkness wherein it was for ever lost.

Then another star fell across the sky, and she hurried ahead,
closing her mind to the strange, incomprehensible pathos that
made an undernote of tears to the starry dark of this land. And
the thought was growing in her mind that, though she had
come into no brimstone pit where horned devils pranced over
flames, yet perhaps it was after all a sort of hell through which
she ran.

Presently in the distance she caught a glimmer of something
bright. The ground dipped after that and she lost it, and
skimmed through a hollow where pale things wavered away
from her into the deepr dark. She never knew what they were,
and was glad. When she came up onto higher ground again
she saw it more clearly, an expanse of dim brilliance ahead.
She hoped it was a lake, and ran more swiftly.

It *was* a lake—a lake that could never have existed outside
some obscure hell like this. She stood on the brink doubtfully,

wondering if this could be the place the light-devil had meant. Black, shining water stretched out before her, heaving gently with a motion unlike that of any water she had ever seen before. And in the depths of it, like fireflies caught in ice, gleamed myriad small lights. They were fixed there immovably, not stirring with the motion of the water. As she watched, something hissed above her and a streak of light split the dark air. She looked up in time to see something bright curving across the sky to fall without a splash into the water, and small ripples of phosphorescence spread sluggishly toward the shore, where they broke at her feet with the queerest whispering sound, as if each succeeding ripple spoke the syllable of a word.

She looked up, trying to locate the origin of the falling lights, but the strange stars looked down upon her blankly. She bent and stared down into the center of the spreading ripples, and where the thing had fallen she thought a new light twinkled through the water. She could not determine what it was, and after a curious moment she gave the question up and began to cast about for the temple the light-devil had spoken of.

After a moment she thought she saw something dark in the center of the lake, and when she had stared for a few minutes it gradually became clearer, an arch of darkness against the starry background of the water. It might be a temple. She strolled slowly along the brim of the lake, trying to get a closer view of it, for the thing was no more than a darkness against the spangles of light, like some void in the sky where no stars shine. And presently she stumbled over something in the grass.

She looked down with startled yellow eyes, and saw a strange, indistinguishable darkness. It had solidity to the feel but scarcely to the eye, for she could not quite focus upon it. It was like trying to see something that did not exist save as a void, a darkness in the grass. It had the shape of a step, and when she followed with her eyes she saw that it was the beginning of a dim bridge stretching out over the lake, narrow and curved and made out of nothingness. It seemed to have no surface, and its edges were difficult to distinguish from the lesser gloom surrounding it. But the thing was tangible—an arch carved out of the solid dark—and it led out in the direction she wished to go. For she was naïvely sure now that the dim blot in the center of the lake was the temple she was searching for. The falling stars had guided her, and she could not have gone astray.

So she set her teeth and gripped her sword and put her foot upon the bridge. It was rock-firm under her, but scarcely more than a foot or so wide, and without rails. When she had gone a step or two she began to feel dizzy; for under her the water heaved with a motion that made her head swim, and the stars twinkled eerily in its depths. She dared not look away for fear of missing her footing on the narrow arch of darkness. It was like walking a bridge flung across the void, with stars underfoot and nothing but an unstable strip of nothingness to bear her up. Half-way across, the heaving of the water and the illusion of vast, constellated spaces beneath and the look her bridge had of being no more than empty space ahead, combined to send her head reeling; and as she stumbled on, the bridge seemed to be wavering with her, swinging in gigantic arcs across the starry void below.

Now she could see the temple more closely, though scarcely more clearly than from the shore. It looked to be no more than an outlined emptiness against the star-crowded brilliance behind it, etching its arches and columns of blankness upon the twinkling waters. The bridge came down in a long dim swoop to its doorway. Jirel took the last few yards at a reckless run and stopped breathless under the arch that made the temple's vague doorway. She stood there panting and staring about narrow-eyed, sword poised in her hand. For though the place was empty and very still she felt a presence even as she set her foot upon the floor of it.

She was staring about a little space of blankness in the starry lake. It seemed to be no more than that. She could see the walls and columns where they were outlined against the water and where they made darknesses in the star-flecked sky, but where there was only dark behind them she could see nothing. It was a tiny place, no more than a few square yards of emptiness upon the face of the twinkling waters. And in its center an image stood.

She stared at it in silence, feeling a curious compulsion

growing within her, like a vague command from something
outside herself. The image was of some substance of nameless
black, unlike the material which composed the building, for
even in the dark she could see it clearly. It was a semi-human
figure, crouching forward with outthrust head, sexless and
strange. Its one central eye was closed as if in rapture, and its
mouth was pursed for a kiss. And though it was but an image
and without even the semblance of life, she felt unmistakably
the presence of something alive in the temple, something so
alien and innominate that instinctively she drew away.

She stood there for a full minute, reluctant to enter the place
where so alien a being dwelt, half conscious of that voiceless
compulsion growing up within her. And slowly she became
aware that all the lines and angles of the half-seen building
were curved to make the image their center and focus. The
very bridge swooped its long arc to complete the centering. As
she watched, it seemed to her that through the arches of the
columns even the stars in lake and sky were grouped in patterns which took the image for their focus. Every line and
curve in the dim world seemed to sweep round toward the
squatting thing before her with its closed eye and expectant
mouth.
Gradually the universal focusing of lines began to exert its
influence upon her. She took a hesitant step forward without
realizing the motion. But that step was all the dormant urge
within her needed. With her one motion forward the compulsion closed down upon her with whirlwind impetuosity. Helplessly she felt herself advancing, helplessly with one small,
sane portion of her mind she realized the madness that was
gripping her, the blind, irresistible urge to do what every
visible line in the temple's construction was made to compel.
With stars swirling around her she advanced across the floor
and laid her hands upon the rounded shoulders of the image
—the sword, forgotten, making a sort of accolade against its
hunched neck—and lifted her red head and laid her mouth
blindly against the pursed lips of the image.
In a dream she took that kiss. In a dream of dizziness and
confusion she seemed to feel the iron-cold lips stirring under

hers. And through the union of that kiss—warm-blooded woman with image of nameless stone—through the meeting of their mouths something entered into her very soul; something cold and stunning; something alien beyond any words. It lay upon her shuddering soul like some frigid weight from the void, a bubble holding something unthinkably alien and dreadful. She could feel the heaviness of it upon some intangible part of her that shrank from the touch. It was like the weight of remorse or despair, only far colder and stranger and —somehow—more ominous, as if this weight were but the egg from which things might hatch too dreadful to put even into thoughts.

The moment of the kiss could have been no longer than a breath's space, but to her it was timeless. In a dream she felt the compulsion falling from her at last. In a dim dream she dropped her hands from its shoulders, finding the sword heavy in her grasp and staring dully at it for a while before clarity began its return to her cloudy mind. When she became completely aware of herself once more she was standing with slack body and dragging head before the blind, rapturous image, that dead weight upon her heart as dreary as an old sorrow, and more coldly ominous than anything she could find words for.

And with returning clarity the most staggering terror came over her, swiftly and suddenly—terror of the image and the temple of darkness, and the coldly spangled lake and of the whole, wide, dim, dreadful world about her. Desperately she longed for home again, even the red fury of hatred and the press of Guillaume's mouth and the hot arrogance of his eyes again. Anything but this. She found herself running without knowing why. Her feet skimmed over the narrow bridge lightly as a gull's wings dipping the water. In a brief instant the starry void of the lake flashed by beneath her and the solid earth was underfoot. She saw the great column of light far away across the dark meadows and beyond it a hill-top

She ran with terror at her heels and devils howling in the rising against the stars. And she ran.

wind her own speed made. She ran from her own curiously alien body, heavy with its weight of inexplicable doom. She

passed through the hollow where pale things wavered away,
she fled over the uneven meadows in a frenzy of terror. She
ran and ran, in those long light bounds the lesser gravity
allowed her, fleeter than a deer, and her own panic choked in
her throat and that weight upon her soul dragged at her too
drearily for tears. She fled to escape it, and could not; and the
ominous certainty that she carried something too dreadful to
think of grew and grew.

For a long while she skimmed over the grass, tirelessly, wing-
heeled, her red hair flying. The panic died after a while, but
that sense of heavy disaster did not die. She felt somehow that
tears would ease her, but something in the frigid darkness of
her soul froze her tears in the ice of that gray and alien chill.

And gradually, through the inner dark, a fierce anticipation
took form in her mind. Revenge upon Guillaume! She had
taken from the temple only a kiss, so it was that which she
must deliver to him. And savagely she exulted in the thought
of what that kiss would release upon him, unsuspecting. She
did not know, but it filled her with fierce joy to guess.

She had passed the column and skirted the morass where the
white, blundering forms still bumped along awkwardly
through the ooze, and was crossing the coarse grass toward the
nearing hill when the sky began to pale along the horizon.
And with that pallor a fresh terror took hold upon her, a wild
horror of daylight in this unholy land. She was not sure if
it was the light itself she so dreaded, or what that light would
reveal in the dark stretches she had traversed so blindly—what
unknown horrors she had skirted in the night. But she knew
instinctively that if she valued her sanity she must be gone
before the light had risen over the land. And she redoubled
her efforts, spurring her wearying limbs to yet more skimming
speed. But it would be a close race, for already the stars were
blurring out, and a flush of curious green was broadening
along the sky, and around her the air was turning to a vague,
unpleasant gray.

She toiled up the steep hillside breathlessly. When she was
half-way up, her own shadow began to take form upon the
rocks, and it was unfamiliar and dreadfully significant of

something just outside her range of understanding. She averted her eyes from it, afraid that at any moment the meaning might break upon her outraged brain.

She could see the top of the hill above her, dark against the paling sky, and she toiled up in frantic haste, clutching her sword and feeling that if she had to look in the full light upon the dreadful little abominations that had snapped around her feet when she first emerged she would collapse into screaming hysteria.

The cave-mouth yawned before her, invitingly black, a refuge from the dawning light behind her. She knew an almost irresistible desire to turn and look back from this vantage-point across the land she had traversed, and gripped her sword hard to conquer the perversive longing. There was a scuffling in the rocks at her feet, and she set her teeth in her underlip and swung viciously in brief arcs, without looking down. She heard small squeakings and the splashy sound of feet upon the stones, and felt her blade shear thrice through semi-solidity, to the click of little vicious teeth. Then they broke and ran off over the hillside, and she stumbled on, choking back the scream that wanted so fiercely to break from her lips.

She fought that growing desire all the way up to the cave-mouth, for she knew that if she gave way she would never cease shrieking until her throat went raw.

Blood was trickling from her bitten lip with the effort at silence when she reached the cave. And there, twinkling upon the stones, lay something small and bright and dearly familiar. With a sob of relief she bent and snatched up the crucifix she had torn from her throat when she came out into this land. And as her fingers shut upon it a vast, protecting darkness swooped around her. Gasping with relief, she groped her way the step or two that separated her from the cave.

Dark lay like a blanket over her eyes, and she welcomed it gladly, remembering how her shadow had lain so awfully upon the hillside as she climbed, remembering the first rays of savage sunlight beating upon her shoulders. She stumbled through the blackness, slowly getting control again over her shaking body and laboring lungs, slowly stilling the panic that the

dawning day had roused so inexplicably within her. And as
that terror died, the dull weight upon her spirit became strong
again. She had all but forgotten it in her panic, but now the
impending and unknown dreadfulness grew heavier and more
oppressive in the darkness of the underground, and she groped
along in a dull stupor of her own depression, slow with the
weight of the strange doom she carried.

Nothing barred her way. In the dullness of her stupor she
scarcely realized it, or expected any of the vague horrors that
peopled the place to leap out upon her. Empty and unmenac-
ing, the way stretched before her blindly stumbling feet. Only
once did she hear the sound of another presence—the rasp of
hoarse breathing and the scrape of a scaly hide against the
stone—but it must have been outside the range of her own
passage, for she encountered nothing.

When she had come to the end and a cold wall rose up before her, it was scarcely more than automatic habit that made
her search along it with groping hand until she came to
the mouth of the shaft. It sloped gently up into the dark. She
crawled in, trailing her sword, until the rising incline and
lowering roof forced her down upon her face. Then with toes
and fingers she began to force herself up the spiral, slippery
way.

Before she had gone very far she was advancing without
effort, scarcely realizing that it was against gravity she moved.
The curious dizziness of the shaft had come over her, the
strange feeling of change in the very substance of her body,
and through the cloudy numbness of it she felt herself sliding
round and round the spirals, without effort. Again, obscurely,
she had the feeling that in the peculiar angles of this shaft was
neither up nor down. And for a long while the dizzy circling
went on.

When the end came at last, and she felt her fingers gripping
the edge of that upper opening which lay beneath the floor of
Joiry's lowest dungeons, she heaved herself up warily and lay
for awhile on the cold floor in the dark, while slowly the
clouds of dizziness passed from her mind, leaving only that

ominous weight within. When the darkness had ceased to circle about her, and the floor steadied, she got up dully and swung the cover back over the opening, her hands shuddering from the feel of the cold, smooth ring which had never seen daylight.

When she turned from this task she was aware of the reason for the lessening in the gloom around her. A guttering light outlined the hole in the wall from which she had pulled the stones—was it a century ago? The brilliance all but blinded her after her long sojourn through blackness, and she stood there awhile, swaying a little, one hand to her eyes, before she went out into the familiar torchlight she knew waited her beyond. Father Gervase, she was sure, anxiously waiting her return. But even he had not dared to follow her through the hole in the wall, down to the brink of the shaft.

Somehow she felt that she should be giddy with relief at this safe homecoming, back to humanity again. But as she stumbled over the upward slope toward light and safety she was conscious of no more than the dullness of whatever unreleased horror it was which still lay so ominously upon her stunned soul.

She came through the gaping hole in the masonry into the full glare of torches awaiting her, remembering with a wry inward smile how wide she had made the opening in anticipation of flight from something dreadful when she came back that way. Well, there was no flight from the horror she bore within her. It seemed to her that her heart was slowing, too, missing a beat now and then and staggering like a weary runner.

She came out into the torchlight, stumbling with exhaustion, her mouth scarlet from the blood of her bitten lip and her bare greaved legs and bare sword-blade foul with the deaths of those little horrors that swarmed around the cave-mouth. From the tangle of red hair her eyes stared out with a bleak, frozen, inward look, as of one who has seen nameless things. That keen, steel-bright beauty which had been hers was as dull and fouled as her sword-blade, and at the look in her eyes Father Gervase shuddered and crossed himself.

5

They were waiting for her in an uneasy group—the priest anxious and dark, Guillaume splendid in the torchlight, tall and arrogant, a handful of men-at-arms holding the guttering lights and shifting uneasily from one foot to the other. When she saw Guillaume the light that flared up in her eyes blotted out for a moment the bleak dreadfulness behind them, and her slowing heart leaped like a spurred horse, sending the blood riotously through her veins. Guillaume, magnificent in his armor, leaning upon his sword and staring down at her from his scornful height, the little black beard jutting. Guillaume, to whom Joiry had fallen. Guillaume.

That which she carried at the core of her being was heavier than anything else in the world, so heavy she could scarcely keep her knees from bending, so heavy her heart labored under its weight. Almost irresistibly she wanted to give way beneath it, to sink down and down under the crushing load, to lie prone and vanquished in the ice-gray, bleak place she was so dimly aware of through the clouds that were rising about her. But there was Guillaume, grim and grinning, and she hated him so very bitterly—she must make the effort. She must, at whatever cost, for she was coming to know that death lay in wait for her if she bore this burden long, that it was a two-edged weapon which could strike at its wielder if the blow were delayed too long. She knew this through the dim mists that were thickening in her brain, and she put all her strength into the immense effort it cost to cross the floor toward him. She stumbled a little, and made one faltering step and then another, and dropped her sword with a clang as she lifted her arms to him.

He caught her strongly, in a hard, warm clasp, and she heard his laugh triumphant and hateful as he bent his head to take the kiss she was raising her mouth to offer. He must have seen, in that last moment before their lips met, the savage glare of victory in her eyes, and been startled. But he did not hesitate. His mouth was heavy upon hers.

It was a long kiss. She felt him stiffen in her arms. She felt a coldness in the lips upon hers, and slowly the dark weight of what she bore lightened, lifted, cleared away from her cloudy mind. Strength flowed back through her richly. The whole world came alive to her once more. Presently she loosed his slack arms and stepped away, looking up into his face with a keen and dreadful triumph upon her own.

She saw the ruddiness of him draining away, and the rigidity of stone coming over his scarred features. Only his eyes remained alive, and there was torment in them, and understanding. She was glad—she had wanted him to understand what it cost to take Joiry's kiss unbidden. She smiled thinly into his tortured eyes, watching. And she saw something cold and alien seeping through him, permeating him slowly with some unnamable emotion which no man could ever have experienced before. She could not name it, but she saw it in his eyes—some dreadful emotion never made for flesh and blood to know, some iron despair such as only an unguessable being from the gray, formless void could ever have felt before—too hideously alien for any human creature to endure. Even she shuddered from the dreadful, cold bleakness looking out of his eyes, and knew as she watched that there must be many emotions and many fears and joys too far outside man's comprehension for any being of flesh to undergo, and live. Grayly she saw it spreading through him, and the very substance of his body shuddered under that iron weight.

And now came a visible, physical change. Watching, she was aghast to think that in her own body and upon her own soul she had borne the seed of this dreadful flowering, and did not wonder that her heart had slowed under the unbearable weight of it. He was standing rigidly with arms half bent, just as he stood when she slid from his embrace. And now great shudders began to go over him, as if he were wavering in the torchlight, some gray-faced wraith in armor with torment in his eyes. She saw the sweat beading his forehead. She saw a trickle of blood from his mouth, as if he had bitten through his lip in the agony of this new, incomprehensible emotion. Then a last shiver went over him violently, and he flung up his head, the little curling beard jutting ceilingward and the muscles of his strong throat corded, and from his lips broke a long, low cry of such utter, inhuman strangeness that Jirel felt coldness rip-

pling through her veins and she put up her hands to her ears
to shut it out. It meant something—it expressed some dreadful
emotion that was neither sorrow nor despair nor anger, but
infinitely alien and infinitely sad. Then his long legs buckled
at the knees and he dropped with a clatter of mail and lay still
on the stone floor.

They knew he was dead. That was unmistakable in the way
he lay. Jirel stood very still, looking down upon him, and
strangely it seemed to her that all the lights in the world had
gone out. A moment before he had been so big and vital, so
magnificent in the torchlight—she could still feel his kiss upon
her mouth, and the hard warmth of his arms. . . .

Suddenly and blindingly it came upon her what she had
done. She knew now why such heady violence had flooded her
whenever she thought of him—knew why the light-devil in her
own form had laughed so derisively—knew the price she must
pay for taking a gift from a demon. She knew that there was
no light anywhere in the world, now that Guillaume was gone.

Father Gervase took her arm gently. She shook him off with
an impatient shrug and dropped to one knee beside Guillaume's body, bending her head so that the red hair fell forward to hide her tears.

Shambleau

*MAN has conquered space before. You may be sure of that.
Somewhere beyond the Egyptians, in that dimness out of which
come echoes of half-mythical names—Atlantis, Mu—somewhere
back of history's first beginnings there must have been an age
when mankind, like us today, built cities of steel to house its
star-roving ships and knew the names of the planets in their
own native tongues—heard Venus' people call their wet world
"Sha-ardol" in that soft, sweet, slurring speech and mimicked
Mars' guttural "Lakkdiz" from the harsh tongues of Mars' dryland dwellers. You may be sure of it. Man has conquered Space
before, and out of that conquest faint, faint echoes run still
through a world that has forgotten the very fact of a civilization which must have been as mighty as our own. There have
been too many myths and legends for us to doubt it. The
myth of the Medusa, for instance, can never have had its roots
in the soil of Earth. That tale of the snake-haired Gorgon
whose gaze turned the gazer to stone never originated about
any creature that Earth nourished. And those ancient Greeks
who told the story must have remembered, dimly and half be-
lieving, a tale of antiquity about some strange being from one
of the outlying planets their remotest ancestors once trod.*

"Shambleau! Ha . . . Shambleau!" The wild hysteria of
the mob rocketed from wall to wall of Lakkdarol's narrow
streets and the storming of heavy boots over the slag-red pavement made an ominous undernote to that swelling bay,
"Shambleau! Shambleau!"

Northwest Smith heard it coming and stepped into the near-

37

est doorway, laying a wary hand on his heat-gun's grip, and
his colorless eyes narrowed. Strange sounds were common
enough in the streets of Earth's latest colony on Mars—a raw,
red little town where anything might happen, and very often
did. But Northwest Smith, whose name is known and respected
in every dive and wild outpost on a dozen wild planets, was a
cautious man, despite his reputation. He set his back against
the wall and gripped his pistol, and heard the rising shout
come nearer and nearer.

Then into his range of vision flashed a red running figure,
dodging like a hunted hare from shelter to shelter in the narrow street. It was a girl—a berry-brown girl in a single tattered
garment whose scarlet burnt the eyes with its brilliance. She
ran wearily, and he could hear her gasping breath from where
he stood. As she came into view he saw her hesitate and lean
one hand against the wall for support, and glance wildly
around for shelter. She must not have seen him in the depths
of the doorway, for as the bay of the mob grew louder and the
pounding of feet sounded almost at the corner she gave a
despairing little moan and dodged into the recess at his very
side.

When she saw him standing there, tall and leather-brown,
hand on his heat-gun, she sobbed once, inarticulately, and collapsed at his feet, a huddle of burning scarlet and bare, brown
limbs.

Smith had not seen her face, but she was a girl, and sweetly
made and in danger; and though he had not the reputation of
a chivalrous man, something in her hopeless huddle at his feet
touched that chord of sympathy for the underdog that stirs
in every Earthman, and he pushed her gently into the corner
behind him and jerked out his gun, just as the first of the running mob rounded the corner.

It was a motley crowd, Earthmen and Martians and a sprin-
kling of Venusian swampmen and strange, nameless denizens
of unnamed planets—a typical Lakkdarol mob. When the first
of them turned the corner and saw the empty street before
them there was a faltering in the rush and the foremost spread
out and began to search the doorways on both sides of the
street.

"Looking for something?" Smith's sardonic call sounded clear above the clamor of the mob.

They turned. The shouting died for a moment as they took in the scene before them—tall Earthman in the space-explorer's leathern garb, all one color from the burning of savage suns save for the sinister pallor of his no-colored eyes in a scarred and resolute face, gun in his steady hand and the scarlet girl crouched behind him, panting.

The foremost of the crowd—a burly Earthman in tattered leather from which the Patrol insignia had been ripped away —stared for a moment with a strange expression of incredulity on his face overspreading the savage exultation of the chase. Then he let loose a deep-throated bellow, "Shambleau!" and lunged forward. Behind him the mob took up the cry again, "Shambleau! Shambleau! Shambleau!" and surged after.

Smith, lounging negligently against the wall, arms folded and gun-hand draped over his left forearm, looked incapable of swift motion, but at the leader's first forward step the pistol swept in a practised half-circle and the dazzle of blue-white heat leaping from its muzzle seared an arc in the slag pavement at his feet. It was an old gesture, and not a man in the crowd but understood it. The foremost recoiled swiftly against the surge of those in the rear, and for a moment there was confusion as the two tides met and struggled. Smith's mouth curled into a grim curve as he watched. The man in the mutilated Patrol uniform lifted a threatening fist and stepped to the very edge of the deadline, while the crowd rocked to and fro behind him.

"Are you crossing that line?" queried Smith in an ominously gentle voice.

"We want that girl!"

"Come and get her!" Recklessly Smith grinned into his face. He saw danger there, but his defiance was not the foolhardy gesture it seemed. An expert psychologist of mobs from long experience, he sensed no murder here. Not a gun had appeared in any hand in the crowd. They desired the girl with an inexplicable bloodthirstiness he was at a loss to understand, but toward himself he sensed no such fury. A mauling he might expect, but his life was in no danger. Guns would have appeared before now if they were coming out at all. So he grinned in the man's angry face and leaned lazily against the wall.

Behind their self-appointed leader the crowd milled impatiently, and threatening voices began to rise again. Smith heard the girl moan at his feet.

"What do you want with her?" he demanded.

"She's Shambleau! Shambleau, you fool! Kick her out of there—we'll take care of her!"

"I'm taking care of her," drawled Smith.

"She's Shambleau, I tell you! Damn your hide, man, we never let those things live! Kick her out here!"

The repeated name had no meaning to him, but Smith's innate stubbornness rose defiantly as the crowd surged forward to the very edge of the arc, their clamor growing louder. "Shambleau! Kick her out here! Give us Shambleau! Shambleau!"

Smith dropped his indolent pose like a cloak and planted both feet wide, swinging up his gun threateningly. "Keep back!" he yelled. "She's mine! Keep back!"

He had no intention of using that heat-beam. He knew by now that they would not kill him unless he started the gunplay himself, and he did not mean to give up his life for any girl alive. But a severe mauling he expected, and he braced himself instinctively as the mob heaved within itself.

To his astonishment a thing happened then that he had never known to happen before. At his shouted defiance the foremost of the mob—those who had heard him clearly—drew back a little, not in alarm but evidently surprised. The ex-Patrolman said, "Yours! She's *yours?*" in a voice from which puzzlement crowded out the anger.

Smith spread his booted legs wide before the crouching figure and flourished his gun.

"Yes," he said. "And I'm keeping her! Stand back there!"

The man stared at him wordlessly, and horror and disgust and incredulity mingled on his weather-beaten face. The incredulity triumphed for a moment and he said again,

"*Yours!*"

Smith nodded defiance.

The man stepped back suddenly, unutterable contempt in his very pose. He waved an arm to the crowd and said loudly, "It's—his!" and the press melted away, gone silent, too, and the look of contempt spread from face to face.

The ex-Patrolman spat on the slag-paved street and turned his back indifferently. "Keep her, then," he advised briefly over one shoulder. "But don't let her out again in this town!"

Smith stared in perplexity almost open-mouthed as the suddenly scornful mob began to break up. His mind was in a whirl. That such bloodthirsty animosity should vanish in a breath he could not believe. And the curious mingling of contempt and disgust on the faces he saw baffled him even more. Lakkdarol was anything but a puritan town—it did not enter his head for a moment that his claiming the brown girl as his own had caused that strangely shocked revulsion to spread through the crowd. No, it was something deeper-rooted than that. Instinctive, instant disgust had been in the faces he saw— they would have looked less so if he had admitted cannibalism or *Pharol*-worship.

And they were leaving his vicinity as swiftly as if whatever unknowing sin he had committed were contagious. The street was emptying as rapidly as it had filled. He saw a sleek Venusian glance back over his shoulder as he turned the corner and sneer, "Shambleau!" and the word awoke a new line of speculation in Smith's mind. Shambleau! Vaguely of French origin, it must be. And strange enough to hear it from the lips of Venusians and Martian drylanders, but it was their use of it that puzzled him more. "We never let those things live," the ex-Patrolman had said. It reminded him dimly of something . . . an ancient line from some writing in his own tongue . . . "Thou shalt not suffer a witch to live." He smiled to himself at the similarity, and simultaneously was aware of the girl at his elbow.

She had risen soundlessly. He turned to face her, sheathing his gun and stared at first with curiosity and then in the entirely frank openness with which men regard that which is not wholly human. For she was not. He knew it at a glance, though the brown, sweet body was shaped like a woman's and she wore

the garment of scarlet—he saw it was leather—with an ease that
few unhuman beings achieve toward clothing. He knew it from
the moment he looked into her eyes, and a shiver of unrest
went over him as he met them. They were frankly green as
young grass, with slit-like, feline pupils that pulsed unceasingly, and there was a look of dark, animal wisdom in their
depths—that look of the beast which sees more than man.

There was no hair upon her face—neither brows nor lashes,
and he would have sworn that the tight scarlet turban bound
around her head covered baldness. She had three fingers and
a thumb, and her feet had four digits apiece too, and all six-
teen of them were tipped with round claws that sheathed back
into the flesh like a cat's. She ran her tongue over her lips—a
thin, pink, flat tongue as feline as her eyes—and spoke with
difficulty. He felt that that throat and tongue had never been
shaped for human speech.

"Not—afraid now," she said softly, and her little teeth were
white and pointed as a kitten's.

"What did they want you for?" he asked her curiously.
"What had you done? Shambleau . . . is that your name?"

"I—not talk your—speech," she demurred hesitantly.

"Well, try to—I want to know. Why were they chasing you?
Will you be safe on the street now, or hadn't you better get
indoors somewhere? They looked dangerous."

"I—go with you." She brought it out with difficulty.

"Say you!" Smith grinned. "What are you, anyhow? You
look like a kitten to me."

"Shambleau." She said it somberly.

"Where d'you live? Are you a Martian?"

"I come from—from far—from long ago—far country——"

"Wait!" laughed Smith. "You're getting your wires crossed.
You're not a Martian?"

She drew herself up very straight beside him, lifting the
turbaned head, and there was something queenly in the poise
of her.

"Martian?" she said scornfully. "My people—are—are—you
have no word. Your speech—hard for me."

"What's yours? I might know it—try me."

She lifted her head and met his eyes squarely, and there was in hers a subtle amusement—he could have sworn it.

"Some day I—speak to you in—my own language," she promised, and the pink tongue flicked out over her lips, swiftly, hungrily.

Approaching footsteps on the red pavement interrupted Smith's reply. A dryland Martian came past, reeling a little and exuding an aroma of *segir*-whisky, the Venusian brand. When he caught the red flash of the girl's tatters he turned his head sharply, and as his *segir*-steeped brain took in the fact of her presence he lurched toward the recess unsteadily, bawling, "Shambleau, by *Pharol!* Shambleau!" and reached out a clutching hand.

Smith struck it aside contemptuously.

"On your way, drylander," he advised.

The man drew back and stared, blear-eyed.

"Yours, eh?" he croaked. "*Zut!* You're welcome to it!" And like the ex-Patrolman before him he spat on the pavement and turned away, muttering harshly in the blasphemous tongue of the drylands.

Smith watched him shuffle off, and there was a crease between his colorless eyes, a nameless unease rising within him.

"Come on," he said abruptly to the girl. "If this sort of thing is going to happen we'd better get indoors. Where shall I take you?"

"With—you," she murmured.

He stared down into the flat green eyes. Those ceaselessly pulsing pupils disturbed him, but it seemed to him, vaguely, that behind the animal shallows of her gaze was a shutter—a closed barrier that might at any moment open to reveal the very deeps of that dark knowledge he sensed there.

Roughly he said again, "Come on, then," and stepped down into the street.

She pattered along a pace or two behind him, making no effort to keep up with his long strides, and though Smith—as men know from Venus to Jupiter's moons—walks as softly as a cat, even in spacemen's boots, the girl at his heels slid like a shadow over the rough pavement, making so little sound that even the lightness of his footsteps was loud in the empty street.

Smith chose the less frequented ways of Lakkdarol, and somewhat shamefacedly thanked his nameless gods that his lodgings were not far away, for the few pedestrians he met turned and stared after the two with that by now familiar mingling of horror and contempt which he was as far as ever from understanding.

The room he had engaged was a single cubicle in a lodging-house on the edge of the city. Lakkdarol, raw camp-town that it was in those days, could have furnished little better anywhere within its limits, and Smith's errand there was not one he wished to advertise. He had slept in worse places than this before, and knew that he would do so again.

There was no one in sight when he entered, and the girl slipped up the stairs at his heels and vanished through the door, shadowy, unseen by anyone in the house. Smith closed the door and leaned his broad shoulders against the panels, regarding her speculatively.

She took in what little the room had to offer in a glance—frowsy bed, rickety table, mirror hanging unevenly and cracked against the wall, unpainted chairs—a typical camp-town room in an Earth settlement abroad. She accepted its poverty in that single glance, dismissed it, then crossed to the window and leaned out for a moment, gazing across the low roof-tops toward the barren countryside beyond, red slag under the late afternoon sun.

"You can stay here," said Smith abruptly, "until I leave town. I'm waiting here for a friend to come in from Venus. Have you eaten?"

"Yes," said the girl quickly. "I shall—need no—food for—a while."

"Well—" Smith glanced around the room. "I'll be in some-time tonight. You can go or stay just as you please. Better lock the door behind me."

With no more formality than that he left her. The door closed and he heard the key turn, and smiled to himself. He did not expect, then, ever to see her again.

He went down the steps and out into the late-slanting sunlight with a mind so full of other matters that the brown girl receded very quickly into the background. Smith's errand in Lakkdarol, like most of his errands, is better not spoken of. Man lives as he must, and Smith's living was a perilous affair outside the law and ruled by the ray-gun only. It is enough to say that the shipping-port and its cargoes outbound interested him deeply just now, and that the friend he awaited was Yarol the Venusian, in that swift little Edsel ship the *Maid* that can flash from world to world with a derisive speed that laughs at Patrol boats and leaves pursuers floundering in the ether far behind. Smith and Yarol and the *Maid* were a trinity that had caused the Patrol leaders much worry and many gray hairs in the past, and the future looked very bright to Smith himself that evening as he left his lodging-house.

Lakkdarol roars by night, as Earthmen's camp-towns have a way of doing on every planet where Earth's outposts are, and it was beginning lustily as Smith went down among the awakening lights toward the center of town. His business there does not concern us. He mingled with the crowds where the lights were brightest, and there was the click of ivory counters and the jingle of silver, and red *segir* gurgled invitingly from black Venusian bottles, and much later Smith strolled home-ward under the moving moons of Mars, and if the street wavered a little under his feet now and then—why, that is only understandable. Not even Smith could drink red *segir* at every bar from the *Martian Lamb* to the *New Chicago* and remain entirely steady on his feet. But he found his way back with very little difficulty—considering—and spent a good five minutes hunting for his key before he remembered he had left it in the inner lock for the girl.

He knocked then, and there was no sound of footsteps from within, but in a few moments the latch clicked and the door swung open. She retreated soundlessly before him as he en-tered, and took up her favorite place against the window, leaning back on the sill and outlined against the starry sky beyond. The room was in darkness.

Smith flipped the switch by the door and then leaned back against the panels, steadying himself. The cool night air had sobered him a little, and his head was clear enough—liquor went to Smith's feet, not his head, or he would never have come this far along the lawless way he had chosen. He lounged against the door now and regarded the girl in the sudden glare of the bulbs, blinding a little as much at the scarlet of her clothing as at the light.

"So you stayed," he said.

"I—waited," she answered softly, leaning farther back against the sill and clasping the rough wood with slim, three-fingered hands, pale brown against the darkness.

"Why?"

She did not answer that, but her mouth curved into a slow smile. On a woman it would have been reply enough—provocative, daring. On Shambleau there was something pitiful and horrible in it—so human on the face of one half-animal. And yet . . . that sweet brown body curving so softly from the tatters of scarlet leather—the velvety texture of that brownness —the white-flashing smile. . . . Smith was aware of a stirring excitement within him. After all—time would be hanging heavy now until Yarol came. . . . Speculatively he allowed the steel-pale eyes to wander over her, with a slow regard that missed nothing. And when he spoke he was aware that his voice had deepened a little. . . .

"Come here," he said.

She came forward slowly, on bare clawed feet that made no slightest sound on the floor, and stood before him with downcast eyes and mouth trembling in that pitifully human smile. He took her by the shoulders—velvety soft shoulders, of a creamy smoothness that was not the texture of human flesh. A little tremor went over her, perceptibly, at the contact of his hands. Northwest Smith caught his breath suddenly and dragged her to him . . . sweet yielding brownness in the circle of his arms . . . heard her own breath catch and quicken as her velvety arms closed about his neck. And then he was looking down into her face, very near, and the green animal eyes met his with the pulsing pupils and the flicker of—something —deep behind their shallows—and through the rising clamor of his blood, even as he stooped his lips to hers, Smith felt something deep within him shudder away—inexplicable, instinc-

tive, revolted. What it might be he had no words to tell, but
the very touch of her was suddenly loathsome—so soft and
velvet and unhuman—and it might have been an animal's face
that lifted itself to his mouth—the dark knowledge looked
hungrily from the darkness of those slit pupils—and for a mad
instant he knew that same wild, feverish revulsion he had seen
in the faces of the mob. . . .

"God!" he gasped, a far more ancient invocation against
evil than he realized, then or ever, and he ripped her arms from
his neck, swung her away with such a force that she reeled half
across the room. Smith fell back against the door, breathing
heavily, and stared at her while the wild revolt died slowly
within him.

She had fallen to the floor beneath the window, and as she
lay there against the wall with bent head he saw, curiously,
that her turban had slipped—the turban that he had been so
sure covered baldness—and a lock of scarlet hair fell below
the binding leather, hair as scarlet as her garment, as unhumanly red as her eyes were unhumanly green. He stared,
and shook his head dizzily and stared again, for it seemed to
him that the thick lock of crimson had moved, *squirmed* of itself against her cheek.

At the contact of it her hands flew up and she tucked it away
with a very human gesture and then dropped her head again
into her hands. And from the deep shadow of her fingers he
thought she was staring up at him covertly.

Smith drew a deep breath and passed a hand across his forehead. The inexplicable moment had gone as quickly as it
came—too swiftly for him to understand or analyze it. "Got to
lay off the *segir*," he told himself unsteadily. Had he imagined
that scarlet hair? After all, she was no more than a pretty
brown girl-creature from one of the many half-human races
peopling the planets. No more than that, after all. A pretty
little thing, but animal. . . . He laughed a little shakily.

"No more of that," he said. "God knows I'm no angel, but
there's got to be a limit somewhere. Here." He crossed to the
bed and sorted out a pair of blankets from the untidy heap,
tossing them to the far corner of the room. "You can sleep
there."

Wordlessly she rose from the floor and began to rearrange the blankets, the uncomprehending resignation of the animal eloquent in every line of her.

Smith had a strange dream that night. He thought he had awakened to a room full of darkness and moonlight and moving shadows, for the nearer moon of Mars was racing through the sky and everything on the planet below her was endued with a restless life in the dark. And something . . . some nameless, unthinkable *thing* . . . was coiled about his throat . . . something like a soft snake, wet and warm. It lay loose and light about his neck . . . and it was moving gently, very gently, with a soft, caressive pressure that sent little thrills of delight through every nerve and fiber of him, a perilous delight—beyond physical pleasure, deeper than joy of the mind. That warm softness was caressing the very roots of his soul with a terrible intimacy. The ecstasy of it left him weak, and yet he knew—in a flash of knowledge born of this impossible dream—that the soul should not be handled. . . . And with that knowledge a horror broke upon him, turning the pleasure into a rapture of revulsion, hateful, horrible—but still most foully sweet. He tried to lift his hands and tear the dream-monstrosity from his throat—tried but half-heartedly; for though his soul was revolted to its very deeps, yet the delight of his body was so great that his hands all but refused the attempt. But when at last he tried to lift his arms a cold shock went over him and he found that he could not stir . . . his body lay stony as marble beneath the blankets, a living marble that shuddered with a dreadful delight through every rigid vein.

The revulsion grew strong upon him as he struggled against the paralyzing dream—a struggle of soul against sluggish body —titanically, until the moving dark was streaked with blankness that clouded and closed about him at last and he sank back into the oblivion from which he had awakened.

Next morning, when the bright sunlight shining through Mars' clear thin air awakened him, Smith lay for a while trying to remember. The dream had been more vivid than reality, but he could not now quite recall . . . only that it had been more sweet and horrible than anything else in life. He lay puzzling for a while, until a soft sound from the corner aroused him from his thoughts and he sat up to see the girl lying in a cat-like coil on her blankets, watching him with round, grave eyes. He regarded her somewhat ruefully.

"Morning," he said. "I've just had the devil of a dream. . . . Well, hungry?"

She shook her head silently, and he could have sworn there was a covert gleam of strange amusement in her eyes.

He stretched and yawned, dismissing the nightmare temporarily from his mind.

"What am I going to do with you?" he inquired, turning to more immediate matters. "I'm leaving here in a day or two and I can't take you along, you know. Where'd you come from in the first place?"

Again she shook her head.

"Not telling? Well, it's your own business. You can stay here until I give up the room. From then on you'll have to do your own worrying."

He swung his feet to the floor and reached for his clothes.

Ten minutes later, slipping the heat-gun into its holster at his thigh, Smith turned to the girl. "There's food-concentrate in that box on the table. It ought to hold you until I get back. And you'd better lock the door again after I've gone."

Her wide, unwavering stare was his only answer, and he was not sure she had understood, but at any rate the lock clicked after him as before, and he went down the steps with a faint grin on his lips.

The memory of last night's extraordinary dream was slipping from him, as such memories do, and by the time he had reached the street the girl and the dream and all of yesterday's happenings were blotted out by the sharp necessities of the present.

Again the intricate business that had brought him here claimed his attention. He went about it to the exclusion of all else, and there was a good reason behind everything he did from the moment he stepped out into the street until the time when he turned back again at evening; though had one chosen to follow him during the day his apparently aimless rambling through Lakkdarol would have seemed very pointless.

He must have spent two hours at the least idling by the space-port, watching with sleepy, colorless eyes the ships that came and went, the passengers, the vessels lying at wait, the cargoes—particularly the cargoes. He made the rounds of the town's saloons once more, consuming many glasses of varied liquors in the course of the day and engaging in idle conversation with men of all races and worlds, usually in their own languages, for Smith was a linguist of repute among his contemporaries. He heard the gossip of the spaceways, news from a dozen planets of a thousand different events. He heard the latest joke about the Venusian Emperor and the latest report on the Chino-Aryan war and the latest song hot from the lips of Rose Robertson, whom every man on the civilized planets adored as "the Georgia Rose." He passed the day quite profitably, for his own purposes, which do not concern us now, and it was not until late evening, when he turned homeward again, that the thought of the brown girl in his room took definite shape in his mind, though it had been lurking there, formless and submerged, all day.

He had no idea what comprised her usual diet, but he bought a can of New York roast beef and one of Venusian frog-broth and a dozen fresh canal-apples and two pounds of that Earth lettuce that grows so vigorously in the fertile canal-soil of Mars. He felt that she must surely find something to her liking in this broad variety of edibles, and—for his day had been very satisfactory—he hummed *The Green Hills of Earth* to himself in a surprisingly good baritone as he climbed the stairs.

The door was locked, as before, and he was reduced to kicking the lower panels gently with his boot, for his arms were full. She opened the door with that softness that was characteristic of her and stood regarding him in the semi-darkness as he stumbled to the table with his load. The room was unlit again.

"Why don't you turn on the lights?" he demanded irritably

after he had barked his shin on the chair by the table in an
effort to deposit his burden there.

"Light and—dark—they are alike—to me," she murmured.

"Cat eyes, eh? Well, you look the part. Here, I've brought
you some dinner. Take your choice. Fond of roast beef? Or
how about a little frog-broth?"

She shook her head and backed away a step.

"No," she said. "I can not—eat your food."

Smith's brows wrinkled. "Didn't you have any of the food-
tablets?"

Again the red turban shook negatively.

"Then you haven't had anything for—why, more than
twenty-four hours! You must be starved."

"Not hungry," she denied.

"What can I find for you to eat, then? There's time yet if
I hurry. You've got to eat, child."

"I shall—eat," she said softly. "Before long—I shall—feed.
Have no—worry."

She turned away then and stood at the window, looking out
over the moonlit landscape as if to end the conversation. Smith
cast her a puzzled glance as he opened the can of roast beef.
There had been an odd undernote in that assurance that,
undefinably, he did not like. And the girl had teeth and tongue
and presumably a fairly human digestive system, to judge from
her human form. It was nonsense for her to pretend that he
could find nothing that she could eat. She must have had some
of the food concentrate after all, he decided, prying up the
thermos lid of the inner container to release the long-sealed
savor of the hot meat inside.

"Well, if you won't eat you won't," he observed philo-
sophically as he poured hot broth and diced beef into the
dish-like lid of the thermos can and extracted the spoon from
its hiding-place between the inner and outer receptacles. She
turned a little to watch him as he pulled up a rickety chair
and sat down to the food, and after a while the realization
that her green gaze was fixed so unwinkingly upon him made
the man nervous, and he said between bites of creamy canal-
apple, "Why don't you try a little of this? It's good."

"The food—I eat is—better," her soft voice told him in its

hesitant murmur, and again he felt rather than heard a faint undernote of unpleasantness in the words. A sudden suspicion struck him as he pondered on that last remark—some vague memory of horror-tales told about campfires in the past—and he swung round in the chair to look at her, a tiny, creeping fear unaccountably arising. There had been that in her words —in her unspoken words, that menaced. . . .

She stood up beneath his gaze demurely, wide green eyes with their pulsing pupils meeting his without a falter. But her mouth was scarlet and her teeth were sharp. . . .

"What food do you eat?" he demanded. And then, after a pause, very softly, "Blood?"

She stared at him for a moment, uncomprehending; then something like amusement curled her lips and she said scornfully, "You think me—vampire, eh? No—I am Shambleau!"

Unmistakably there were scorn and amusement in her voice at the suggestion, but as unmistakably she knew what he meant —accepted it as a logical suspicion—vampires! Fairy-tales—but fairy-tales this unhuman, outland creature was most familiar with. Smith was not a credulous man, nor a superstitious one, but he had seen too many strange things himself to doubt that the wildest legend might have a basis of fact. And there was something namelessly strange about her. . . .

He puzzled over it for a while between deep bites of the canal-apple. And though he wanted to question her about a great many things, he did not, for he knew how futile it would be.

He said nothing more until the meat was finished and another canal-apple had followed the first, and he had cleared away the meal by the simple expedient of tossing the empty can out of the window. Then he lay back in the chair and surveyed her from half-closed eyes, colorless in a face tanned like saddle-leather. And again he was conscious of the brown, soft curves of her, velvety—subtle arcs and planes of smooth flesh under the tatters of scarlet leather. Vampire she might be, unhuman she certainly was, but desirable beyond words as she sat submissive beneath his low regard, her red-turbaned head bent, her clawed fingers lying in her lap. They sat very still for a while, and the silence throbbed between them.

She was so like a woman—an Earth woman—sweet and submissive and demure, and softer than soft fur, if he could forget the three-fingered claws and the pulsing eyes—and that
deeper strangeness beyond words. . . . (Had he dreamed that
red lock of hair that moved? Had it been *segir* that woke the
wild revulsion he knew when he held her in his arms? Why
had the mob so thirsted for her?) He sat and stared, and
despite the mystery of her and the half-suspicions that thronged
his mind—for she was so beautifully soft and curved under
those revealing tatters—he slowly realized that his pulses were
mounting, became aware of a kindling within . . . brown
girl-creature with downcast eyes . . . and then the lids lifted
and the green flatness of a cat's gaze met his, and last night's
revulsion woke swiftly again, like a warning bell that clanged
as their eyes met—animal, after all, too sleek and soft for humanity, and that inner strangeness. . . .

Smith shrugged and sat up. His failings were legion, but the
weakness of the flesh was not among the major ones. He mo-
tioned the girl to her pallet of blankets in the corner and
turned to his own bed.

From deeps of sound sleep he awoke much later. He awoke
suddenly and completely, and with that inner excitement that
presages something momentous. He awoke to brilliant moonlight, turning the room so bright that he could see the scarlet
of the girl's rags as she sat up on her pallet. She was awake,
she was sitting with her shoulder half turned to him and her
head bent, and some warning instinct crawled coldly up his
spine as he watched what she was doing. And yet it was a very
ordinary thing for a girl to do—any girl, anywhere. She was
unbinding her turban. . . .

He watched, not breathing, a presentiment of something
horrible stirring in his brain, inexplicably. . . . The red folds
loosened, and—he knew then that he had not dreamed—again
a scarlet lock swung down against her cheek . . . a hair, was
it? a lock of hair? . . . thick as a thick worm it fell, plumply,
against that smooth cheek . . . more scarlet than blood and
thick as a crawling worm . . . and like a worm it crawled.

Smith rose on an elbow, not realizing the motion, and fixed

an unwinking stare, with a sort of sick, fascinated incredulity,
on that—that lock of hair. He had not dreamed. Until now he
had taken it for granted that it was the *segir* which had made
it seem to move on that evening before. But now . . . it was
lengthening, stretching, moving of itself. It must be hair, but
it *crawled;* with a sickening life of its own it squirmed down
against her cheek, caressingly, revoltingly, impossibly. . . .
Wet, it was, and round and thick and shining. . . .

She unfastened the fast fold and whipped the turban off.
From what he saw then Smith would have turned his eyes away
—and he had looked on dreadful things before, without flinch-
ing—but he could not stir. He could only lie there on his elbow
staring at the mass of scarlet, squirming—worms, hairs, what?
—that writhed over her head in a dreadful mockery of ringlets.
And it was lengthening, falling, somehow growing before his
eyes, down over her shoulders in a spilling cascade, a mass that
even at the beginning could never have been hidden under the
skull-tight turban she had worn. He was beyond wondering,
but he realized that. And still it squirmed and lengthened and
fell, and she shook it out in a horrible travesty of a woman
shaking out her unbound hair—until the unspeakable tangle
of it—twisting, writhing, obscenely scarlet—hung to her waist
and beyond, and still lengthened, an endless mass of crawling
horror that until now, somehow, impossibly, had been hidden
under the tight-bound turban. It was like a nest of blind, restless red worms . . . it was—it was like naked entrails endowed
with an unnatural aliveness, terrible beyond words.

Smith lay in the shadows, frozen without and within in a sick
numbness that came of utter shock and revulsion.

She shook out the obscene, unspeakable tangle over her
shoulders, and somehow he knew that she was going to turn in
a moment and that he must meet her eyes. The thought of that
meeting stopped his heart with dread, more awfully than anything else in this nightmare horror; for nightmare it must be,
surely. But he knew without trying that he could not wrench
his eyes away—the sickened fascination of that sight held him
motionless, and somehow there was a certain beauty. . . .

Her head was turning. The crawling awfulnesses rippled
and squirmed at the motion, writhing thick and wet and shin-

ing over the soft brown shoulders about which they fell now in obscene cascades that all but hid her body. Her head was turning. Smith lay numb. And very slowly he saw the round of her cheek foreshorten and her profile come into view, all the scarlet horrors twisting ominously, and the profile shortened in turn and her full face came slowly round toward the bed—moonlight shining brilliantly as day on the pretty girl-face, demure and sweet, framed in tangled obscenity that crawled. . . .

The green eyes met his. He felt a perceptible shock, and a shudder rippled down his paralyzed spine, leaving an icy numbness in its wake. He felt the goose-flesh rising. But that numbness and cold horror he scarcely realized, for the green eyes were locked with his in a long, long look that somehow presaged nameless things—not altogether unpleasant things—the voiceless voice of her mind assailing him with little murmurous promises. . . .

For a moment he went down into a blind abyss of submission; and then somehow the very sight of that obscenity in eyes that did not then realize they saw it, was dreadful enough to draw him out of the seductive darkness . . . the sight of her crawling and alive with unnamable horror.

She rose, and down about her in a cascade fell the squirming scarlet of—of what grew upon her head. It fell in a long, alive cloak to her bare feet on the floor, hiding her in a wave of dreadful, wet, writhing life. She put up her hands and like a swimmer she parted the waterfall of it, tossing the masses back over her shoulders to reveal her own brown body, sweetly curved. She smiled exquisitely, and in starting waves back from her forehead and down about her in a hideous background writhed the snaky wetness of her living tresses. And Smith knew that he looked upon Medusa.

The knowledge of that—the realization of vast backgrounds reaching into misted history—shook him out of his frozen horror for a moment, and in that moment he met her eyes again, smiling, green as glass in the moonlight, half hooded under drooping lids. Through the twisting scarlet she held out her arms. And there was something soul-shakingly desirable about her, so that all the blood surged to his head suddenly and he stumbled to his feet like a sleeper in a dream as she swayed toward him, infinitely graceful, infinitely sweet in her cloak of living horror.

And somehow there was beauty in it, the wet scarlet writhings with moonlight sliding and shining along the thick, worm-round tresses and losing itself in the masses only to glint again and move silvery along writhing tendrils—an awful, shuddering beauty more dreadful than any ugliness could be.

But all this, again, he but half realized, for the insidious murmur was coiling again through his brain, promising, caressing, alluring, sweeter than honey; and the green eyes that held his were clear and burning like the depths of a jewel, and behind the pulsing slits of darkness he was staring into a greater dark that held all things. . . . He had known—dimly he had known when he first gazed into those flat animal shallows that behind them lay this—all beauty and terror, all horror and delight, in the infinite darkness upon which her eyes opened like windows, paned with emerald glass.

Her lips moved, and in a murmur that blended indistinguishably with the silence and the sway of her body and the dreadful sway of her—her hair—she whispered—very softly, very passionately, "I shall—speak to you now—in my own tongue—oh, beloved!".

And in her living cloak she swayed to him, the murmur swelling seductive and caressing in his innermost brain—promising, compelling, sweeter than sweet. His flesh crawled to the horror of her, but it was a perverted revulsion that clasped what it loathed. His arms slid round her under the sliding cloak, wet, wet and warm and hideously alive—and the sweet velvet body was clinging to his, her arms locked about his neck —and with a whisper and a rush the unspeakable horror closed about them both.

In nightmares until he died he remembered that moment when the living tresses of Shambleau first folded him in their embrace. A nauseous, smothering odor as the wetness shut around him—thick, pulsing worms clasping every inch of his body, sliding, writhing, their wetness and warmth striking through his garments as if he stood naked to their embrace.

All this in a graven instant—and after that a tangled flash of conflicting sensation before oblivion closed over him. For he

remembered the dream—and knew it for nightmare reality
now, and the sliding, gently moving caresses of those wet,
warm worms upon his flesh was an ecstasy above words—that
deeper ecstasy that strikes beyond the body and beyond the
mind and tickles the very roots of the soul with unnatural delight. So he stood, rigid as marble, as helplessly stony as any
of Medusa's victims in ancient legends were, while the terrible
pleasure of Shambleau thrilled and shuddered through every
fiber of him; through every atom of his body and the intangible atoms of what men call the soul, through all that was
Smith the dreadful pleasure ran. And it was truly dreadful.
Dimly he knew it, even as his body answered to the root-deep
ecstasy, a foul and dreadful wooing from which his very soul
shuddered away—and yet in the innermost depths of that soul
some grinning traitor shivered with delight. But deeply, behind all this, he knew horror and revulsion and despair beyond telling, while the intimate caresses crawled obscenely in
the secret places of his soul—knew that the soul should not be
handled—and shook with the perilous pleasure through it all.

And this conflict and knowledge, this mingling of rapture
and revulsion all took place in the flashing of a moment while
the scarlet worms coiled and crawled upon him, sending deep,
obscene tremors of that infinite pleasure into every atom that
made up Smith. And he could not stir in that slimy, ecstatic
embrace—and a weakness was flooding that grew deeper after
each succeeding wave of intense delight, and the traitor in his
soul strengthened and drowned out the revulsion—and something within him ceased to struggle as he sank wholly into a
blazing darkness that was oblivion to all else but that devouring rapture. . . .

The young Venusian climbing the stairs to his friend's lodg-
ing-room pulled out his key absent-mindedly, a pucker forming between his fine brows. He was slim, as all Venusians are,
as fair and sleek as any of them, and as with most of his coun-
trymen the look of cherubic innocence on his face was wholly
deceptive. He had the face of a fallen angel, without Lucifer's
majesty to redeem it; for a black devil grinned in his eyes and
there were faint lines of ruthlessness and dissipation about his

mouth to tell of the long years behind him that had run the
gamut of experiences and made his name, next to Smith's, the
most hated and the most respected in the records of the Patrol.

He mounted the stairs now with a puzzled frown between his
eyes. He had come into Lakkdarol on the noon liner—the *Maid*
in her hold very skillfully disguised with paint and otherwise
—to find in lamentable disorder the affairs he had expected to
be settled. And cautious inquiry elicited the information that
Smith had not been seen for three days. That was not like his
friend—he had never failed before, and the two stood to lose
not only a large sum of money but also their personal safety
by the inexplicable lapse on the part of Smith. Yarol could
think of one solution only: fate had at last caught up with his
friend. Nothing but physical disability could explain it.

Still puzzling, he fitted his key in the lock and swung the
door open.

In that first moment, as the door opened, he sensed something very wrong. . . . The room was darkened, and for a
while he could see nothing, but at the first breath he scented
a strange, unnamable odor, half sickening, half sweet. And
deep stirrings of ancestral memory awoke within him—ancient
swamp-born memories from Venusian ancestors far away and
long ago. . . .

Yarol laid his hand on his gun, lightly, and opened the door
wider. In the dimness all he could see at first was a curious
mound in the far corner. . . . Then his eyes grew accustomed
to the dark, and he saw it more clearly, a mound that somehow heaved and stirred within itself. . . . A mound of—he
caught his breath sharply—a mound like a mass of entrails,
living, moving, writhing with an unspeakable aliveness. Then
a hot Venusian oath broke from his lips and he cleared the
door-sill in a swift stride, slammed the door and set his back
against it, gun ready in his hand, although his flesh crawled
—for he *knew*. . . .

"Smith!" he said softly, in a voice thick with horror. "Northwest!"

The moving mass stirred—shuddered—sank back into crawling quiescence again.

"Smith! Smith!" The Venusian's voice was gentle and in-sistent, and it quivered a little with terror.

An impatient ripple went over the whole mass of aliveness in the corner. It stirred again, reluctantly, and then tendril by writhing tendril it began to part itself and fall aside, and very slowly the brown of a spaceman's leather appeared beneath it, all slimed and shining.

"Smith! Northwest!" Yarol's persistent whisper came again, urgently, and with a dream-like slowness the leather garments moved . . . a man sat up in the midst of the writhing worms, a man who once, long ago, might have been Northwest Smith. From head to foot he was slimy from the embrace of the crawl-ing horror about him. His face was that of some creature beyond humanity—dead-alive, fixed in a gray stare, and the look of terrible ecstasy that overspread it seemed to come from somewhere far within, a faint reflection from immeasurable distances beyond the flesh. And as there is mystery and magic in the moonlight which is after all but a reflection of the every-day sun, so in that gray face turned to the door was a terror unnamable and sweet, a reflection of ecstasy beyond the un-derstanding of any who have known only earthly ecstasy them-selves. And as he sat there turning a blank, eyeless face to Yarol the red worms writhed ceaselessly about him, very gently, with a soft, caressive motion that never slacked.

"Smith . . . come here! Smith . . . get up . . . Smith, Smith!" Yarol's whisper hissed in the silence, commanding, urgent—but he made no move to leave the door.

And with a dreadful slowness, like a dead man rising, Smith stood up in the nest of slimy scarlet. He swayed drunkenly on his feet, and two or three crimson tendrils came writhing up his legs to the knees and wound themselves there, support-ingly, moving with a ceaseless caress that seemed to give him some hidden strength, for he said then, without inflection,

"Go away. Go away. Leave me alone." And the dead ecstatic face never changed.

"Smith!" Yarol's voice was desperate. "Smith, listen! Smith, can't you hear me?"

"Go away," the monotonous voice said. "Go away. Go away. Go—"

"Not unless you come too. Can't you hear? Smith! Smith! I'll—"

He hushed in mid-phrase, and once more the ancestral prickle of race-memory shivered down his back, for the scarlet mass was moving again, violently, rising. . . .

Yarol pressed back against the door and gripped his gun, and the name of a god he had forgotten years ago rose to his lips unbidden. For he knew what was coming next, and the knowledge was more dreadful than any ignorance could have been.

The red, writhing mass rose higher, and the tendrils parted and a human face looked out—no, half human, with green cat-eyes that shone in that dimness like lighted jewels, compellingly. . . .

Yarol breathed "Shar!" again, and flung up an arm across his face, and the tingle of meeting that green gaze for even an instant went thrilling through him perilously.

"Smith!" he called in despair. "Smith, can't you hear me?"

"Go away," said that voice that was not Smith's. "Go away."

And somehow, although he dared not look, Yarol knew that the—the other—had parted those worm-thick tresses and stood there in all the human sweetness of the brown, curved woman's body, cloaked in living horror. And he felt the eyes upon him, and something was crying insistently in his brain to lower that shielding arm. . . . He was lost—he knew it, and the knowledge gave him that courage which comes from despair. The voice in his brain was growing, swelling, deafening him with a roaring command that all but swept him before it—command to lower that arm—to meet the eyes that opened upon darkness—to submit—and a promise, murmurous and sweet and evil beyond words, of pleasure to come. . . .

But somehow he kept his head—somehow, dizzily, he was gripping his gun in his upflung hand—somehow, incredibly, crossing the narrow room with averted face, groping for Smith's shoulder. There was a moment of blind fumbling in emptiness, and then he found it, and gripped the leather that was slimy and dreadful and wet—and simultaneously he felt something loop gently about his ankle and a shock of repulsive pleasure went through him, and then another coil, and another, wound about his feet. . . .

Yarol set his teeth and gripped the shoulder hard, and his hand shuddered of itself, for the feel of that leather was slimy as the worms about his ankles, and a faint tingle of obscene delight went through him from the contact.

That caressive pressure on his legs was all he could feel, and the voice in his brain drowned out all other sounds, and his body obeyed him reluctantly—but somehow he gave one heave of tremendous effort and swung Smith, stumbling, out of that nest of horror. The twining tendrils ripped loose with a little sucking sound, and the whole mass quivered and reached after, and then Yarol forgot his friend utterly and turned his whole being to the hopeless task of freeing himself. For only a part of him was fighting, now—only a part of him struggled against the twining obscenities, and in his innermost brain the sweet, seductive murmur sounded, and his body clamored to surrender. . . .

"*Shar! Shar y'danis . . . Shar mor'la-rol—*" prayed Yarol, gasping and half unconscious that he spoke, boy's prayers that he had forgotten years ago, and with his back half turned to the central mass he kicked desperately with his heavy boots at the red, writhing worms about him. They gave back before him, quivering and curling themselves out of reach, and though he knew that more were reaching for his throat from behind, at least he could go on struggling until he was forced to meet those eyes. . . .

He stamped and kicked and stamped again, and for one instant he was free of the slimy grip as the bruised worms curled back from his heavy feet, and he lurched away dizzily, sick with revulsion and despair as he fought off the coils, and then he lifted his eyes and saw the cracked mirror on the wall. Dimly in its reflection he could see the writhing scarlet horror behind him, cat face peering out with its demure girl-smile, dreadfully human, and all the red tendrils reaching after him. And remembrance of something he had read long ago swept incongruously over him, and the gasp of relief and hope that he gave shook for a moment the grip of the command in his brain.

Without pausing for a breath he swung the gun over his shoulder, the reflected barrel in line with the reflected horror in the mirror, and flicked the catch.

In the mirror he saw its blue flame leap in a dazzling spate across the dimness, full into the midst of that squirming, reaching mass behind him. There was a hiss and a blaze and a high, thin scream of inhuman malice and despair—the flame cut a wide arc and went out as the gun fell from his hand, and Yarol pitched forward to the floor.

Northwest Smith opened his eyes to Martian sunlight streaming thinly through the dingy window. Something wet and cold was slapping his face, and the familiar fiery sting of *segir*-whisky burnt his throat.

"Smith!" Yarol's voice was saying from far away. "N. W.! Wake up, damn you! Wake up!"

"I'm—awake," Smith managed to articulate thickly. "Wha's matter?"

Then a cup-rim was thrust against his teeth and Yarol said irritably, "Drink it, you fool!"

Smith swallowed obediently and more of the fire-hot *segir* flowed down his grateful throat. It spread a warmth through his body that awakened him from the numbness that had gripped him until now, and helped a little toward driving out the all-devouring weakness he was becoming aware of slowly. He lay still for a few minutes while the warmth of the whisky went through him, and memory sluggishly began to permeate his brain with the spread of the *segir*. Nightmare memories . . . sweet and terrible . . . memories of—

"God!" gasped Smith suddenly, and tried to sit up. Weakness smote him like a blow, and for an instant the room wheeled as he fell back against something firm and warm—Yarol's shoulder. The Venusian's arm supported him while the room steadied, and after a while he twisted a little and stared into the other's black gaze.

Yarol was holding him with one arm and finishing the mug of *segir* himself, and the black eyes met his over the rim and crinkled into sudden laughter, half hysterical after that terror that was passed.

"By *Pharol!*" gasped Yarol, choking into his mug. "By *Pharol,* N. W.! I'm never gonna let you forget this! Next time you have to drag me out of a mess I'll say—"

"Let it go," said Smith. "What's been going on? How—"

"Shambleau." Yarol's laughter died. "Shambleau! What were you doing with a thing like that?"

"What was it?" Smith asked soberly.

"Mean to say you didn't know? But where'd you find it? How—"

"Suppose you tell me first what you know," said Smith firmly. "And another swig of that *segir,* too, please. I need it."

"Can you hold the mug now? Feel better?"

"Yeah—some. I can hold it—thanks. Now go on."

"Well—I don't know just where to start. They call them Shambleau—"

"Good God, is there more than one?"

"It's a—a sort of race, I think, one of the very oldest. Where they come from nobody knows. The name sounds a little French, doesn't it? But it goes back beyond the start of history. There have always been Shambleau."

"I never heard of 'em."

"Not many people have. And those who know don't care to talk about it much."

"Well, half this town knows. I hadn't any idea what they were talking about, then. And I still don't understand, but—"

"Yes, it happens like this, sometimes. They'll appear, and the news will spread and the town will get together and hunt them down, and after that—well, the story doesn't get around very far. It's too—too unbelievable."

"But—my God, Yarol!—what was it? Where'd it come from? How—"

"Nobody knows just where they come from. Another planet —maybe some undiscovered one. Some say Venus—I know there are some rather awful legends of them handed down in our family—that's how I've heard about it. And the minute I opened that door, awhile back—I—I think I knew that smell. . . ."

"But—what *are* they?"

"God knows. Not human, though they have the human

form. Or that may be only an illusion . . . or maybe I'm crazy.
I don't know. They're a species of the vampire—or maybe the
vampire is a species of—of them. Their normal form must be
that—that mass, and in that form they draw nourishment from
the—I suppose the life-forces of men. And they take some form
—usually a woman form, I think, and key you up to the highest
pitch of emotion before they—begin. That's to work the life-
force up to intensity so it'll be easier. . . . And they give,
always, that horrible, foul pleasure as they—feed. There are
some men who, if they survive the first experience, take to it
like a drug—can't give it up—keep the thing with them all
their lives—which isn't long—feeding it for that ghastly satisfaction. Worse than smoking *ming* or—or 'praying to *Pharol*.' "

"Yes," said Smith. "I'm beginning to understand why that
crowd was so surprised and—and disgusted when I said—well,
never mind. Go on."

"Did you get to talk to—to it?" asked Yarol.

"I tried to. It couldn't speak very well. I asked it where it
came from and it said—'from far away and long ago'—something like that."

"I wonder. Possibly some unknown planet—but I think not.
You know there are so many wild stories with some basis of
fact to start from, that I've sometimes wondered—mightn't
there be a lot more of even worse and wilder superstitions
we've never even heard of? Things like this, blasphemous and
foul, that those who know have to keep still about? Awful,
fantastic things running around loose that we never hear
rumors of at all!

"These things—they've been in existence for countless ages.
No one knows when or where they first appeared. Those
who've seen them, as we saw this one, don't talk about it. It's
just one of those vague, misty rumors you find half hinted at
in old books sometimes. . . . I believe they are an older race
than man, spawned from ancient seed in times before ours,
perhaps on planets that have gone to dust, and so horrible to
man that when they are discovered the discoverers keep still
about it—forget them again as quickly as they can.

"And they go back to time immemorial. I suppose you recognized the legend of Medusa? There isn't any question that

the ancient Greeks knew of them. Does it mean that there
have been civilizations before yours that set out from Earth
and explored other planets? Or did one of the Shambleau
somehow make its way into Greece three thousand years ago?
If you think about it long enough you'll go off your head! I
wonder how many other legends are based on things like this
—things we don't suspect, things we'll never know.

"The Gorgon, Medusa, a beautiful woman with—with snakes
for hair, and a gaze that turned men to stone, and Perseus
finally killed her—I remembered this just by accident, N. W.,
and it saved your life and mine—Perseus killed her by using
a mirror as he fought to reflect what he dared not look at
directly. I wonder what the old Greek who first started that
legend would have thought if he'd known that three thousand
years later his story would save the lives of two men on another planet. I wonder what that Greek's own story was, and
how he met the thing, and what happened. . . .

"Well, there's a lot we'll never know. Wouldn't the records
of that race of—of *things,* whatever they are, be worth reading!
Records of other planets and other ages and all the beginnings
of mankind! But I don't suppose they've kept any records. I
don't suppose they've even any place to keep them—from what
little I know, or anyone knows about it, they're like the Wandering Jew, just bobbing up here and there at long intervals,
and where they stay in the meantime I'd give my eyes to
know! But I don't believe that terribly hypnotic power they
have indicates any superhuman intelligence. It's their means
of getting food—just like a frog's long tongue or a carnivorous
flower's odor. Those are physical because the frog and the
flower eat physical food. The Shambleau uses a—a mental reach
to get mental food. I don't quite know how to put it. And just
as a beast that eats the bodies of other animals acquires with
each meal greater power over the bodies of the rest, so the
Shambleau, stoking itself up with the life-forces of men, in-
creases its power over the minds and the souls of other men.
But I'm talking about things I can't define—things I'm not
sure exist.

"I only know that when I felt—when those tentacles closed
around my legs—I didn't want to pull loose, I felt sensations

that—that—oh, I'm fouled and filthy to the very deepest part of me by that—pleasure—and yet—"

"I know," said Smith slowly. The effect of the *segir* was beginning to wear off, and weakness was washing back over him in waves, and when he spoke he was half meditating in a low voice, scarcely realizing that Yarol listened. "I know it—much better than you do—and there's something so indescribably awful that the thing emanates, something so utterly at odds with everything human—there aren't any words to say it. For a while I was a part of it, literally, sharing its thoughts and memories and emotions and hungers, and—well, it's over now and I don't remember very clearly, but the only part left free was that part of me that was all but insane from the—the obscenity of the thing. And yet it was a pleasure so sweet—I think there must be some nucleus of utter evil in me—in everyone—that needs only the proper stimulus to get complete control; because even while I was sick all through from the touch of those—things—there was something in me that was—was simply gibbering with delight. . . . Because of that I saw things—and knew things—horrible, wild things I can't quite remember—visited unbelievable places, looked backward through the memory of that—creature—I was one with, and saw—God, I wish I could remember!"

"You ought to thank your God you can't," said Yarol soberly.

His voice roused Smith from the half-trance he had fallen into, and he rose on his elbow, swaying a little from weakness. The room was wavering before him, and he closed his eyes, not to see it, but he asked, "You say they—they don't turn up again? No way of finding—another?"

Yarol did not answer for a moment. He laid his hands on the other man's shoulders and pressed him back, and then sat staring down into the dark, ravaged face with a new, strange, undefinable look upon it that he had never seen there before—whose meaning he knew, too well.

"Smith," he said finally, and his black eyes for once were steady and serious, and the little grinning devil had vanished from behind them, "Smith, I've never asked your word on anything before, but I've—I've earned the right to do it now, and I'm asking you to promise me one thing."

Smith's colorless eyes met the black gaze unsteadily. Irresolution was in them, and a little fear of what that promise might be. And for just a moment Yarol was looking, not into his friend's familiar eyes, but into a wide gray blankness that held all horror and delight—a pale sea with unspeakable pleasures sunk beneath it. Then the wide stare focused again and Smith's eyes met his squarely and Smith's voice said, "Go ahead. I'll promise."

"That if you ever should meet a Shambleau again—ever, anywhere—you'll draw your gun and burn it to hell the instant you realize what it is. Will you promise me that?"

There was a long silence. Yarol's somber black eyes bored relentlessly into the colorless ones of Smith, not wavering. And the veins stood out on Smith's tanned forehead. He never broke his word—he had given it perhaps half a dozen times in his life, but once he had given it, he was incapable of breaking it. And once more the gray seas flooded in a dim tide of memories, sweet and horrible beyond dreams. Once more Yarol was staring into blankness that hid nameless things. The room was very still.

The gray tide ebbed. Smith's eyes, pale and resolute as steel, met Yarol's levelly.

"I'll—try," he said. And his voice wavered.

Black God's Shadow

THROUGH Jirel's dreams a faraway voice went wailing. She opened yellow eyes upon darkness and lay still for a while, wondering what had waked her and staring into the gloom of her tower chamber, listening to the familiar night sounds of the sentry on the battlements close overhead, the rattle of armor and the soft shuffle of feet in the straw laid down to muffle the sound so that Joiry's lady might sleep in peace.

And as she lay there in the dark, quite suddenly the old illusion came over her again. She felt the pressure of strong mailed arms and the weight of a bearded mouth insolently upon hers, and she closed her red lips on an oath at her own weakness and knew again the sting of helpless tears behind her eyelids.

She lay quiet, remembering. Guillaume—so hatefully magnificent in his armor, grinning down upon her from her own dais in her own castle hall where her own dead soldiers lay scattered about upon the bloody flags. Guillaume—his arms hard about her, his mouth heavy upon her own. Even now anger swept like a flame across her memory in answer to the arrogance and scorn of that conqueror's kiss. Yet was it anger? —was it hatred? And how had she to know, until he lay dead at last at her vengeful feet, that it was not hate which bubbled up so hotly whenever she remembered the insolence of his arms, or that he had defeated her men and conquered unconquerable Joiry? For she had been the commander of the strongest fortress in the kingdom, and called no man master, and it was her proudest boast that Joiry would never fall, and that no lover dared lay hands upon her save in answer to her smile.

No, it had not been hatred which answered Guillaume's overwhelming arrogance. Not hate, though the fire and fury of it had gone storming like madness through her. So many loves had blown lightly through her life before—how was she to know this surge of heady violence for what it was, until too late? Well, it was ended now.

She had gone down the secret way that she and one other knew, down into that dark and nameless hell which none who wore a cross might enter, where God's dominion ended at the portals, and who could tell what strange and terrible gods held sway instead? She remembered the starry darkness of it, and the voices that cried along the wind, and the brooding perils she could not understand. No other thing than the flame of her—hatred?—could have driven her down, and nothing but its violence could have sustained her along the dark ways she went seeking a weapon worthy to slay Guillaume.

Well, she had found it. She had taken the black god's kiss. Heavy and cold upon her soul she had carried it back, feeling the terrible weight bearing down upon some intangible part of her that shuddered and shrank from the touch. She had fouled her very soul with that burden, but she had not guessed what terrible potentialities it bore within it, like some egg of hell's spawning to slay the man she loved.

Her weapon was a worthy one. She smiled grimly, remembering that—remembering her return, and how triumphantly he had accepted that kiss from hell, not understanding. . . . Again she saw the awful fruition of her vengeance, as the chill of her soul's burden shifted, through the meeting of their mouths, from her soul to his. Again she saw the spreading of that nameless emotion from Beyond through his shuddering body, an iron despair which no flesh and blood could endure.

Yes, a worthy weapon. She had periled her soul in the seeking of it, and slain him with a god-cursed kiss, and known too late that she would never love another man. Guillaume—tall and splendid in his armor, the little black beard split by the whiteness of his grin, and arrogance sneering from his scarred and scornful face. Guillaume—whose kiss would haunt her all

the nights of her life. Guillaume—who was dead. In the dark
she hid her face upon her bent arm, and the red hair fell forward to smother her sobs.

When sleep came again she did not know. But presently she
was alone in a dim, formless place through whose mists the far-
away voice wailed fretfully. It was a familiar voice with
strange, plaintive overtones—a sad little lost voice wailing
through the dark.

"Oh, Jirel," it moaned reedily, the tiniest thread of sound.
"Oh, Jirel—my murderess. . . ."

And in the dream her heart stood still, and—though she
had killed more men than one—she thought she knew that
voice, tiny and thin though it was in the bodiless dark of her
sleep. And she held her breath, listening. It came again, "Oh,
Jirel! It is Guillaume calling—Guillaume, whom you slew. Is
there no end to your vengeance? Have mercy, oh my murderess!
Release my soul from the dark god's torment. Oh Jirel—Jirel—
I pray your mercy!"

Jirel awoke wet-eyed and lay there staring into the dark, re-
calling that pitiful little reedy wail which had once been
Guillaume's rich, full-throated voice. And wondering. The
dark god? True, Guillaume had died unshriven, with all his
sins upon him, and because of this she had supposed that his
soul plunged straight downward to the gates of hell.

Yet—could it be? By the power of that infernal kiss which she
had braved the strange dark place underground to get as a
weapon against him—by the utter strangeness of it, and the
unhuman death he died, it must be that now his naked soul
wandered, lost and lonely, through that nameless hell lit by
strange stars, where ghosts moved in curious forms through the
dark. And he asked her mercy—Guillaume, who in life had
asked mercy of no living creature.

She heard the watch changing on the battlements above,
and dropped again into an uneasy slumber, and once more
entered the dim place where the little voice cried through the
mist, wailing piteously for mercy from her vengeance. Guillaume—the proud Guillaume, with his deep voice and scornful eyes. Guillaume's lost soul wailing through her dreams

. . . "Have mercy upon me, oh my murderess!" . . . and
again she woke with wet eyes and started up, staring wildly
around her in the gloom and thinking that surely she heard
yet the echo of the little lost voice crying. And as the sound
faded from her ears she knew that she must go down again.

For a while she lay there, shivering a little and forcing herself into the knowledge. Jirel was a brave woman and a savage
warrior, and the most reckless soldier of all her men-at-arms.
There was not a man for miles about who did not fear and
respect Joiry's commander—her sword-keen beauty and her
reckless courage and her skill at arms. But at the thought of
what she must do to save Guillaume's soul the coldness of
terror blew over her and her heart contracted forebodingly.
To go down again—down into the perilous, star-lit dark among
dangers more dreadful than she could put words to—dared she?
Dared she go?

She rose at last, cursing her own weakness. The stars through
the narrow windows watched her pull on her doeskin shirt
and the brief tunic of linked mail over it. She buckled the
greaves of a long-dead Roman legionary on her slim, strong
legs, and, as on that unforgettable night not long since when
she had dressed for this same journey, she took her two-edged
sword unsheathed in her hand.

Again she went down through the dark of the sleeping castle.
Joiry's dungeons are deep, and she descended a long way
through the oozing, dank corridors underground, past cells
where the bones of Joiry's enemies rotted in forgotten chains.
And she, who feared no living man, was frightened in that
haunted dark, and gripped her sword closer and clutched the
cross at her neck with nervous fingers. The silence hurt her
ears with its weight, and the dark was like a bandage over her
straining eyes.

At the end of the last oozing passage, far underground, she
came to a wall. With her free hand she set to work pulling the
unmortared stones from their places, making an opening to
squeeze through—trying not to remember that upon this spot
that dreadful night tall Guillaume had died, with the black
god's kiss burning upon his mouth and unnamable torment
in his eyes. Here upon these stones. Against the darkness

vividly she could see that torch-lit scene, and Guillaume's long,
mailed body sprawled across the floor. She would never forget
that. Perhaps even after she died she would remember the
smoky, acrid smell of the torches, and the coldness of the stones
under her bare knees as she knelt beside the body of the man
she had killed; the choke in her throat, and the brush of the
red hair against her cheek, falling forward to mask her tears
from the stolid men-at-arms. And Guillaume—Guillaume . . .

She took her lip between her teeth resolutely, and turned her
mind to the pulling out of stones. Presently there was a hole
big enough for her slim height, and she pushed through into
the solid dark beyond. Her feet were upon a ramp, and she
went down cautiously, feeling her way with exploring toes.
When the floor leveled she dropped to her knees and felt for
the remembered circle in the pavement. She found that, and
the curious cold ring in its center, of some nameless metal
which daylight had never shone upon, metal so smooth and
cold and strange that her fingers shuddered as she gripped it
and heaved. That lid was heavy. As before, she had to take
her sword in her teeth, for she dared not lay it down, and use
both hands to lift the stone circle. It rose with an odd little
sighing sound, as if some suction from below had gripped it
and were released.

She sat on the edge for a moment, swinging her feet in the
opening and gathering all her courage for the plunge. When
she dared hesitate no longer, for fear she would never descend
if she delayed another instant, she caught her breath and
gripped her sword hard and plunged.

It must have been the strangest descent that the world has
known—not a shaft but a spiral twisting down in smooth, cork-
screw loops, a spiral made for no human creature to travel, yet
into whose sides in some forgotten era a nameless human had
cut notches for hands and feet, so that Jirel went down more
slowly than if she had had to take an unbroken plunge. She
slipped smoothly along down the spirals, barely braking her
passage now and again by grasping at the notches in the wall
when she felt herself sliding too fast.

Presently the familiar sickness came over her—that strange,
inner dizziness as if the spiral were taking her not only through

space but through dimensions, and the very structure of her
body were altering and shifting with the shifting spirals. And
it seemed, too, that down any other shaft she would have fallen
more swiftly. This was not a free glide downward—she scarcely
seemed to be falling at all. In the spiral there was neither up
nor down, and the sickness intensified until in the whirling
loops and the whirling dizziness she lost all count of time and
distance, and slid through the dark in a stupor of her own
misery.

At long last the spiral straightened and began to incline less
steeply, and she knew that she approached the end. It was hard
work then, levering herself along the gentle slope on hands and
knees, and when she came out at last into open darkness she
scrambled to her feet and stood panting, sword in hand, straining her eyes against the impenetrable dark of this place that
must be without counterpart anywhere in the world, or outside
it. There were perils here, but she scarcely thought of them as
she set out through the dark, for remembering those greater
perils beyond.

She went forward warily for all that, swinging her sword in
cautious arcs before her that she might not run full-tilt into
some invisible horror. It was an unpleasant feeling, this groping through blackness, knowing eyes upon her, feeling presences near her, watching. Twice she heard hoarse breathing,
and once the splat of great wet feet upon stone, but nothing
touched her or tried to bar her passage.

Nevertheless she was shaking with tension and terror when
at last she reached the end of the passage. There was no visible
sign to tell her that it was ended, but as before, suddenly she
sensed that the oppression of those vast weights of earth on all
sides had lifted. She was standing at the threshold of some
mighty void. The very darkness had a different quality—and
at her throat something constricted.

Jirel gripped her sword a little more firmly and felt for the
crucifix at her neck—found it—lifted the chain over her head.

Instantly a burst of blinding radiance smote her dark-accus-
tomed eyes more violently than a blow. She stood at a cave
mouth, high on the side of a hill, staring out over the most

blazing day she had ever seen. Heat and light shimmered in
the dazzle: strangely colored light, heat that danced and shook.
Day, over a dreadful land.

Jirel cried out inarticulately and clapped a hand over her
outraged eyes, groping backward step by step into the shelter-
ing dark of the cave. Night in this land was terrible enough,
but day—no, she dared not look upon the strange hell save
when darkness veiled it. She remembered that other journey,
when she had raced the dawn up the hillside, shuddering,
averting her eyes from the terror of her own misshapen
shadow forming upon the stones. No, she must wait, how long
she could not guess; for though it had been night above
ground when she left, here was broad day, and it might be that
day in this land was of a different duration from that she
knew.

She drew back farther into the cave, until that dreadful
day was no more than a blur upon the darkness, and sat down
with her back to the rock and the sword across her bare knees,
waiting. That blurred light upon the walls had a curious tinge
of color such as she had never seen in any earthly daylight. It
seemed to her that it shimmered—paled and deepened and
brightened again as if the illumination were not steady. It had
almost the quality of firelight in its fluctuations.

Several times something seemed to pass across the cave-
mouth, blotting out the light for an instant, and once she saw
a great, stooping shadow limned upon the wall, as if something had paused to peer within the cave. And at the thought
of what might rove this land by day Jirel shivered as if in a
chill wind, and groped for her crucifix before she remembered
that she no longer wore it.

She waited for a long while, clasping cold hands about her
knees, watching that blur upon the wall in fascinated anticipation. After a time she may have dozed a little, with the light,
unresting sleep of one poised to wake at the tiniest sound or
motion. It seemed to her that eternities went by before the
light began to pale upon the cave wall.

She watched it fading. It did not move across the wall as
sunlight would have done. The blur remained motionless, dim-
ming slowly, losing its tinge of unearthly color, taking on the

blueness of evening. Jirel stood up and paced back and forth to limber her stiffened body. But not until that blur had faded so far that no more than the dimmest glimmer of radiance lay upon the stone did she venture out again toward the cave mouth.

Once more she stood upon the hilltop, looking out over a land lighted by strange constellations that sprawled across the sky in pictures whose outlines she could not quite trace, though there was about them a dreadful familiarity. And, looking up upon the spreading patterns in the sky, she realized afresh that this land, whatever it might be, was no underground cavern of whatever vast dimensions. It was open air she breathed, and stars in a celestial void she gazed upon, and however she had come here, she was no longer under the earth.

Below her the dim country spread. And it was not the same landscape she had seen on that other journey. No mighty column of shadowless light swept skyward in the distance. She caught the glimmer of a broad river where no river had flowed before, and the ground here and there was patched and checkered with pale radiance, like luminous fields laid out orderly upon the darkness.

She stepped down the hill delicately, poised for the attack of those tiny, yelping horrors that had raved about her knees once before. They did not come. Surprised, hoping against hope that she was to be spared that nauseating struggle, she went on. The way down was longer than she remembered. Stones turned under her feet, and coarse grass slashed at her knees. She was wondering as she descended where her search was to begin, for in all the dark, shifting land she saw nothing to guide her, and Guillaume's voice was no more than a fading memory from her dream. She could not even find her way back to the lake where the black god crouched, for the whole landscape was changed unrecognizably.

So when, unmolested, she reached the foot of the hill, she set off at random over the dark earth, running as before with that queer dancing lightness, as if the gravity pull of this place were less than that to which she was accustomed, so that the ground seemed to skim past under her flying feet. It was like a dream, this effortless glide through the darkness, fleet as the wind.

Presently she began to near one of those luminous patches that resembled fields, and saw now that they were indeed a sort of garden. The luminosity rose from myriads of tiny, darting lights planted in even rows, and when she came near enough she saw that the lights were small insects, larger than fireflies, and with luminous wings which they beat vainly upon the air, darting from side to side in a futile effort to be free. For each was attached to its little stem, as if they had sprung living from the soil. Row upon row of them stretched into the dark.

She did not even speculate upon who had sowed such seed here, or toward what strange purpose. Her course led her across a corner of the field, and as she ran she broke several of the stems, releasing the shining prisoners. They buzzed up around her instantly, angrily as bees, and wherever a luminous wing brushed her a hot pain stabbed. She beat them off after a while and ran on, skirting other fields with new wariness.

She crossed a brook that spoke to itself in the dark with a queer, whispering sound so near to speech that she paused for an instant to listen, then thought she had caught a word or two of such dreadful meaning that she ran on again, wondering if it could have been only an illusion.

Then a breeze sprang up and brushed the red hair from her ears, and it seemed to her that she caught the faintest, far wailing. She stopped dead-still, listening, and the breeze stopped too. But she was almost certain she had heard that voice again, and after an instant's hesitation she turned in the direction from which the breeze had blown.

It led toward the river. The ground grew rougher, and she began to hear water running with a subdued, rushing noise, and presently again the breeze brushed her face. Once more she thought she could hear the dimmest echo of the voice that had cried in her dreams.

When she came to the brink of the water she paused for a moment, looking down to where the river rushed between steep banks. The water had a subtle difference in appearance

from water in the rivers she knew—somehow thicker, for all its
swift flowing. When she leaned out to look, her face was mirrored monstrously upon the broken surface, in a way that no
earthly water would reflect, and as the image fell upon its
torrent the water broke there violently, leaping upward and
splashing as if some hidden rock had suddenly risen in its bed.
There was a hideous eagerness about it, as if the water were
ravening for her, rising in long, hungry leaps against the rocky
walls to splash noisily and run back into the river. But each
leap came higher against the wall, and Jirel started back in
something like alarm, a vague unease rising within her at the
thought of what might happen if she waited until the striving
water reached high enough.

At her withdrawal the tumult lessened instantly, and after
a moment or so she knew by the sound that the river had
smoothed over its broken place and was flowing on undis-
turbed. Shivering a little, she went on upstream whence the
fitful breeze seemed to blow.

Once she stumbled into a patch of utter darkness and fought
through in panic fear of walking into the river in her blindness, but she won free of the curious air-pocket without mishap. And once the ground under her skimming feet quaked
like jelly, so that she could scarcely keep her balance as she
fled on over the unstable section. But ever the little breeze blew
and died away and blew again, and she thought the faint echo
of a cry was becoming clearer. Almost she caught the far-away
sound of "Jirel—" moaning upon the wind, and quickened
her pace.

For some while now she had been noticing a growing pallor
upon the horizon, and wondering uneasily if night could be so
short here, and day already about to dawn. But no—for she
remembered that upon that other terrible dawn which she had
fled so fast to escape, the pallor had ringed the whole horizon
equally, as if day rose in one vast circle clear around the nameless land. Now it was only one spot on the edge of the sky
which showed that unpleasant, dawning light. It was faintly
tinged with green that strengthened as she watched, and presently above the hills in the distance rose the rim of a vast
green moon. The stars paled around it. A cloud floated across

its face, writhed for an instant as if in some skyey agony, then puffed into a mist and vanished, leaving the green face clear again.

And it was a mottled face across which dim things moved very slowly. Almost it might have had an atmosphere of its own, and dark clouds floating sluggishly; and if that were so it must have been self-luminous, for these slow masses dimmed its surface and it cast little light despite its hugeness. But there was light enough so that in the land through which Jirel ran great shadows took shape upon the ground, writhing and shifting as the moon-clouds obscured and revealed the green surface, and the whole night scene was more baffling and un-real than a dream. And there was something about the green luminance that made her eyes ache.

She waded through shadows as she ran now, monstrous shadows with a hideous dissimilarity to the things that cast them, and no two alike, however identical the bodies which gave them shape. Her own shadow, keeping pace with her along the ground, she did not look at after one shuddering glance. There was something so unnatural about it, and yet—yet it was like her, too, with a dreadful likeness she could not fathom. And more than once she saw great shadows drifting across the ground without any visible thing to cast them—nothing but the queerly shaped blurs moving soundlessly past her and melting into the farther dark. And that was the worst of all.

She ran on upwind, ears straining for a repetition of the far crying, skirting the shadows as well as she could and shudder-ing whenever a great dark blot drifted noiselessly across her path. The moon rose slowly up the sky, tinting the night with a livid greenness, bringing it dreadfully to life with moving shadows. Sometimes the sluggishly moving darknesses across its face clotted together and obscured the whole great disk, and she ran on a few steps thankfully through the unlighted dark before the moon-clouds parted again and the dead green face looked blankly down once more, the cloud-masses crawl-ing across it like corruption across a corpse's face.

During one of these darknesses something slashed viciously at her leg, and she heard the grate of teeth on the greave she

wore. When the moon unveiled again she saw a long bright
scar along the metal, and a drip of phosphorescent venom
trickling down. She gathered a handful of grass to wipe it off
before it reached her unprotected foot, and the grass withered
in her hand when the poison touched it.

All this while the river had been rushing past her and away,
and as she ran it began to narrow and diminish; so she knew
she must be approaching its head. When the wind blew she
was sure now that she heard her own name upon it, in the
small wail which had once been Guillaume's scornful voice.
Then the ground began to rise, and down the hillside she
mounted, the river fell tinkling, a little thread of water no
larger than a brook.

The tinkling was all but articulate now. The river's rush had
been no more than a roaring threat, but the voice of the brook
was deliberately clear, a series of small, bright notes like
syllables, saying evil things. She tried not to listen, for fear of
understanding.

The hill rose steeper, and the brook's voice sharpened and
clarified and sang delicately in its silverly poisonous tones,
and above her against the stars she presently began to discern
something looming on the very height of the hill, something
like a hulking figure motionless as the hill it crowned. She
gripped her sword and slackened her pace a little, skirting the
dark thing warily. But when she came near enough to make it
out in the green moonlight she saw that it was no more than
an image crouching there, black as darkness, giving back a
dull gleam from its surface where the lividness of the moon
struck it. Its shadow moved uneasily upon the ground.

The guiding wind had fallen utterly still now. She stood in
a breathless silence before the image, and the stars sprawled
their queer patterns across the sky and the sullen moonlight
poured down upon her and nothing moved anywhere but
those quivering shadows that were never still.

The image had the shape of a black, shambling thing with
shallow head sunk between its shoulders and great arms dragging forward on the ground. But something about it, something indefinable and obscene, reminded her of Guillaume.

Some aptness of line and angle parodied in the ugly hulk the
long, clean lines of Guillaume, the poise of his high head,
the scornful tilt of his chin. She could not put a finger on any
definite likeness, but it was unmistakably there. And it was all
the ugliness of Guillaume—she saw it as she stared. All his
cruelty and arrogance and brutish force. The image might
have been a picture of Guillaume's sins, with just enough of
his virtues left in to point its dreadfulness.

For an instant she thought she could see behind the black
parody, rising from it and irrevocably part of it, a nebulous
outline of the Guillaume she had never known, the scornful
face twisted in despair, the splendid body writhing futilely
away from that obscene thing which was himself—Guillaume's
soul, rooted in the uglinesses which the image personified. And
she knew his punishment—so just, yet so infinitely unjust.

And what subtle torment the black god's kiss had wrought
upon him! To dwell in the full, frightful realization of his own
sins, chained to the actual manifestation, suffering eternally
in the obscene shape that was so undeniably himself—his
worst and lowest self. It was just, in a way. He had been a harsh
and cruel man in life. But the very fact that such punishment
was agony to him proved a higher self within his complex soul
—something noble and fine which writhed away from the unspeakable thing—himself. So the very fineness of him was a
weapon to torture his soul, turned against him even as his sins
were turned.

She understood all this in the timeless while she stood there
with eyes fixed motionless upon the hulking shape of the
image, wringing from it the knowledge of what its ugliness
meant. And something in her throat swelled and swelled, and
behind her eyelids burnt the sting of tears. Fiercely she fought
back the weakness, desperately cast about for some way in
which she might undo what she had unwittingly inflicted upon
him.

And then all about her something intangible and grim began to form. Some iron presence that manifested itself only
by the dark power she felt pressing upon her, stronger and
stronger. Something coldly inimical to all things human. The

black god's presence. The black god, come to defend his victim against one who was so alien to all his darkness—one who wept and trembled, and was warm with love and sorrow and desperate with despair.

She felt the inexorable force tightening around her, freezing her tears, turning the warmth and tenderness of her into gray ice, rooting her into a frigid immobility. The air dimmed about her, gray with cold, still with the utter deadness of the black god's unhuman presence. She had a glimpse of the dark place into which he was drawing her—a moveless, twilight place, deathlessly still. And an immense weight was pressing her down. The ice formed upon her soul, and the awful, iron despair which has no place among human emotions crept slowly through the fibers of her innermost self.

She felt herself turning into something cold and dark and rigid—a black image of herself—a black, hulking image to prison the spark of consciousness that still burned.

Then, as from a long way off in another time and world, came the memory of Guillaume's arms about her and the scornful press of his mouth over hers. It had not happened to her. It had happened to someone else, someone human and alive, in a far-away place. But the memory of it shot like fire through the rigidness of the body she had almost forgotten was hers, so cold and still it was—the memory of that curious, raging fever which was both hate and love. It broke the ice that bound her, for a moment only, and in that moment she fell to her knees at the dark statue's feet and burst into shuddering sobs, and the hot tears flowing were like fire to thaw her soul.

Slowly that thawing took place. Slowly the ice melted and the rigidity gave way, and the awful weight of the despair which was no human emotion lifted by degrees. The tears ran hotly between her fingers. But all about her she could feel, as tangibly as a touch, the imminence of the black god, waiting. And she knew her humanity, her weakness and transience, and the eternal, passionless waiting she could never hope to outlast. Her tears must run dry—and then—

She sobbed on, knowing herself in hopeless conflict with the vastness of death and oblivion, a tiny spark of warmth and life fighting vainly against the dark engulfing it; the perishable

spark, struggling against inevitable extinction. For the black
god was all death and nothingness, and the powers he drew
upon were without limit—and all she had to fight him with was
the flicker within her called life.

But suddenly in the depths of her despair she felt something
stirring. A long, confused blurring passed over her, and another, and another, and the strangest emotions tumbled
through her mind and vanished. Laughter and mirth, sorrow
and tears and despair, love, envy, hate. She felt somehow a
lessening in the oppressive peril about her, and she lifted her
face from her hands.

Around the dark image a mist was swirling. It was tenuous
and real by turns, but gradually she began to make out a ring
of figures—girls' figures, more unreal than a vision—dancing
girls who circled the crouching statue with flying feet and
tossing hair—girls who turned to Jirel her own face in as many
moods as there were girls. Jirel laughing, Jirel weeping, Jirel
convulsed with fury, Jirel honey-sweet with love. Faster they
swirled, a riot of flashing limbs, a chaos of tears and mirth and
all humanity's moods. The air danced with them in shimmering waves, so that the land was blurred behind them and the
image seemed to shiver within itself.

And she felt those waves of warmth and humanity beating
insistently against the hovering chill which was the black god's
presence. Life and warmth, fighting back the dark nothingness
she had thought unconquerable. She felt it wavering about her
as a canopy wavers in the wind. And slowly she felt it melting.
Very gradually it lifted and dissipated, while the wild figures
of gayety and grief and all kindred emotions whirled about the
image and the beat of their aliveness pulsed through the air in
heatwaves against the grayness of the god's cold.

And something in Jirel knew warmly that the image of life
as a tiny spark flickering out in limitless black was a false one
—that without light there can be no darkness—that death and
life are interdependent, one upon the other. And that she,
armored in the warmth of her aliveness, was the black god's
equal, and a worthy foe. It was an even struggle. She called up
the forces of life within her, feeling them hurled against the
darkness, beating strongly upon the cold and silence of ob-

livion. Strength flowed through her, and she knew herself
immortal in the power of life.

How long this went on she never knew. But she felt victory
pulsing like wine through her veins even before the cold pall
lifted. And it lifted quite suddenly. In a breath, without warning, the black god's presence was not. In that breath the
swirling dancers vanished, and the night was empty about her,
and the singing of triumph ran warmly through her body.

But the image—the image! The queerest change was coming
over it. The black, obscene outlines were unstable as mist. They
quavered and shook, and ran together and somehow melted.
. . . The green moon veiled its face again with clouds, and
when the light returned the image was no more than a black
shadow running fluidly upon the ground; a shadow which bore
the outlines of Guillaume—or what might have been Guillaume. . . .

The moon-shadows moved across the livid disk, and the
shadow on the ground moved too, a monstrous shadow latent
with a terrible implication of the horrors dormant within the
being which cast the shadow, dreadful things that Guillaume
might have been and done. She knew then why the misshapen
shadows were so monstrous. They were a dim, leering hinting
at what might have been—what might yet be—frightful suggestions of the dreadfulnesses dormant within every living being.
And the insane suggestions they made were the more terrible
because, impossible beyond nightmares though they seemed,
yet the mind intuitively recognized their truth. . . .

A little breeze sprang up fitfully, and the shadow moved,
slipping over the stones without a sound. She found herself
staggering after it on legs that shook, for the effort of that
battle with the god had drained her of all strength. But the
shadow was gliding faster now, and she dared not lose it. It
floated on without a sound, now fast, now slow, its monstrous
outlines shifting continually into patterns each more terribly
significant than the last. She stumbled after it, the sword a dead
weight in her hand, her red head hanging.

In five minutes she had lost all sense of direction. Beyond
the hilltop the river ceased. The moving moonlight confused

her and the stars traced queer pictures across the sky, from
which she could get no bearings. The moon was overhead by
now, and in those intervals when its clouds obscured the surface and the night was black around her, Guillaume's misshapen shadow vanished with the rest, and she suffered agonies
of apprehension before the light came out again and she took
up the chase anew.

The dark blot was moving now over a rolling meadowland
dotted with queerly shaped trees. The grass over which she ran
was velvet-soft, and she caught whiffs of perfume now and
again from some tree that billowed with pale bloom in the
moonlight. The shadow wavering ahead of her moved forward
to pass one tall tree a little apart from the rest, its branches
hanging in long, shaking streamers from its central crown. She
saw the dark shape upon the ground pause as it neared the tree,
and shiver a little, and then melt imperceptibly into the
shadow cast by its branches. That tree-shadow, until Guillaume's touched it, had borne the shape of a monster with
crawling tentacles and flattened, thrusting head, but at the
moment of conjunction the two melted into one—all the
tentacles leaped forward to embrace the newcomer, and the two
merged into an unnamably evil thing that lay upon the ground
and heaved with a frightful aliveness of its own.

Jirel paused at its edge, looking down helplessly. She dis-
liked to set her foot even upon the edge of that hideous black
shape, though she knew intuitively that it could not harm her.
The joined shadows were alive with menace and evil, but only
to things in their own plane. She hesitated under the tree,
wondering vainly how to part her lover's shade from the thing
that gripped it. She felt somehow that his shadow had not
joined the other altogether willingly. It was rather as if the
evil instinct in the tree-shape had reached out to the evil in
Guillaume, and by that evil held him, though the fineness that
was still his revolted to the touch.

Then something brushed her shoulder gently, and lapped
around her arm, and she leaped backward in a panic, too late.
The tree's swinging branches had writhed round toward her,
and one already was wrapped about her body. That shadow
upon the ground had been a clear warning of the danger

a tentacled monster, lying in wait. Up swung her sword in a
dormant within the growth, had she only realized it before—
flash of green-tinged moonlight, and she felt the gripping
branch yield like rubber under the blow. It gave amazingly
and sprang back again, jerking her almost off her feet. She
turned the blade against it, hewing desperately as she saw
other branches curling around toward her. One had almost
come within reach of her sword-arm, and was poising for the
attack, when she felt her blade bite into the rubbery surface
at last. Then with a root-deep shudder through all its members
the tree loosed its hold and the severed limb fell writhing to
the ground. Thick black sap dripped from the wound. And
all the branches hung motionless, but upon the ground the
shadow flung wildly agonized tentacles wide, and from the released grip Guillaume's shadow sprang free and glided away
over the grass. Shaking with reaction, Jirel followed.

She gave more attention to the trees they passed now. There
was one little shrub whose leaves blew constantly in shivering
ripples, even when there was no wind, and its shadow was the
shadow of a small leaping thing that hurled itself time and
again against some invisible barrier and fell back, only to leap
once more in panic terror. And one slim, leafless tree writhed
against the stars with a slow, unceasing motion. It made no
sound, but its branches twisted together and shuddered and
strained in an agony more eloquent than speech. It seemed to
wring its limbs together, agonized, dumb, with a slow anguish
that never abated. And its shadow, dimly, was the shadow of
a writhing woman.

And one tree, a miracle of bloom in the moonlight, swayed
its ruffled branches seductively, sending out wave upon wave
of intoxicating perfume and making a low, delightful humming, somehow like the melody of bees. Its shadow upon the
ground was the shadow of a coiled serpent, lifting to strike.

Jirel was glad when they left the region of the trees and
curved to the left down a long hill slope across which other
shadows, without form, blew unceasingly with nothing to cast
them. They raced noiselessly by, like wind-driven clouds.
Among them she lost and found and lost again the shape she

followed, until she grew dizzy from trying to keep her footing upon a ground that quavered with the blowing shadows so that she never knew upon what her feet were stepping, and the dim thing she followed was a nothingness that threaded its way in and out of the cloud-shapes bafflingly.

She had the idea now that the shadow of her lover was heading toward some definite goal. There was purpose in its dim gliding, and she looked ahead for some sign of the place it aimed toward. Below the hill the land stretched away featurelessly, cloud-mottled in the livid moonlight. Drifts of mist obscured it, and there were formless dark patches and pale blotches upon the night, and here and there a brook crawled across the blackness. She was completely lost now, for the river had long since vanished and she saw no hill which might have been the one upon which she had emerged.

They crossed another belt of quaking land, and the shadow gained upon her as she staggered over the jelly-like surface. They came to a pale brook across which the shadow glided without a pause. It was a narrow, swift brook whose water chuckled thickly to itself in the dark. One stepping-stone broke the surface in the center of the stream, and she held her breath and leaped for it, not daring to slacken her pace. The stone gave under her foot like living flesh, and she thought she heard a groan, but she had gained the farther bank and did not pause to listen.

Then they were hurrying down another slope, the shadow gliding faster now, and more purposefully. And the slope went down and down, steeply, until it became the side of a ravine and the rocks began to roll under her stumbling feet. She saw the fleeting shadow slip over a ledge and down a steep bank and then plunge into the darkness which lay like water along the bottom of the gully, and she gave a little sob of despair, for she knew now that she had lost it. But she struggled on into the dark that swallowed her up.

It was like wading deeper and deeper into a tangible oblivion. The blackness closed over her head, and she was groping through solid night. It filled the hollow in a thick flood, and in the depths of it she could not even see the stars overhead. There was a moment of this blindness and groping, and then the moon rose.

Like a great leprous face it swung over the ravine's edge, the moon-clouds crawling across its surface. And that green light was an agony to her eyes, obscurely, achingly. It was like no mortal moonlight. It seemed endowed with a poisonous quality that was essentially a part of the radiance, and that unearthly, inexplicable light had an effect upon the liquid dark in the gully's bottom which no earthly moonlight could have had. It penetrated the blackness, broke it up into myriad struggling shadows that did not lie flat upon the ground, as all shadows should, but stood upright and three-dimensional and danced about her in a dizzy riot of nothingness taken shape. They brushed by her and through her without meeting obstruction, because for all their seeming solidity they were no more than shadows, without substance.

Among them danced the shape of Guillaume, and the outlines of it made her faint with terror, they were so like—and so dreadfully unlike—the Guillaume she had known, so leeringly suggestive of all the evil in him, and all the potential evil of mankind. The other shapes were ugly too, but they were the shapes of things whose real form she did not know, so that the implications latent in them she did not understand. But she missed no subtle half-tone of the full dreadfulness which was Guillaume, and her mind staggered with the suggestions the shadow-form made.

"Guillaume—" she heard herself sobbing, "Guillaume!" and realized that it was the first articulate sound which had passed her lips since she entered here. At her voice the reeling shadow slowed a little and hesitated, and then very reluctantly began to drift toward her through the spinning shades.

And then without warning something immeasurably cold and still closed down around her once more. The black god's presence. Again she felt herself congealing, through and through, as the ice of eternal nothingness thickened upon her soul and the gray, dim, formless place she remembered took shape about her and the immense weight of that iron despair descended again upon her shuddering spirit. If she had had warning she could have struggled, but it came so suddenly that

before she could marshal her forces for the attack she was frigid
to the core with the chill of unhumanity, and her body did
not belong to her, and she was turning slowly into a black
shadow that reeled among shadows in a dreadful, colorless
void. . . .

Sharply through this stabbed the fire-hot memory that had
wakened her before—the weight of a man's bearded mouth
upon hers, the grip of his mailed arms. And again she knew
the flash of violence that might have been hate or love, and
warmth flowed through her again in a sustaining tide.

And she fought. All the deeps of warmth and humanity in
her she drew upon to fight the cold, all the violence of emotion to combat the terrible apathy which had gripped her once
and was stretching out again for her soul.

It was not an easy victory. There were moments when the
chill all but conquered, and moments when she felt herself
drawn tenuously out of the congealing body which was hers to
reel among the other shadows—a dim thing whose shape hinted
at unspeakable possibilities, a shadow with form and depth
and no reality. She caught remote beats of the insane harmony
they danced to, and though her soul was fainting, her unreal
shade went whirling on with the rest. She shared their torment
for long minutes together.

But always she pulled herself free again. Always she fought
back somehow into the ice-fettered body and shook off the
frigid apathy that bound it, and hurled her weapons of life
and vitality against the dark god's frosty presence.

And though she knew she would win this time, a little creeping doubt had entered her mind and would not be ousted.
She could beat the god off, but she could never destroy him.
He would always return. She dared not destroy him—a vision
of her thought-picture came back to her, of the tiny life-spark
burning against eternal darkness. And though if there were no
light there could be no dark, yet it was true in reverse too, and
if the power upon which the black god drew were destroyed—
if the dark were dissipated, then there would be no light. No
life. Interdependence, and eternal struggle. . . .

All this she was realizing with a remote part of herself as

she fought. She realized it very vaguely, for her mind had not been trained to such abstractions. With her conscious self she was calling up the memories of love and hate and terror, the exultation of battle, the exaltation of joy. Everything that was alive and pulsing and warm she flung against the black god's chill, feeling her thoughts rise up in a protecting wall about her, to shut out all menace.

Victory, as before, came very suddenly. Without warning a blaze of light sprang up around her. The dark presence melted into oblivion. In that abrupt glare she closed her dazzled eyes, and when she opened them again familiar moonlight was flooding the glen. The fluid dark had vanished, the shadows no longer danced. That light had blasted them out of existence, and as it died she stared round the dim ravine with startled eyes, searching for the thing that was all she had seen of Guillaume. It was gone with the rest. The tangible dark which had brimmed the place was utterly gone. Not a shadow moved anywhere. But on the wind that was blowing down the ravine a small voice wailed.

And so again the weary chase went on. But she had less than ever to guide her now—only a fitful crying in the dark. "Jirel—" it wailed, "Jirel—Jirel—" and by that calling she followed. She could see nothing. Guillaume was no more than a voice now, and she could follow him by ear alone. Emptily the landscape stretched before her.

She had come out of the ravine's end upon a broad fan-shaped slope which tilted downward into darkness. Water was falling somewhere near, but she could not see it. She ran blindly, ears strained for the small wailing cry. It led out over the slope and skirted the foot of a hill and passed by the place where water fell in a thin cascade down a cliffside, and whispered evilly to itself as it fell.

The sound obscured the sound she followed, and when she had passed beyond the whisper of the falls she had to stop and listen for a long time, while her heart thudded and the land around her crept with small, inexplicable noises, before she caught the far-away wail, "Jirel—Jirel—"

She set off in the direction from which the sound came, and

presently heard it again more clearly, "Jirel! Jirel, my murderess!"

It was a heart-breaking course she ran, with no more than a fitful wailing to guide her and unknown perils lurking all about in the dark, and her own body and soul so drained of all strength by that second struggle with the god that the misty darkness wavered before her eyes and the ground underfoot heaved up to meet her time after time.

Once she fell, and lay still for a second to catch her struggling breath. But it seemed to her that the ground against her body was too warm, somehow, and moving gently as if with leisured breathing. So she leaped up again in swift alarm, and went skimming on with that dream-like speed over the dark grass.

It seemed to her that, as the shadow she had pursued had fled through shadowy places where she all but lost it time and again, now the fleeing voice led her through noisy places where she could scarcely hear it above the talking of brooks and the rush of falls and the blowing of the wind. She heard sounds she had never heard before—small, tenuous voices murmuring in the wind, the whispering of grass saying things in a murmurous language, the squeak of insects brushing past her face and somehow almost articulate. She had heard no birds here, though once a great, dark, shapeless thing flapped heavily through the air a little distance ahead. But there were frog voices from the swamps she skirted, and hearing these she remembered what she had met in another swamp on her first visit here, and a little chill went down her back.

In every sound she heard ran the thread of evil inextricably tangled with a thread of purest despair—a human despair even through the grasses' rustling and in the murmur of the wind— voices wailing so hopelessly that more than once tears started unbidden to her eyes, but so indistinctly that she could never be sure she had heard. And always through the wailing rippled the chuckle of dim evils without any names in human languages. And with all these sounds she heard many others that meant nothing to her and upon whose origins she dared not speculate.

Through this welter of incomprehensible noises she fol-

lowed the one far crying that had meaning for her. It led in
a long arc across rolling ground, over muttering brooks that
talked morbidly in the dark. Presently she began to catch faint
strains of the most curious music. It did not have the quality
of composition, or even unity, but seemed to consist of single
groups of notes, like sprays of music, each unrelated to the rest,
as if thousands of invisible creatures were piping tiny, primitive tunes, every one deaf to the songs of his fellows. The sound
grew louder as she advanced, and she saw that she was coming
to a luminous patch upon the dark ground. When she reached
the edge she paused in wonder.

The music was rising from the earth, and it rose visibly. She
could actually see the separate strains wavering upward
through the still air. She could never have described what she
saw, for the look of that visible music was beyond any human
words. Palely the notes rose, each singing its tiny, simple tune.
There seemed to be no discords, for all the non-unity of the
sounds. She had the mad fancy that the music was growing—
that if she wished she could wade through the ranks of it and
gather great sheaves of sound—perhaps bouquets which, if
they were carefully selected, would join together and play a
single complex melody.

But it was not music she dared listen to long. There was in
it the queerest little gibbering noise, and as she lingered that
sound intensified and ran through her brain in small, giggling
undernotes, and she caught herself laughing senselessly at
nothing at all. Then she took fright, and listened for the
voice that was Guillaume. And terrifyingly she heard it strongly
in the very midst of the little mad jinglings. It deepened and
grew, and drowned out the smaller sounds, and the whole field
was one vast roar of insane laughter that thundered through
her head in destroying waves—a jarring laughter that threatened to shake her very brain into a jelly, and shivered through
her body irresistibly and wrung tears from her eyes even as she
laughed.

"Guillaume!" she called again in the midst of her agony.
"Oh Guillaume!" and at the sound of her voice all laughter
ceased and a vast, breathless silence fell upon the whole dark
world. Through that silence the tiniest wail threaded itself

reedily, "Jirel—." Then other sounds came back to life, and
the wind blew and the wail diminished in the distance. Again
the chase went on.

By now the moon's dead, crawling face had sunk nearly to
the horizon, and the shadows lay in long patterns across the
ground. It seemed to her that around the broad ring of the
sky a pallor was rising. In her weariness and despair she did
not greatly care now, knowing though she did that should day
catch her here it meant a death more terrible than any man
can die on earth, and an eternity, perhaps, of torment in one
of the many shapes she had seen and recognized as the spirits
of the damned. Perhaps a writhing tree—or imprisonment in
an obscenely revelatory image, like Guillaume—or no more
than a wailing along the wind for ever. She was too tired to
care. She stumbled on hopelessly, hearing the voice that cried
her name grow fainter and fainter in the distance.

The end of the chase came very suddenly. She reached a
stream that flowed smoothly under the arch of a low, dark
bridge, and crossed over it, seeing her face look up at her from
the water with a wild mouthing of soundless cries, though her
own lips were closed. She met her reflected eyes and read warning and despair and the acutest agony in their depths, and saw
her own face writhing all out of familiarity with anguish and
hopelessness. It was a frightful vision, but she scarcely saw it,
and ran on without heeding the image in the water or the
landscape around her or even the broadening dawn around
the horizon.

Then close ahead of her sounded the thin small voice she
followed, and she woke out of her stupor and stared around.
That bridge had not ended upon the far side of the brook,
but somehow had arched up its sides and broadened its floor
and become a dark temple around whose walls ran a more
bestial sculpture than anything imagined even in dreams. Here
in this carved and columned building was the epitome of the
whole dim hell through which she had been running. Here in
these sculptures she read all the hideous things the shadows
had hinted at, all the human sorrow and despair and hopelessness she had heard in the wind's crying, all the chuckling evil

that the water spoke. In the carvings she could trace the
prisoned souls of men and beasts, tormented in many ways,
some of which she had already seen, but many that she had
not, and which she mercifully could not understand. It was not
clear for what they were punished, save that the torture was
tinged just enough with justice so that it seemed the more
hideously unjust in its exaggerations. She closed her eyes and
stood swaying a little, feeling the triumphant evil of the temple
pulsing around her, too stunned and sick even to wonder what
might come next.

Then the small voice was beating around her head. Almost
she felt the desperate hammering of wings, as if some little,
frantic bird were flying against her face. "Jirel!—Jirel!" it cried
in the purest agony, over and over, a final, wild appeal. And
she did not know what to do. Helplessly she stood there, feeling it beating round her head, feeling the temple's obscene
triumph surging through her.

And without warning, for the third time the black god's
presence folded like a cloak about her. Almost she welcomed
it. Here was something she knew how to fight. As from a long
distance away she heard the small voice crying in diminishing
echoes, and the frigid twilight was forming about her, and the
gray ice thickened upon her soul. She called up the memories
of hate and love and anger to hurl against it, thinking as she
did so that perhaps one who had lived less violently than herself and had lesser stores of passions to recall might never be
able to combat the god's death-chill. She remembered laughter,
and singing and gayety—she remembered slaughter and blood
and the wild clang of mail—she remembered kisses in the
dark, and the hard grip of men's arms about her body.

But she was weary, and the dawn was breaking terribly
along the sky, and the dark god's power was rooted in a changeless oblivion that never faltered. And she began to realize
failure. The memories she flung out had no power against the
gray pall of that twilight place wherein he dwelt, and she
knew the first seeping of the iron despair through her brain.
Gradually the will to struggle congealed with her congealing
body, until she was no longer a warm, vital thing of flesh and

blood, but something rigid and ice-bound, dwelling bodilessly
in the twilight.

There was one small spark of her that the god could not
freeze. She felt him assailing it. She felt him driving it out of
the cold thing that had been her body—drawing it forth irresistibly—she was a thin, small crying in the dark. . . . Helplessly she felt herself whirling to and fro upon currents she
had never felt before, and dashing against unseen obstacles,
wailing wordlessly. She had no substance, and the world had
faded from around her. She was aware of other things—dim,
vague, like beating pulses, that were whirling through the
dark, small lost things like herself, bodiless and unprotected,
buffeted by every current that blew; little wailing things,
shrieking through the night.

Then one of the small vaguenesses blew against her and
through her, and in the instant of its passage she caught the
faint vibration of her name, and knew that this was the voice
that had summoned her out of her dreams, the voice she had
pursued: Guillaume. And with that instant's union something
as sustaining as life itself flashed through her wonderfully, a
bright spark that swelled and grew and blazed, and—

She was back again in her body amidst the bestial carvings
of the temple—a thawing, warming body from which the
shackles of icy silence were falling, and that hot blaze was
swelling still, until all of her being was suffused and pulsing
with it, and the frigid pall of dark melted away unresistingly
before the hot, triumphant blaze that dwelt within her.

In her ecstasy of overwhelming warmth she scarcely realized
her victory. She did not greatly care. Something very splendid
was happening. . . .

Then the air trembled, and all about her small, thin sounds
went shivering upward, as if ribbons of high screams were
rippling past her across a background of silence. The blaze
within her faded slowly, paled, imperceptibly died away, and
the peace of utter emptiness flooded into her soul. She turned
wearily backward across the bridge. Behind her the temple
stood in a death-like quiet. The evil that had beat in long
pulses through it was stilled for a while by something stun-

ningly splendid which had no place in the starry hell; something human and alive, something compounded of love and
longing, near-despair and sacrifice and triumph.

Jirel did not realize how great a silence she left behind, nor
very clearly what she had done. Above her against the paling
sky she saw a familiar hilltop, and dimly knew that in all her
long night of running she had been circling round toward her
starting-place. She was too numb to care. She was beyond
relief or surprise.

She began the climb passionlessly, with no triumph in the
victory she knew was hers at last. For she had driven Guillaume out of the image and into the shadow, and out of the
shadow into the voice, and out of the voice into—clean death,
perhaps. She did not know. But he had found peace, for his
insistences no longer beat upon her consciousness. And she
was content.

Above her the cave mouth yawned. She toiled up the slope,
dragging her sword listlessly, weary to the very soul, but quite
calm now, with a peace beyond all understanding.

Black Thirst

NORTHWEST SMITH leant his head back against the warehouse wall and stared up into the black night-sky of Venus. The waterfront street was very quiet tonight, very dangerous. He could hear no sound save the eternal slap-slap of water against the piles, but he knew how much of danger and sudden death dwelt here voiceless in the breathing dark, and he may have been a little homesick as he stared up into the clouds that masked a green star hanging lovely on the horizon—Earth and home. And if he thought of that he must have grinned wryly to himself in the dark, for Northwest Smith had no home, and Earth would not have welcomed him very kindly just then.

He sat quietly in the dark. Above him in the warehouse wall a faintly lighted window threw a square of pallor upon the wet street. Smith drew back into his angle of darkness under the slanting shaft, hugging one knee. And presently he heard footsteps softly on the street.

He may have been expecting footsteps, for he turned his head alertly and listened, but it was not a man's feet that came so lightly over the wooden quay, and Smith's brow furrowed. A woman, here, on this black waterfront by night? Not even the lowest class of Venusian street-walker dared come along the waterfronts of Ednes on the nights when the space-liners were not in. Yet across the pavement came clearly now the light tapping of a woman's feet.

Smith drew farther back into the shadows and waited. And presently she came, a darkness in the dark save for the triangular patch of pallor that was her face. As she passed under the light falling dimly from the window overhead he understood suddenly how she dared walk here and who she was. A long black cloak hid her, but the light fell upon her face, heart-shaped under the little three-cornered velvet cap that Venusian women wear, fell on ripples of half-hidden bronze hair; and by that sweet triangular face and shining hair he knew her for one of the Minga maids—those beauties that from the beginning of history have been bred in the Minga stronghold for loveliness and grace, as race-horses are bred on Earth, and reared from earliest infancy in the art of charming men. Scarcely a court on the three planets lacks at least one of these exquisite creatures, long-limbed, milk-white, with their bronze hair and lovely brazen faces—if the lord of that court has the wealth to buy them. Kings from many nations and races have poured their riches into the Minga gateway, and girls like pure gold and ivory have gone forth to grace a thousand palaces, and this has been so since Ednes first rose on the shore of the Greater Sea.

This girl walked here unafraid and unharmed because she wore the beauty that marked her for what she was. The heavy hand of the Minga stretched out protectingly over her bronze head, and not a man along the wharf-fronts but knew what dreadful penalties would overtake him if he dared so much as to lay a finger on the milk-whiteness of a Minga maid— terrible penalties, such as men whisper of fearfully over *segir-* whisky mugs in the waterfront dives of many nations—mysterious, unnamable penalties more dreadful than any knife or gun-flash could inflict.

And these dangers, too, guarded the gates of the Minga castle. The chastity of the Minga girls was proverbial, a trade boast. This girl walked in peace and safety more sure than that attending the steps of a nun through slum streets by night on Earth.

But even so, the girls went forth very rarely from the gates of the castle, never unattended. Smith had never seen one before, save at a distance. He shifted a little now, to catch a better glimpse as she went by, to look for the escort that must surely walk a pace or two behind, though he heard no footsteps save her own. The slight motion caught her eye. She stopped.

She peered closer into the dark, and said in a voice as sweet and smooth as cream,

"How would you like to earn a goldpiece, my man?"

A flash of perversity twisted Smith's reply out of its usual slovenly dialect, and he said in his most cultured voice, in his most perfect High Venusian,

"Thank you, no."

For a moment the woman stood quite still, peering through the darkness in a vain effort to reach his face. He could see her own, a pale oval in the window light, intent, surprised. Then she flung back her cloak and the dim light glinted on the case of a pocket flash as she flicked the catch. A beam of white radiance fell blindingly upon his face.

For an instant the light held him—lounging against the wall in his spaceman's leather, the burns upon it, the tatters, ray-gun in its holster low on his thigh, and the brown scarred face turned to hers, eyes the colorless color of pale steel narrowed to the glare. It was a typical face. It belonged here, on the waterfront, in these dark and dangerous streets. It belonged to the type that frequents such places, those lawless men who ride the spaceways and live by the rule of the ray-gun, recklessly, warily outside the Patrol's jurisdiction. But there was more than that in the scarred brown face turned to the light. She must have seen it as she held the flash unwavering, some deep-buried trace of breeding and birth that made the cultured accents of the High Venusian not incongruous. And the colorless eyes derided her.

"No," she said, flicking off the light. "Not one gold-piece, but a hundred. And for another task that I meant."

"Thank you," said Smith, not rising. "You must excuse me."

"Five hundred," she said without a flicker of emotion in her creamy voice.

In the dark Smith's brows knit. There was something fantastic in the situation. Why—?

She must have sensed his reaction almost as he realized it himself, for she said,

"Yes, I know. It sounds insane. You see—I knew you in the light just now. Will you?—can you?—I can't explain here on the street. . . ."

Smith held the silence unbroken for thirty seconds, while a lightning debate flashed through the recesses of his wary mind. Then he grinned to himself in the dark and said, "I'll come." Belatedly he got to his feet. "Where?"

"The Palace Road on the edge of the Minga. Third door from the central gate, to the left. Say to the door-warden— 'Vaudir.' "

"That is—?"

"Yes, my name. You will come, in half an hour?"

An instant longer Smith's mind hovered on the verge of refusal. Then he shrugged.

"Yes."

"At the third bell, then." She made the little Venusian gesture of parting and wrapped her cloak about her. The blackness of it, and the softness of her footfalls, made her seem to melt into the darkness without a sound, but Smith's trained ears heard her footsteps very softly on the pavement as she went on into the dark.

He sat there until he could no longer detect any faintest sound of feet on the wharf. He waited patiently, but his mind was a little dizzy with surprise. Was the traditional inviolability of the Minga a fraud? Were the close-guarded girls actually allowed sometimes to walk unattended by night, making assignations as they pleased? Or was it some elaborate hoax? Tradition for countless centuries had declared the gates in the Minga wall to be guarded so relentlessly by strange dangers that not even a mouse could slip through without the knowledge of the Alendar, the Minga's lord. Was it then by order of the Alendar that the door would open to him when he whispered "Vaudir" to the warden? Or would it open? Was the girl perhaps the property of some Ednes lord, deceiving him for obscure purposes of her own? He shook his head a little and grinned to himself. After all, time would tell.

He waited a while longer in the dark. Little waves lapped the piles with sucking sounds, and once the sky lit up with the long, blinding roar of a space-ship splitting the dark.

At last he rose and stretched his long body as if he had been sitting there for a good while. Then he settled the gun on his leg and set off down the black street. He walked very lightly in his spaceman's boots.

A twenty-minute walk through dark byways, still and deserted, brought him to the outskirts of that vast city-within-a-city called the Minga. The dark, rough walls of it towered over him, green with the lichen-like growths of the Hot Planet. On the Palace Road one deeply-sunk central gateway opened upon the mysteries within. A tiny blue light burned over the arch. Smith went softly through the dimness to the left of it, counting two tiny doors half hidden in deep recesses. At the third he paused. It was painted a rusty green, and a green vine spilling down the wall half veiled it, so that if he had not been searching he would have passed it by.

Smith stood for a long minute, motionless, staring at the green panels deep-sunk in rock. He listened. He even sniffed the heavy air. Warily as a wild beast he hesitated in the dark. But at last he lifted his hand and tapped very lightly with his fingertips on the green door.

It swung open without a sound. Pitch-blackness confronted him, an archway of blank dark in the dimly seen stone wall. And a voice queried softly, *"Qu'a lo' val?"*

"Vaudir," murmured Smith, and grinned to himself involuntarily. How many romantic youths must have stood at these doors in nights gone by, breathing hopefully the names of bronze beauties to doormen in dark archways! But unless tradition lied, no man before had ever passed. He must be the first in many years to stand here invited at a little doorway in the Minga wall and hear the watchman murmur, "Come."

Smith loosened the gun at his side and bent his tall head under the arch. He stepped into blackness that closed about him like water as the door swung shut. He stood there with quickened heart-beats, hand on his gun, listening. A blue light, dim and ghostly, flooded the place without warning and he saw that the doorman had crossed to a switch at the far side of the tiny chamber wherein he stood. The man was one of the Minga eunuchs, a flabby creature, splendid in crimson velvet. He carried a cloak of purple over his arm, and made a splash of royal colors in the dimness. His sidelong eyes regarded Smith from under lifted brows, with a look that the

Earthman could not fathom. There was amusement in it, and a touch of terror and a certain reluctant admiration.

Smith looked about him in frank curiosity. The little entry was apparently hollowed out of the enormously thick wall itself. The only thing that broke its bareness was the ornate bronze door set in the far wall. His eyes sought the eunuch's in mute inquiry.

The creature came forward obsequiously, murmuring, "Permit me—" and flung the purple cloak he carried over Smith's shoulders. Its luxurious folds, faintly fragrant, swept about him like a caress. It covered him, tall as he was, to the very boot-soles. He drew back in faint distaste as the eunuch lifted his hands to fasten the jeweled clasp at his throat. "Please to draw up the hood also," murmured the creature without apparent resentment, as Smith snapped the fastening himself. The hood covered his sun-bleached hair and fell in thick folds about his face, casting it into deep shadow.

The eunuch opened the bronze inner door and Smith stared down a long hallway curving almost imperceptibly to the right. The paradox of elaborately decorated simplicity was illustrated in every broad polished panel of the wall, so intricately and exquisitely carved that it gave at first the impression of a strange, rich plainness.

His booted feet sank sensuously into the deep pile of the carpet at every step as he followed the eunuch down the hall. Twice he heard voices murmuring behind lighted doors, and his hand lay on the butt of the ray-gun under the folds of his robe, but no door opened and the hall lay empty and dim before them. So far it had been amazingly easy. Either tradition lied about the impregnability of the Minga, or the girl Vaudir had bribed with incredible lavishness or—that thought again, uneasily—it was with the Alendar's consent that he walked here unchallenged. But why?

They came to a door of silver grille at the end of the curved corridor, and passed through it into another hallway slanting up, as exquisitely voluptuous as the first. A flight of stairs wrought from dully gleaming bronze curved at the end of it. Then came another hall lighted with rosy lanterns that swung from the arched ceiling, and beyond another stairway, this time of silvery metal fretwork, spiraling down again.

And in all that distance they met no living creature. Voices hummed behind closed doors, and once or twice strains of music drifted faintly to Smith's ears, but either the corridors had been cleared by a special order, or incredible luck was attending them. And he had the uncomfortable sensation of eyes upon his back more than once. They passed dark hallways and open, unlighted doors, and sometimes the hair on his neck bristled with the feeling of human nearness, inimical, watching.

For all of twenty minutes they walked through curved corridors and up and down spiral stairs until even Smith's keen senses were confused and he could not have said at what height above the ground he was, or in what direction the corridor led into which they at last emerged. At the end of that time his nerves were tense as steel wire and he restrained himself only by force from nervous, over-the-shoulder glances each time they passed an open door. An air of languorous menace brooded almost visibly over the place, he thought. The sound of soft voices behind doors, the feel of eyes, of whispers in the air, the memory of tales half heard in waterfront dives about the secrets of the Minga, the nameless dangers of the Minga. . . .

Smith gripped his gun as he walked through the splendor and the dimness, every sense assailed by voluptuous appeals, but his nerves strained to wire and his flesh crawled as he passed unlighted doors. This was too easy. For so many centuries the tradition of the Minga had been upheld, a byword of impregnability, a stronghold guarded by more than swords, by greater dangers than the ray-gun—and yet here he walked, unquestioned, into the deepest heart of the place, his only disguise a velvet cloak, his only weapon a holstered gun, and no one challenged him, no guards, no slaves, not even a passer-by to note that a man taller than any dweller here should be strode unquestioned through the innermost corridors of the inviolable Minga. He loosened the ray-gun in its sheath.

The eunuch in his scarlet velvet went on confidently ahead. Only once did he falter. They had reached a dark passageway, and just as they came opposite its mouth the sound of a soft, slithering scrape, as of something over stones, draggingly, reached their ears. He saw the eunuch start and half glance back, and then hurry on at a quicker pace, nor did he slacken until they had put two gates and a length of lighted corridor between them and that dark passage.

So they went on, through halls half lighted, through scented air and empty dimness where the doorways closed upon murmurous mysteries within or opened to dark and the feel of watching eyes. And they came at last, after endless, winding progress, into a hallway low-ceiled and paneled in mother-of-pearl, pierced and filigreed with carving, and all the doors were of silver grille. And as the eunuch pushed open the silver gate that led into this corridor the thing happened that his taut nerves had been expecting ever since the start of the fantastic journey. One of the doors opened and a figure stepped out and faced them.

Under the robe Smith's gun slid soundlessly from its holster. He thought he saw the eunuch's back stiffen a little, and his step falter, but only for an instant. It was a girl who had come out, a slave-girl in a single white garment, and at the first glimpse of the tall, purple-robed figure with hooded face, towering over her, she gave a little gasp and slumped to her knees as if under a blow. It was obeisance, but so shocked and terrified that it might have been a faint. She laid her face to the very carpet, and Smith, looking down in amazement on the prostrate figure, saw that she was trembling violently.

The gun slid back into its sheath and he paused for a moment over her shuddering homage. The eunuch twisted round to beckon with soundless violence, and Smith caught a glimpse of his face for the first time since their journey began. It was glistening with sweat, and the sidelong eyes were bright and shifting, like a hunted animal's. Smith was oddly reassured by the sight of the eunuch's obvious panic. There was danger then—danger of discovery, the sort of peril he knew and could fight. It was that creeping sensation of eyes watching, of unseen things slithering down dark passages, that had strained his nerves so painfully. And yet, even so, it had been too easy. . . .

The eunuch had paused at a silver door half-way down the hall and was murmuring something very softly, his mouth against the grille. A panel of green brocade was stretched across the silver door on the inside, so they could see nothing within the room, but after a moment a voice said, "Good!" in a breathing whisper, and the door quivered a little and swung open six inches. The eunuch genuflected in a swirl of scarlet robes, and Smith caught his eye swiftly, the look of terror not yet faded, but amusement there too, and a certain respect. And then the door opened wider and he stepped inside.

He stepped into a room green as a sea-cave. The walls were paneled in green brocade, low green couches circled the room, and, in the center, the blazing bronze beauty of the girl Vaudir. She wore a robe of green velvet cut in the startling Venusian fashion to loop over one shoulder and swathe her body in tight, molten folds, and the skirt of it was slit up one side so that at every other motion the long white leg flashed bare.

He saw her for the first time in a full light, and she was lovely beyond belief with her bronze hair cloudy on her shoulders and the pale, lazy face smiling. Under deep lashes the sidelong black eyes of her race met his.

He jerked impatiently at the hampering hood of the cloak. "May I take this off?" he said. "Are we safe here?"

She laughed with a short, metallic sound. "Safe!" she said ironically. "But take it off if you must. I've gone too far now to stop at trifles."

And as the rich folds parted and slid away from his leather brownness she in turn stared in quickened interest at what she had seen only in a half-light before. He was almost laughably incongruous in this jewel-box room, all leather and sunburn and his scarred face keen and wary in the light of the lantern swinging from its silver chain. She looked a second time at that face, its lean, leathery keenness and the scars that ray-guns had left, and the mark of knife and talon, and the tracks of wild years along the spaceways. Wariness and resolution were instinct in that face, there was ruthlessness in every line of it, and when she met his eyes a little shock went over her. Pale, pale as bare steel, colorless in the sunburnt face.

Steady and clear and no-colored, expressionless as water.
Killer's eyes.

And she knew that this was the man she needed. The name
and fame of Northwest Smith had penetrated even into these
mother-of-pearl Minga halls. In its way it had spread into
stranger places than this, by strange and devious paths and for
strange, devious reasons. But even had she never heard the
name (nor the deed she connected it with, which does not
matter here), she would have known from this scarred face,
these cold and steady eyes, that here stood the man she wanted,
the man who could help her if any man alive could.

And with that thought, others akin to it flashed through
her mind like blades crossing, and she dropped her milk-white
lids over the sword-play to hide its deadliness, and said, "Northwest . . . Smith," in a musing murmur.

"To be commanded," said Smith in the idiom of her own
tongue, but a spark of derision burned behind the courtly
words.

Still she said nothing, but looked him up and down with
slow eyes. He said at last,

"Your desire—?" and shifted impatiently.

"I had need of a wharfman's services," she said, still in that
breathing whisper. "I had not seen you, then. . . . There are
many wharfmen along the seafront, but only one of you, oh
man of Earth—" and she lifted her arms and swayed toward
him exactly as a reed sways to a lake breeze, and her arms lay
lightly on his shoulders and her mouth was very near. . . .

Smith looked down into the veiled eyes. He knew enough
of the breed of Venus to guess the deadly sword-flash of motive
behind anything a Venusian does, and he had caught a glimpse
of that particular sword-flash before she lowered her lids. And
if her thoughts were sword-play, his burnt like heat-beams
straight to their purpose. In the winking of an eye he knew a
part of her motive—the most obvious part. And he stood there
unanswering in the circle of her arms.

She looked up at him, half incredulous not to feel a leather
embrace tighten about her.

"Qu'a lo'val?" she murmured whimsically. "So cold, then, Earthman? Am I not desirable?"

Wordlessly he looked down at her, and despite himself the blood quickened in him. Minga girls for too many centuries had been born and bred to the art of charming men for North-west Smith to stand here in the warm arms of one and feel no answer to the invitation in her eyes. A subtle fragrance rose from her brazen hair, and the velvet molded a body whose whiteness he could guess from the flash of the long bare thigh her slashed skirt showed. He grinned a little crookedly and stepped away, breaking the clasp of her hands behind his neck.

"No," he said. "You know your art well, my dear, but your motive does not flatter me."

She stood back and regarded him with a wry, half-appreciative smile.

"What do you mean?"

"I'll have to know much more about all this before I commit myself as far as—that."

"You fool," she smiled. "You're in over your head now, as deeply as you could ever be. You were the moment you crossed the door-sill at the outer wall. There is no drawing back."

"Yet it was so easy—so very easy, to come in," murmured Smith.

She came forward a step and looked up at him with narrowed eyes, the pretense of seduction dropped like a cloak.

"You saw that, too?" she queried in a half-whisper. "It seemed so—to you? Great Shar, if I could be *sure*. . . ." And there was terror in her face.

"Suppose we sit down and you tell me about it," suggested Smith practically.

She laid a hand—white as cream, soft as satin—on his arm and drew him to the low divan that circled the room. There was inbred, generations-old coquetry in the touch, but the white hand shook a little.

"What is it you fear so?" queried Smith curiously as they sank to the green velvet. "Death comes only once, you know."

She shook her bronze head contemptuously.

"Not that," she said. "At least—no, I wish I knew just what

it is I do fear—and that is the most dreadful part of it. But I wish—I wish it had not been so easy to get you here."

"The place was deserted," he said thoughtfully. "Not a soul along the halls. Not a guard anywhere. Only once did we see any other creature, and that was a slave-girl in the hall just outside your door."

"What did she—do?" Vaudir's voice was breathless.

"Dropped to her knees as if she'd been shot. You might have thought me the devil himself by the way she acted."

The girl's breath escaped in a sigh.

"Safe, then," she said thankfully. "She must have thought you the—the Alendar." Her voice faltered a little over the name, as if she half feared to pronounce it. "He wears a cloak like that you wore when he comes through the halls. But he comes so very seldom. . . ."

"I've never seen him," said Smith, "but, good Lord, is he such a monster? The girl dropped as if she'd been hamstrung."

"Oh, hush, hush!" Vaudir agonized. "You mustn't speak of him so. He's—he's—of course she knelt and hid her face. I wish to heaven I had. . . ."

Smith faced her squarely and searched the veiled dark eyes with a gaze as bleak as empty seas. And he saw very clearly behind the veils the stark, nameless terror at their depths.

"What is it?" he demanded.

She drew her shoulders together and shivered a little, and her eyes were furtive as she glanced around the room.

"Don't you feel it?" she asked in that half-whisper to which her voice sank so caressingly. And he smiled to himself to see how instinctively eloquent was the courtezan in her—alluring gestures though her hands trembled, soft voice huskily seductive even in its terror. "—always, always!" she was saying. "The soft, hushed, hovering menace! It haunts the whole place. Didn't you feel it as you came in?"

"I think I did," Smith answered slowly. "Yes—that feel of something just out of sight, hiding in dark doorways . . . a sort of tensity in the air. . . ."

"Danger," she whispered, "terrible, nameless danger . . .

oh, I feel it wherever I go . . . it's soaked into me and through me until it's a part of me, body and soul. . . ."

Smith heard the note of rising hysteria in her voice, and said quickly,

"Why did you come to me?"

"I didn't, consciously." She conquered the hysteria with an effort and took up her tale a little more calmly. "I was really looking for a wharfman, as I said, and for quite another reason than this. It doesn't matter, now. But when you spoke, when I flashed my light and saw your face, I knew you. I'd heard of you, you see, and about the—the Lakkmanda affair, and I knew in a moment that if anyone alive could help me, it would be you."

"But what is it? Help you in what?"

"It's a long story," she said, "and too strange, almost, to believe, and too vague for you to take seriously. And yet I *know*. . . . Have you heard the history of the Minga?"

"A little of it. It goes back very far."

"Back into the beginning—and farther. I wonder if you can understand. You see, we on Venus are closer to our beginnings than you. Life here developed faster, of course, and along lines more different than Earthmen realize. On Earth civilization rose slowly enough for the—the elementals—to sink back into darkness. On Venus—oh, it's bad, *bad* for men to develop too swiftly! Life rises out of dark and mystery and things too strange and terrible to be looked upon. Earth's civilization grew slowly, and by the time men were civilized enough to look back they were sufficiently far from their origins not to see, not to know. But we here who look back see too clearly, sometimes, too nearly and vividly the black beginning. . . . Great Shar defend me, what I have seen!"

White hands flashed up to hide sudden terror in her eyes, and hair in a brazen cloud fell fragrantly over her fingers. And even in that terror was an inbred allure as natural as breathing.

In the little silence that followed, Smith caught himself glancing furtively over his shoulder. The room was ominously still. . . .

Vaudir lifted her face from her hands, shaking back her

hair. The hands trembled. She clasped them on her velvet knee and went on.

"The Minga," she said, and her voice was resolutely steady, "began too long ago for anyone to name the date. It began before dates. When Far-thursa came out of the sea-fog with his men and founded this city at the mountain's foot he built it around the walls of a castle already here. The Minga castle. And the Alendar sold Minga girls to the sailors and the city began. All that is myth, but the Minga had always been here.

"The Alendar dwelt in his stronghold and bred his golden girls and trained them in the arts of charming men, and guarded them with—with strange weapons—and sold them to kings at royal prices. There has always been an Alendar. I have seen him, once. . . .

"He walks the halls on rare occasions, and it is best to kneel and hide one's face when he comes by. Yes, it is best. . . . But I passed him one day, and—and—he is tall, tall as you, Earthman, and his eyes are like—the space between the worlds. I looked into his eyes under the hood he wore—I was not afraid of devil or man, then. I looked him in the eyes before I made obeisance, and I—I shall never be free of fear again. I looked into evil as one looks into a pool. Blackness and blankness and raw evil. Impersonal, not malevolent. Elemental . . . the elemental dreadfulness that life rose from. And I know very surely, now, that the first Alendar sprang from no mortal seed. There were races before man. . . . Life goes back very dreadfully through many forms and evils, before it reaches the wellspring of its beginning. And the Alendar had not the eyes of a human creature, and I met them—and I am damned!"

Her voice trailed softly away and she sat quiet for a space, staring before her with remembering eyes.

"I am doomed and damned to a blacker hell than any of Shar's priests threaten," she resumed. "No, wait—this is not hysteria. I haven't told you the worst part. You'll find it hard to believe, but it's truth—truth—Great Shar, if I could hope it were not!

"The origin of it is lost in legend. But why, in the beginning, did the first Alendar dwell in the misty sea-edge castle, alone and unknown, breeding his bronze girls?—not for sale,

then. Where did he get the secret of producing the invariable
type? And the castle, legend says, was age-old when Far-thursa
found it. The girls had a perfected, consistent beauty that
could be attained only by generations of effort. How long had
the Minga been built, and by whom? Above all, why? What
possible reason could there be for dwelling there absolutely
unknown, breeding civilized beauties in a world half-savage?
Sometimes I think I have guessed the reason. . . ."

Her voice faded into a resonant silence, and for a while she
sat staring blindly at the brocaded wall. When she spoke
again it was with a startling shift of topic.

"Am I beautiful, do you think?"

"More so than any I have ever seen before," answered Smith
without flattery.

Her mouth twisted.

"There are girls here now, in this building, so much lovelier
than I that I am humbled to think of them. No mortal man
has ever seen them, except the Alendar, and he—is not wholly
mortal. No mortal man will ever see them. They are not for
sale. Eventually they will disappear. . . .

"One might think that feminine beauty must reach an apex
beyond which it can not rise, but this is not true. It can in-
crease and intensify until—I have no words. And I truly believe
that there is no limit to the heights it can reach, in the hands
of the Alendar. And for every beauty we know and hear of,
through the slaves that tend them, gossip says there are as many
more, too immortally lovely for mortal eyes to see. Have you
ever considered that beauty might be refined and intensified
until one could scarcely bear to look upon it? We have tales
here of such beauty, hidden in some of the secret rooms of the
Minga.

"But the world never knows of these mysteries. No monarch
on any planet known is rich enough to buy the loveliness
hidden in the Minga's innermost rooms. It is not for sale. For
countless centuries the Alendars of the Minga have been breeding beauty, in higher and higher degrees, at infinite labor and
cost—beauty to be locked in secret chambers, guarded most
terribly, so that not even a whisper of it passes the outer walls,

beauty that vanishes, suddenly, in a breath—like that! Where? Why? How? No one knows.

"And it is that I fear. I have not a fraction of the beauty I speak of, yet a fate like that is written for me—somehow I know. I have looked into the eyes of the Alendar, and—I know. And I am sure that I must look again into those blank black eyes, more deeply, more dreadfully. . . . I know—and I am sick with terror of what more I shall know, soon. . . .

"Something dreadful is waiting for me, drawing nearer and nearer. Tomorrow, or the next day, or a little while after, I shall vanish, and the girls will wonder and whisper a little, and then forget. It has happened before. Great Shar, what shall I do?"

She wailed it, musically and hopelessly, and sank into a little silence. And then her look changed and she said reluctantly,

"And I have dragged you in with me. I have broken every tradition of the Minga in bringing you here, and there has been no hindrance—it has been too easy, too easy. I think I have sealed your death. When you first came I was minded to trick you into committing yourself so deeply that perforce you must do as I asked to win free again. But I know now that through the simple act of asking you here I have dragged you in deeper than I dreamed. It is a knowledge that has come to me somehow, out of the air tonight. I can feel knowledge beating upon me—compelling me. For in my terror to get help I think I have precipitated damnation upon us both. I know now—I have known in my soul since you entered so easily, that you will not go out alive—that—*it*—will come for me and drag you down too. . . . Shar, Shar, what have I done!"

"But what, what?" Smith struck his knee impatiently. "What is it we face? Poison? Guards? Traps? Hypnotism? Can't you give me even a guess at what will happen?"

He leaned forward to search her face commandingly, and saw her brows knit in an effort to find words that would cloak the mysteries she had to tell. Her lips parted irresolutely.

"The Guardians," she said. "The—Guardians. . . ."

And then over her hesitant face swept a look of such horror that his hand clenched on his knee and he felt the hairs rise along his neck. It was not horror of any material thing, but an inner dreadfulness, a terrible awareness. The eyes that had met his glazed and escaped his commanding stare without shifting their focus. It was as if they ceased to be eyes and became dark windows—vacant. The beauty of her face set like a mask, and behind the blank windows, behind the lovely set mask, he could sense dimly the dark command flowing in. . . .

She put out her hands stiffly and rose. Smith found himself on his feet, gun in hand, while his hackles lifted shudderingly and something pulsed in the air as tangibly as the beat of wings. Three times that nameless shudder stirred the air, and then Vaudir stepped forward like an automaton and faced the door. She walked in her dream of masked dreadfulness, stiffly, through the portal. As she passed him he put out a hesitant hand and laid it on her arm, and a little stab of pain shot through him at the contact, and once more he thought he felt the pulse of wings in the air. Then she passed by without hesitation, and his hand fell.

He made no further effort to arouse her, but followed after on cat-feet, delicately as if he walked on eggs. He was crouching a little, unconsciously, and his gun-hand held a tense finger on the trigger.

They went down the corridor in a breathing silence, an empty corridor where no lights showed beyond closed doors, where no murmur of voices broke the live stillness. But little shudders seemed to shake in the air somehow, and his heart was pounding suffocatingly.

Vaudir walked like a mechanical doll, tense in a dream of horror. When they reached the end of the hall he saw that the silver grille stood open, and they passed through without pausing. But Smith noted with a little qualm that a gateway opening to the right was closed and locked, and the bars across it were sunk firmly into wall-sockets. There was no choice but to follow her.

The corridor slanted downward. They passed others branching to right and left, but the silver gateways were closed and barred across each. A coil of silver stairs ended the passage, and the girl went stiffly down without touching the rails. It was a long spiral, past many floors, and as they descended, the rich, dim light lessened and darkened and a subtle smell of moisture and salt invaded the scented air. At each turn where the stairs opened on successive floors, gates were barred across the outlets; and they passed so many of these that Smith knew, as they went down and down, that however high the green jewel-box room had been, by now they were descending deep into the earth. And still the stair wound downward. The stories that opened beyond the bars like honeycomb layers became darker and less luxurious, and at last ceased altogether and the silver steps wound down through a well of rock, lighted so dimly at wide intervals that he could scarcely see the black polished walls circling them in. Drops of moisture began to appear on the dark surface, and the smell was of black salt seas and dank underground.

And just as he was beginning to believe that the stairs went on and on into the very black, salt heart of the planet, they came abruptly to the bottom. A flourish of slim, shining rails ended the stairs, at the head of a hallway, and the girl's feet turned unhesitatingly to follow its dark length. Smith's pale eyes, searching the dimness, found no trace of other life than themselves; yet eyes were upon him—he knew it surely.

They came down the black corridor to a gateway of wrought metal set in bars whose ends sank deep into the stone walls. She went through, Smith at her heels raking the dark with swift, unresting eyes like a wild animal's, wary in a strange jungle. And beyond the great gates a door hung with sweeping curtains of black ended the hall. Somehow Smith felt that they had reached their destination. And nowhere along the whole journey had he had any choice but to follow Vaudir's unerring, unseeing footsteps. Grilles had been locked across every possible outlet. But he had his gun. . . .

Her hands were white against the velvet as she pushed aside the folds. Very bright she stood for an instant—all green and gold and white—against the blackness. Then she passed through and the folds swept to behind her—candle-flame extinguished in dark velvet. Smith hesitated the barest instant before he parted the curtains and peered within.

He was looking into a room hung in black velvet that ab-

sorbed the light almost hungrily. That light radiated from a
single lamp swinging from the ceiling directly over an ebony
table. It shone softly on a man—a very tall man.

He stood darkly under it, very dark in the room's darkness,
his head bent, staring up from under level black brows. His
eyes in the half-hidden face were pits of blackness, and under
the lowered brows two pinpoint gleams stabbed straight—not
at the girl—but at Smith hidden behind the curtains. It held
his eyes as a magnet holds steel. He felt the narrow glitter
plunging blade-like into his very brain, and from the keen,
burning stab something within him shuddered away involuntarily. He thrust his gun through the curtains, stepped through
quietly, and stood meeting the sword-gaze with pale, unwavering eyes.

Vaudir moved forward with a mechanical stiffness that
somehow could not hide her grace—it was as if no power
existing could ever evoke from that lovely body less than
loveliness. She came to the man's feet and stopped there. Then
a long shudder swept her from head to foot and she dropped
to her knees and laid her forehead to the floor.

Across the golden loveliness of her the man's eyes met
Smith's, and the man's voice, deep, deep, like black waters
flowing smoothly, said,

"I am the Alendar."

"Then you know me," said Smith, his voice harsh as iron in
the velvet dimness.

"You are Northwest Smith," said the smooth, deep voice dis-
passionately. "An outlaw from the planet Earth. You have
broken your last law, Northwest Smith. Men do not come here
uninvited—and live. You perhaps have heard tales. . . ."

His voice melted into silence, lingeringly.

Smith's mouth curled into a wolfish grin, without mirth,
and his gun hand swung up. Murder flashed bleakly from his
steel-pale eyes. And then with stunning abruptness the world
dissolved about him. A burst of coruscations flamed through
his head, danced and wheeled and drew slowly together in a
whirling darkness until they were two pinpoint sparks of
light—a dagger stare under level brows. . . .

When the room steadied about him he was standing with slack arms, the gun hanging from his fingers, an apathetic numbness slowly withdrawing from his body. A dark smile curved smoothly on the Alendar's mouth.

The stabbing gaze slid casually away, leaving him dizzy in sudden vertigo, and touched the girl prostrate on the floor. Against the black carpet her burnished bronze curls sprayed out exquisitely. The green robe folded softly back from the roundness of her body, and nothing in the universe could have been so lovely as the creamy whiteness of her on the dark floor. The pit-black eyes brooded over her impassively. And then, in his smooth, deep voice the Alendar asked, amazingly, matter-of-factly,

"Tell me, do you have such girls on Earth?"

Smith shook his head to clear it. When he managed an answer his voice had steadied, and in the receding of that dizziness even the sudden drop into casual conversation seemed not unreasonable.

"I have never seen such a girl anywhere," he said calmly.

The sword gaze flashed up and pierced him.

"She has told you," said the Alendar. "You know I have beauties here that outshine her as the sun does a candle. And yet . . . she has more than beauty, this Vaudir. You have felt it, perhaps?"

Smith met the questioning gaze, searching for mockery, but finding none. Not understanding—a moment before the man had threatened his life—he took up the conversation.

"They all have more than beauty. For what other reason do kings buy the Minga girls?"

"No—not that charm. She has it too, but something more subtle than fascination, much more desirable than loveliness. She has courage, this girl. She has intelligence. Where she got it I do not understand. I do not breed my girls for such things. But I looked into her eyes once, in the hallway, as she told you —and saw there more arousing things than beauty. I summoned her—and you come at her heels. Do you know why? Do you know why you did not die at the outer gate or anywhere along the hallways on your way in?"

Smith's pale stare met the dark one questioningly. The voice flowed on.

"Because there are—interesting things in your eyes too. Courage and ruthlessness and a certain—power, I think. Intensity is in you. And I believe I can find a use for it, Earthman."

Smith's eyes narrowed a little. So calm, so matter-of-fact, this talk. But death was coming. He felt it in the air—he knew that feel of old. Death—and worse things than that, perhaps. He remembered the whispers he had heard.

On the floor the girl moaned a little, and stirred. The Alendar's quiet, pinpoint eyes flicked her, and he said softly, "Rise." And she rose, stumbling, and stood before him with bent head. The stiffness was gone from her. On an impulse Smith said suddenly, "Vaudir!" She lifted her face and met his gaze, and a thrill of horror rippled over him. She had regained consciousness, but she would never be the same frightened girl he had known. Black knowledge looked out of her eyes, and her face was a strained mask that covered horror barely—barely! It was the face of one who has walked through a blacker hell than any of humanity's understanding, and gained knowledge there that no human soul could endure knowing and live.

She looked him full in the face for a long moment, silently, and then turned away to the Alendar again. And Smith thought, just before her eyes left his, he had seen in them one wild flash of hopeless, desperate appeal. . . .

"Come," said the Alendar.

He turned his back—Smith's gun-hand trembled up and then fell again. No, better wait. There was always a bare hope, until he saw death closing in all around.

He stepped out over the yielding carpet at the Alendar's heels. The girl came after with slow steps and eyes downcast in a horrible parody of meditation, as if she brooded over the knowledge that dwelt so terribly behind her eyes.

The dark archway at the opposite end of the room swallowed them up. Light failed for an instant—a breath-stopping instant while Smith's gun leaped up involuntarily, like a live thing in his hand, futilely against invisible evil, and his brain rocked at the utter blackness that enfolded him. It was over in the wink of an eye, and he wondered if it had ever been as his gun-hand fell again. But the Alendar said across one shoulder,

"A barrier I have placed to guard my—beauties. A mental barrier that would have been impassable had you not been with me, yet which—but you understand now, do you not, my Vaudir?" And there was an indescribable leer in the query that injected a note of monstrous humanity into the inhuman voice.

"I understand," echoed the girl in a voice as lovely and toneless as a sustained musical note. And the sound of those two inhuman voices proceeding from the human lips of his companions sent a shudder thrilling along Smith's nerves.

They went down the long corridor thereafter in silence, Smith treading soundlessly in his spaceman's boots, every fiber of him tense to painfulness. He found himself wondering, even in the midst of his strained watchfulness, if any other creature with a living human soul had ever gone down this corridor before—if frightened golden girls had followed the Alendar thus into blackness, or if they too had been drained of humanity and steeped in that nameless horror before their feet followed their master through the black barrier.

The hallway led downward, and the salt smell became clearer and the light sank to a glimmer in the air, and in a silence that was not human they went on.

Presently the Alendar said—and his deep, liquid voice did nothing to break the stillness, blending with it softly so that not even an echo roused,

"I am taking you into a place where no other man than the Alendar has ever set foot before. It pleases me to wonder just how your unaccustomed senses will react to the things you are about to see. I am reaching an—an age"—he laughed softly—"where experiment interests me. Look!"

Smith's eyes blinked shut before an intolerable blaze of sudden light. In the streaked darkness of that instant while the glare flamed through his lids he thought he felt everything shift unaccountably about him, as if the very structure of the atoms that built the walls were altered. When he opened his eyes he stood at the head of a long gallery blazing with a soft, delicious brilliance. How he had got there he made no effort even to guess.

Very beautifully it stretched before him. The walls and floor and ceiling were of sheeny stone. There were low couches along the walls at intervals, and a blue pool broke the floor, and the air sparkled unaccountably with golden light. And figures were moving through that champagne sparkle. . . .

Smith stood very still, looking down the gallery. The Alendar watched him with a subtle anticipation upon his face, the pinpoint glitter of his eyes sharp enough to pierce the Earthman's very brain. Vaudir with bent head brooded over the black knowledge behind her drooping lids. Only Smith of the three looked down the gallery and saw what moved through the golden glimmer of the air.

They were girls. They might have been goddesses—angels haloed with bronze curls, moving leisurely through a golden heaven where the air sparkled like wine. There must have been a score of them strolling up and down the gallery in twos and threes, lolling on the couches, bathing in the pool. They wore the infinitely graceful Venusian robe with its looped shoulder and slit skirt, in soft, muted shades of violet and blue and jewel-green, and the beauty of them was breath-stopping as a blow. Music was in every gesture they made, a flowing, singing grace that made the heart ache with its sheer loveliness.

He had thought Vaudir lovely, but here was beauty so exquisite that it verged on pain. Their sweet, light voices were pitched to send little velvety burrs along his nerves, and from a distance the soft sounds blended so musically that they might have been singing together. The loveliness of their motion made his heart contract suddenly, and the blood pounded in his ears. . . .

"You find them beautiful?" The Alendar's voice blended into the humming lilt of voices as perfectly as it had blended with silence. His dagger-glitter of eyes was fixed piercingly on Smith's pale gaze, and he smiled a little, faintly. "Beautiful? Wait!"

He moved down the gallery, tall and very dark in the rainbow light. Smith, following after, walked in a haze of wonder.

It is not given to every man to walk through heaven. He felt
the air tingle like wine, and a delicious perfume caressed him
and the haloed girls drew back with wide, amazed eyes fixed
on him in his stained leather and heavy boots as he passed.
Vaudir paced quietly after, her head bent, and from her the
girls turned away their eyes, shuddering a little.

He saw now that their faces were as lovely as their bodies,
languorously, colorfully. They were contented faces, unconscious of beauty, unconscious of any other existence than their
own—soulless. He felt that instinctively. Here was beauty incarnate, physically, tangibly; but he had seen in Vaudir's face
—before—a sparkle of daring, a tenderness of remorse at having
brought him here, that gave her an indefinable superiority
over even this incredible beauty, soulless.

They went down the gallery in a sudden hush as the musical
voices fell silent from very amazement. Apparently the Alendar
was a familiar figure here, for they scarcely glanced at him,
and from Vaudir they turned away in a shuddering revulsion
that preferred not to recognize her existence. But Smith was
the first man other than the Alendar whom they had ever seen,
and the surprise of it struck them dumb.

They went on through the dancing air, and the last lovely,
staring girls fell behind, and an ivory gateway opened before
them, without a touch. They went downstairs from there, and
along another hallway, while the tingle died in the air and a
hum of musical voices sprang up behind them. They passed
beyond the sound. The hallway darkened until they were
moving again through dimness.

Presently the Alendar paused and turned.

"My more costly jewels," he said, "I keep in separate settings.
As here—"

He stretched out his arm, and Smith saw that a curtain hung
against the wall. There were others, farther on, dark blots
against the dimness. The Alendar drew back black folds, and
light from beyond flowed softly through a pattern of bars to
cast flowery shadows on the opposite wall. Smith stepped forward and stared.

He was looking through a grille window down into a room

lined with dark velvet. It was quite plain. There was a low couch against the wall opposite the window, and on it—Smith's heart gave a stagger and paused—a woman lay. And if the girls in the gallery had been like goddesses, this woman was lovelier than men have ever dared to imagine even in legends. She was beyond divinity—long limbs white against the velvet, sweet curves and planes of her rounding under the robe, bronze hair spilling like lava over one white shoulder, and her face calm as death with closed eyes. It was a passive beauty, like alabaster shaped perfectly. And charm, a fascination all but tangible, reached out from her like a magic spell. A sleeping charm, magnetic, powerful. He could not wrench his eyes away. He was like a wasp caught in honey. . . .

The Alendar said something across Smith's shoulder, in a vibrant voice that thrilled the air. The closed lids rose. Life and loveliness flowed into the calm face like a tide, lighting it unbearably. That heady charm wakened and brightened to a dangerous liveness—tugging, pulling. . . . She rose in one long glide like a wave over rocks; she smiled (Smith's senses reeled to the beauty of that smile) and then sank in a deep salaam, slowly, to the velvet floor, her hair rippling and falling all about her, until she lay abased in a blaze of loveliness under the window.

The Alendar let the curtain fall, and turned to Smith as the dazzling sight was blotted out. Again the pinpoint glitter stabbed into Smith's brain. The Alendar smiled again.

"Come," he said, and moved down the hall.

They passed three curtains, and paused at a fourth. Afterward Smith remembered that the curtain must have been drawn back and he must have bent forward to stare through the window bars, but the sight he saw blasted every memory of it from his mind. The girl who dwelt in this velvet-lined room was stretching on tiptoe just as the drawn curtain caught her, and the beauty and grace of her from head to foot stopped Smith's breath as a ray-stab to the heart would have done. And the irresistible, wrenching charm of her drew him forward until he was clasping the bars with white-knuckled hands, unaware of anything but her compelling, soul-destroying desirability. . . .

She moved, and the dazzle of grace that ran like a song through every motion made his senses ache with its pure, unattainable loveliness. He knew, even in his daze of rapture, that he might hold the sweet, curved body in his arms for ever, yet hunger still for the fulfilment which the flesh could never wring from her. Her loveliness aroused a hunger in the soul more maddening than the body's hunger could ever be. His brain rocked with the desire to possess that intangible, irresistible loveliness that he knew he could never possess, never reach with any sense that was in him. That bodiless desire raged like madness through him, so violently that the room reeled and the white outlines of the beauty unattainable as the stars wavered before him. He caught his breath and choked and drew back from the intolerable, exquisite sight.

The Alendar laughed and dropped the curtain.

"Come," he said again, the subtle amusement clear in his voice, and Smith in a daze moved after him down the hall.

They went a long way, past curtains hanging at regular intervals along the wall. When they paused at last, the curtain before which they stopped was faintly luminous about the edges, as if something dazzling dwelt within. The Alendar drew back the folds.

"We are approaching," he said, "a pure clarity of beauty, hampered only a little by the bonds of flesh. Look."

One glance only Smith snatched of the dweller within. And the exquisite shock of that sight went thrilling like torture through every nerve of him. For a mad instant his reason staggered before the terrible fascination beating out from that dweller in waves that wrenched at his very soul—incarnate loveliness tugging with strong fingers at every sense and every nerve and intangibly, irresistibly, at deeper things than these, groping among the roots of his being, dragging his soul out. . . .

Only one glance he took, and in the glance he felt his soul answer that dragging, and the terrible desire tore futilely through him. Then he flung up an arm to shield his eyes and reeled back into the dark, and a wordless sob rose to his lips and the darkness reeled about him.

The curtain fell. Smith pressed the wall and breathed in

long, shuddering gasps, while his heart-beats slowed gradually
and the unholy fascination ebbed from about him. The
Alendar's eyes were glittering with a green fire as he turned
from the window, and a nameless hunger lay shadowily on his
face. He said,

"I might show you others, Earthman. But it could only
drive you mad, in the end—you were very near the brink for a
moment just now—and I have another use for you. . . . I
wonder if you begin to understand, now, the purpose of all
this?"

The green glow was fading from that dagger-sharp gaze as
the Alendar's eyes stabbed into Smith's. The Earthman gave
his head a little shake to clear away the vestiges of that devouring desire, and took a fresh grip on the butt of his gun. The
familiar smoothness of it brought him a measure of reassurance, and with it a reawakening to the peril all around. He
knew now that there could be no conceivable mercy for him,
to whom the innermost secrets of the Minga had been unaccountably revealed. Death was waiting—strange death, as soon
as the Alendar wearied of talking—but if he kept his ears open
and his eyes alert it might not—please God—catch him so
quickly that he died alone. One sweep of that blade-blue flame
was all he asked, now. His eyes, keen and hostile, met the
dagger-gaze squarely. The Alendar smiled and said,

"Death in your eyes, Earthman. Nothing in your mind but
murder. Can that brain of yours comprehend nothing but
battle? Is there no curiosity there? Have you no wonder of
why I brought you here? Death awaits you, yes. But a not unpleasant death, and it awaits all, in one form or another.
Listen, let me tell you—I have reason for desiring to break
through that animal shell of self-defense that seals in your
mind. Let me look deeper—if there are depths. Your death
will be—useful, and in a way, pleasant. Otherwise—well, the
black beasts hunger. And flesh must feed them, as a sweeter
drink feeds me. . . . Listen."

Smith's eyes narrowed. A sweeter drink. . . . Danger, danger
—the smell of it in the air—instinctively he felt the peril of
opening his mind to the plunging gaze of the Alendar, the

force of those compelling eyes beating like strong lights into his brain. . . .

"Come," said the Alendar softly, and moved off soundlessly through the gloom. They followed, Smith painfully alert, the girl walking with lowered, brooding eyes, her mind and soul afar in some wallowing darkness whose shadow showed so hideously beneath her lashes.

The hallway widened to an arch, and abruptly, on the other side, one wall dropped away into infinity and they stood on the dizzy brink of a gallery opening on a black, heaving sea. Smith bit back a startled oath. One moment before the way had led through low-roofed tunnels deep underground; the next instant they stood on the shore of a vast body of rolling darkness, a tiny wind touching their faces with the breath of unnamable things.

Very far below, the dark waters rolled. Phosphorescence lighted them uncertainly, and he was not even sure it was water that surged there in the dark. A heavy thickness seemed to be inherent in the rollers, like black slime surging.

The Alendar looked out over the fire-tinged waves. He waited for an instant without speaking, and then, far out in the slimy surges, something broke the surface with an oily splash, something mercifully veiled in the dark, then dived again, leaving a wake of spreading ripples over the surface.

"Listen," said the Alendar, without turning his head. "Life is very old. There are older races than man. Mine is one. Life rose out of the black slime of the sea-bottoms and grew toward the light along many diverging lines. Some reached maturity and deep wisdom when man was still swinging through the jungle trees.

"For many centuries, as mankind counts time, the Alendar has dwelt here, breeding beauty. In later years he has sold some of his lesser beauties, perhaps to explain to mankind's satisfaction what it could never understand were it told the truth. Do you begin to see? My race is very remotely akin to those races which suck blood from man, less remotely to those which drink his life-forces for nourishment. I refine taste even more than that. I drink—beauty. I live on beauty. Yes, literally.

"Beauty is as tangible as blood, in a way. It is a separate, distinct force that inhabits the bodies of men and women. You must have noticed the vacuity that accompanies perfect beauty in so many women . . . the force so strong that it drives out all other forces and lives vampirishly at the expense of intelligence and goodness and conscience and all else.

"In the beginning, here—for our race was old when this world began, spawned on another planet, and wise and ancient —we woke from slumber in the slime, to feed on the beauty force inherent in mankind even in cave-dwelling days. But it was meager fare, and we studied the race to determine where the greatest prospects lay, then selected specimens for breeding, built this stronghold and settled down to the business of evolving mankind up to its limit of loveliness. In time we weeded out all but the present type. For the race of man we have developed the ultimate type of loveliness. It is interesting to see what we have accomplished on other worlds, with utterly different races. . . .

"Well, there you have it. Women, bred as a spawning-ground for the devouring force of beauty on which we live.

"But—the fare grows monotonous, as all food must without change. Vaudir I took because I saw in her a sparkle of something that except in very rare instances has been bred out of the Minga girls. For beauty, as I have said, eats up all other qualities but beauty. Yet somehow intelligence and courage survived latently in Vaudir. It decreases her beauty, but the tang of it should be a change from the eternal sameness of the rest. And so I thought until I saw you.

"I realized then how long it had been since I tasted the beauty of man. It is so rare, so different from female beauty, that I had all but forgotten it existed. And you have it, very subtly, in a raw, harsh way. . . .

"I have told you all this to test the quality of that—that harsh beauty in you. Had I been wrong about the deeps of your mind, you would have gone to feed the black beasts, but I see that I was not wrong. Behind your animal shell of self-preservation are depths of that force and strength which nourish the roots of male beauty. I think I shall give you a while to let it grow, under the forcing methods I know, before I—drink. It will be delightful. . . .

The voice trailed away in a murmurous silence, the pin-point glitter sought Smith's eyes. And he tried half-heartedly to avoid it, but his eyes turned involuntarily to the stabbing gaze, and the alertness died out of him, gradually, and the compelling pull of those glittering points in the pits of dark-ness held him very still.

And as he stared into the diamond glitter he saw its bril-liance slowly melt and darken, until the pinpoints of light had changed to pools that dimmed, and he was looking into black evil as elemental and vast as the space between the worlds, a dizzying blankness wherein dwelt unnamable hor-ror . . . deep, deep . . . all about him the darkness was cloud-ing. And thoughts that were not his own seeped into his mind out of that vast, elemental dark . . . crawling, writhing thoughts . . . until he had a glimpse of that dark place where Vaudir's soul wallowed, and something sucked him down and down into a waking nightmare he could not fight. . . .

Then somehow the pull broke for an instant. For just that instant he stood again on the shore of the heaving sea and gripped a gun with nerveless fingers—then the darkness closed about him again, but a different, uneasy dark that had not quite the all-compelling power of that other nightmare—it left him strength enough to fight.

And he fought, a desperate, moveless, soundless struggle in a black sea of horror, while worm-thoughts coiled through his straining mind and the clouds rolled and broke and rolled again about him. Sometimes, in the instants when the pull slackened, he had time to feel a third force struggling here be-tween that black, blind downward suck that dragged at him and his own sick, frantic effort to fight clear, a third force that was weakening the black drag so that he had moments of lucidity when he stood free on the brink of the ocean and felt the sweat roll down his face and was aware of his laboring heart and how gaspingly breath tortured his lungs, and he knew he was fighting with every atom of himself, body and mind and soul, against the intangible blackness sucking him down.

And then he felt the force against him gather itself in a final effort—he sensed desperation in that effort—and come rolling over him like a tide. Bowled over, blinded and dumb and deaf, drowning in utter blackness, he floundered in the deeps of that nameless hell where thoughts that were alien and slimy squirmed through his brain. Bodiless he was, and unstable, and as he wallowed there in the ooze more hideous than any earthly ooze, because it came from black, inhuman souls and out of ages before man, he became aware that the worm-thoughts a-squirm in his brain were forming slowly into monstrous meanings—knowledge like a formless flow was pouring through his bodiless brain, knowledge so dreadful that consciously he could not comprehend it, though subconsciously every atom of his mind and soul sickened and writhed futilely away. It was flooding over him, drenching him, permeating him through and through with the very essence of dreadfulness—he felt his mind melting away under the solvent power of it, melting and running fluidly into new channels and fresh molds—horrible molds. . . .

And just at that instant, while madness folded around him and his mind rocked on the verge of annihilation, something snapped, and like a curtain the dark rolled away, and he stood sick and dizzy on the gallery above the black sea. Everything was reeling about him, but they were stable things that shimmered and steadied before his eyes, blessed black rock and tangible surges that had form and body—his feet pressed firmness and his mind shook itself and was clean and his own again.

And then through the haze of weakness that still shrouded him a voice was shrieking wildly, "Kill! . . . kill!" and he saw the Alendar staggering against the rail, all his outlines unaccountably blurred and uncertain, and behind him Vaudir with blazing eyes and face wrenched hideously into life again, screaming "Kill!" in a voice scarcely human.

Like an independent creature his gun-hand leaped up—he had gripped that gun through everything that happened—and he was dimly aware of the hardness of it kicking back against his hand with the recoil, and of the blue flash flaming from its muzzle. It struck the Alendar's dark figure full, and there was a hiss and a dazzle. . . .

Smith closed his eyes tight and opened them again, and stared with a sick incredulity; for unless that struggle had unhinged his brain after all, and the worm-thoughts still dwelt slimily in his mind, tingeing all he saw with unearthly horror —unless this was true, he was looking not at a man just rayed through the lungs, and who should be dropping now in a bleeding, collapsed heap to the floor, but at—at—God, what *was* it? The dark figure had slumped against the rail, and instead of blood gushing, a hideous, nameless, formless black poured sluggishly forth—a slime like the heaving sea below. The whole dark figure of the man was melting, slumping farther down into the pool of blackness forming at his feet on the stone floor.

Smith gripped his gun and watched in numb incredulity, and the whole body sank slowly down and melted and lost all form—hideously, gruesomely—until where the Alendar had stood a heap of slime lay viscidly on the gallery floor, hideously alive, heaving and rippling and striving to lift itself into a semblance of humanity again. And as he watched, it lost even that form, and the edges melted revoltingly and the mass flattened and slid down into a pool of utter horror, and he became aware that it was pouring slowly through the rails into the sea. He stood watching while the whole rolling, shimmering mound melted and thinned and trickled through the bars, until the floor was clear again, and not even a stain marred the stone.

A painful constriction of his lungs roused him, and he realized he had been holding his breath, scarcely daring to realize. Vaudir had collapsed against the wall, and he saw her knees give limply, and staggered forward on uncertain feet to catch her as she fell.

"Vaudir, Vaudir!" he shook her gently. "Vaudir, what's happened? Am I dreaming? Are we safe now? Are you—awake again?"

Very slowly her white lids lifted, and the black eyes met his. And he saw shadowily there the knowledge of that wallowing void he had dimly known, the shadow that could never be cleared away. She was steeped and foul with it. And the look of her eyes was such that involuntarily he released her and stepped away. She staggered a little and then regained her balance and regarded him from under bent brows. The level inhumanity of her gaze struck into his soul, and yet he thought he saw a spark of the girl she had been, dwelling in torture amid the blackness. He knew he was right when she said, in a far-away, toneless voice,

"Awake? . . . No, not ever now, Earthman. I have been down too deeply into hell . . . he had dealt me a worse torture than he knew, for there is just enough humanity left within me to realize what I have become, and to suffer. . . .

"Yes, he is gone, back into the slime that bred him. I have been a part of him, one with him in the blackness of his soul, and I know. I have spent eons since the blackness came upon me, dwelt for eternities in the dark, rolling seas of his mind, sucking in knowledge . . . and as I was one with him, and he now gone, so shall I die; yet I will see you safely out of here if it is in my power, for it was I who dragged you in. If I can remember—if I can find the way. . . ."

She turned uncertainly and staggered a step back along the way they had come. Smith sprang forward and slid his free arm about her, but she shuddered away from the contact.

"No, no—unbearable—the touch of clean human flesh—and it breaks the chord of my remembering. . . . I can not look back into his mind as it was when I dwelt there, and I must, I must. . . ."

She shook him off and reeled on, and he cast one last look at the billowing sea, and then followed. She staggered along the stone floor on stumbling feet, one hand to the wall to support herself, and her voice was whispering gustily, so that he had to follow close to hear, and then almost wished he had not heard,

"—black slime—darkness feeding on light—everything wavers so—slime, slime and a rolling sea—he rose out of it, you know, before civilization began here—he is age-old—there never has been but one Alendar. . . . And somehow—I could not see just how, or remember why—he rose from the rest, as some of his race on other planets had done, and took the man-form and stocked his breeding-pens. . . ."

They went on up the dark hallway, past curtains hiding incarnate loveliness, and the girl's stumbling footsteps kept time to her stumbling, half-incoherent words.

"—has lived all these ages here, breeding and devouring beauty—vampire-thirst, a hideous delight in drinking in that beauty-force—I felt it and remembered it when I was one with him—wrapping black layers of primal slime about—quenching human loveliness in ooze, sucking—blind black thirst. . . . And his wisdom was ancient and dreadful and full of power— so he could draw a soul out through the eyes and sink it in hell, and drown it there, as he would have done mine if I had not had, somehow, a difference from the rest. Great Shar, I wish I had not! I wish I were drowned in it and did not feel in every atom of me the horrible uncleanness of—what I know. But by virtue of that hidden strength I did not surrender wholly, and when he had turned his power to subduing you I was able to struggle, there in the very heart of his mind, making a disturbance that shook him as he fought us both— making it possible to free you long enough for you to destroy the human flesh he was clothed in—so that he lapsed into the ooze again. I do not quite understand why that happened— only that his weakness, with you assailing him from without and me struggling strongly in the very center of his soul was such that he was forced to draw on the power he had built up to maintain himself in the man form, and weakened it enough so that he collapsed when the man-form was assailed. And he fell back into the slime again—whence he rose—black slime —heaving—oozing. . . ."

Her voice trailed away in murmurs, and she stumbled, all but falling. When she regained her balance she went on ahead of him at a greater distance, as if his very nearness were repugnant to her, and the soft babble of her voice drifted back in broken phrases without meaning.

Presently the air began to tingle again, and they passed the silver gate and entered that gallery where the air sparkled like champagne. The blue pool lay jewel-clear in its golden setting. Of the girls there was no sign.

When they reached the head of the gallery the girl paused, turning to him a face twisted with the effort at memory.

"Here is the trial," she said urgently. "If I can remember—" She seized her head in clutching hands, shaking it savagely.

"I haven't the strength, now—can't—can't—" the piteous little murmur reached his ears incoherently. Then she straightened resolutely, swaying a little, and faced him, holding out her hands. He clasped them hesitantly, and saw a shiver go through her at the contact, and her face contort painfully, and then a shudder communicated itself through that clasp and he too winced in revolt. He saw her eyes go blank and her face strain in lines of tensity, and a fine dew broke out on her forehead. For a long moment she stood so, her face like death, and strong shudders went over her body and her eyes were blank as the void between the planets.

And as each shudder swept her it went unbroken through the clasping of their hands to him, and they were black waves of dreadfulness, and again he saw the heaving sea and wallowed in the hell he had fought out of on the gallery, and he knew for the first time what torture she must be enduring who dwelt in the very deeps of that uneasy dark. The pulses came faster, and for moments together he went down into the blind blackness and the slime, and felt the first wriggling of the worm-thoughts tickling the roots of his brain. . . .

And then suddenly a clean darkness closed round them and again everything shifted unaccountably, as if the atoms of the gallery were changing, and when Smith opened his eyes he was standing once more in the dark, slanting corridor with the smell of salt and antiquity heavy in the air.

Vaudir moaned softly beside him, and he turned to see her reeling against the wall and trembling so from head to foot that he looked to see her fall the next moment.

"Better—in a moment," she gasped. "It took—nearly all my strength to—to get us through—wait. . . ."

So they halted there in the darkness and the dead salt air, until the trembling abated a little and she said, "Come," in her little whimpering voice. And again the journey began. It was only a short way, now, to the barrier of black blankness that guarded the door into the room where they had first seen the Alendar. When they reached the place she shivered a little and paused, then resolutely held out her hands. And as he took them he felt once more the hideous slimy waves course through him, and plunged again into the heaving hell. And as before the clean darkness flashed over them in a breath, and then she dropped his hands and they were standing in the archway looking into the velvet-hung room they had left—it seemed eons ago.

He watched as waves of blinding weakness flooded over her from that supreme effort. Death was visible in her face as she turned to him at last.

"Come—oh, come quickly," she whispered, and staggered forward.

At her heels he followed, across the room, past the great iron gateway, down the hall to the foot of the silver stairs. And here his heart sank, for he felt sure she could never climb the long spiral distances to the top. But she set her foot on the step and went upward resolutely, and as he followed he heard her murmuring to herself,

"Wait—oh, wait—let me reach the end—let me undo this much—and then—no, no! Please Shar, not the black slime again. . . . Earthman, Earthman!"

She paused on the stair and turned to face him, and her haggard face was frantic with desperation and despair.

"Earthman, promise—do not let me die like this! When we reach the end, ray me! Burn me clean, or I shall go down for eternity into the black sinks from which I dragged you free. Oh, promise!"

"I will," Smith's voice said quietly. "I will."

And they went on. Endlessly the stairs spiraled upward and endlessly they climbed. Smith's legs began to ache intolerably, and his heart was pounding like a wild thing, but Vaudir seemed not to notice weariness. She climbed steadily and no more unsurely than she had come along the halls. And after eternities they reached the top.

And there the girl fell. She dropped like a dead woman at the head of the silver spiral. Smith thought for a sick instant that he had failed her and let her die uncleansed, but in a moment or two she stirred and lifted her head and very slowly dragged herself to her feet.

"I will go on—I will, I will," she whispered to herself. "—come this far—must finish—" and she reeled off down the lovely, rosily-lit hallway paneled in pearl.

He could see how perilously near she was to her strength's
end, and he marveled at the tenacity with which she clung
to life though it ebbed away with every breath and the pulse
of darkness flowed in after it. So with bulldog stubbornness
she made her wavering way past door after door of carven
shell, under rosy lights that flushed her face with a ghastly
mockery of health, until they reached the silver gateway at
the end. The lock had been removed from it by now, and
the bar drawn.

She tugged open the gate and stumbled through.

And the nightmare journey went on. It must be very near
morning, Smith thought, for the halls were deserted, but did
he not sense a breath of danger in the still air? . . .

The girl's gasping voice answered that half-formed query
as if, like the Alendar, she held the secret of reading men's
minds.

"The—Guardians—still rove the halls, and unleashed now—
so keep your ray-gun ready, Earthman. . . ."

After that he kept his eyes alert as they retraced, stumbling
and slow, the steps he had taken on his way in. And once
he heard distinctly the soft slither of—something—scraping
over the marble pavement, and twice he smelt with shocking
suddenness in this scented air a whiff of salt, and his mind
flashed back to a rolling black sea. . . . But nothing molested
them.

Step by faltering step the hallways fell behind them, and
he began to recognize landmarks, and the girl's footsteps
staggered and hesitated and went on gallantly, incredibly,
beating back oblivion, fighting the dark surges rolling over
her, clinging with tenacious fingers to the tiny spark of life
that drove her on.

And at long last, after what seemed hours of desperate effort,
they reached the blue-lit hallway at whose end the outer
door opened. Vaudir's progress down it was a series of dizzy
staggers, interspersed with pauses while she hung to the carven
doors with tense fingers and drove her teeth into a bloodless
lip and gripped that last flicker of life. He saw the shudders
sweep over her, and knew what waves of washing dark must

be rising all about her, and how the worm-thoughts writhed through her brain. . . . But she went on. Every step now was a little tripping, as if she fell from one foot to the other, and at each step he expected that knee to give way and pitch her down into the black deeps that yawned for her. But she went on.

She reached the bronze door, and with a last spurt of effort she lifted the bar and swung it open. Then that tiny spark flickered out like a lamp. Smith caught one flash of the rock room within—and something horrible on the floor—before he saw her pitch forward as the rising tide of slimy oblivion closed at last over her head. She was dying as she fell, and he whipped the ray-gun up and felt the recoil against his palm as a blue blaze flashed forth and transfixed her in midair. And he could have sworn her eyes lighted for a flickering instant and the gallant girl he had known looked forth, cleansed and whole, before death—clean death—glazed them.

She slumped down in a huddle at his feet, and he felt a sting of tears beneath his eyelids as he looked down on her, a huddle of white and bronze on the rug. And as he watched, a film of defilement veiled the shining whiteness of her—decay set in before his eyes and progressed with horrible swiftness, and in less time than it takes to tell he was staring with horrified eyes at a pool of black slime across which green velvet lay bedraggled.

Northwest Smith closed his pale eyes, and for a moment struggled with memory, striving to wrest from it the long-forgotten words of a prayer learned a score of years ago on another planet. Then he stepped over the pitiful, horrible heap on the carpet and went on.

In the little rock room of the outer wall he saw what he had glimpsed when Vaudir opened the door. Retribution had overtaken the eunuch. The body must have been his, for tatters of scarlet velvet lay about the floor, but there was no way to recognize what its original form had been. The smell of salt was heavy in the air, and a trail of black slime snaked across the floor toward the wall. The wall was solid, but it ended there. . . .

Smith laid his hand on the outer door, drew the bar, swung it open. He stepped out under the hanging vines and filled his lungs with pure air, free, clear, untainted with scent or salt. A pearly dawn was breaking over Ednes.

The Tree of Life

OVER time-ruined Illar the searching planes swooped and circled. Northwest Smith, peering up at them with a steel-pale stare from the shelter of a half-collapsed temple, thought of vultures wheeling above carrion. All day long now they had been raking these ruins for him. Presently, he knew, thirst would begin to parch his throat and hunger to gnaw at him. There was neither food nor water in these ancient Martian ruins, and he knew that it could be only a matter of time before the urgencies of his own body would drive him out to signal those wheeling Patrol ships and trade his hard-won liberty for food and drink. He crouched lower under the shadow of the temple arch and cursed the accuracy of the Patrol gunner whose flame-blast had caught his dodging ship just at the edge of Illar's ruins.

Presently it occurred to him that in most Martian temples of the ancient days an ornamental well had stood in the outer court for the benefit of wayfarers. Of course all water in it would be a million years dry now, but for lack of anything better to do he rose from his seat at the edge of the collapsed central dome and made his cautious way by still intact corridors toward the front of the temple. He paused in a tangle of wreckage at the courtyard's edge and looked out across the sun-drenched expanse of pavement toward that ornate well that once had served travelers who passed by here in the days when Mars was a green planet.

It was an unusually elaborate well, and amazingly well preserved. Its rim had been inlaid with a mosaic pattern whose symbolism must once have borne deep meaning, and above it in a great fan of time-defying bronze an elaborate grille-work portrayed the inevitable tree-of-life pattern which so often appears in the symbolism of the three worlds. Smith looked at it a bit incredulously from his shelter, it was so miraculously preserved amidst all this chaos of broken stone, casting a delicate tracery of shadow on the sunny pavement as perfectly as it must have done a million years ago when dusty travelers paused here to drink. He could picture them filing in at noontime through the great gates that—

The vision vanished abruptly as his questing eyes made the circle of the ruined walls. There had been no gate. He could not find a trace of it anywhere around the outer wall of the court. The only entrance here, as nearly as he could tell from the foundations that remained, had been the door in whose ruins he now stood. Queer. This must have been a private court, then, its great grille-crowned well reserved for the use of the priests. Or wait—had there not been a priest-king Illar after whom the city was named? A wizard-king, so legend said, who ruled temple as well as palace with an iron hand. This elaborately patterned well, of material royal enough to withstand the weight of ages, might well have been sacrosanct for the use of that long-dead monarch. It might—

Across the sun-bright pavement swept the shadow of a plane. Smith dodged back into deeper hiding while the ship circled low over the courtyard. And it was then, as he crouched against a crumbled wall and waited, motionless, for the danger to pass, that he became aware for the first time of a sound that startled him so he could scarcely credit his ears—a recurrent sound, choked and sorrowful—the sound of a woman sobbing.

The incongruity of it made him forgetful for a moment of the peril hovering overhead in the sun-hot outdoors. The dimness of the temple ruins became a living and vital place for that moment, throbbing with the sound of tears. He looked about half in incredulity, wondering if hunger and thirst were playing tricks on him already, or if these broken halls might be haunted by a million-years-old sorrow that wept along the corridors to drive its hearers mad. There were tales of such haunters in some of Mars' older ruins. The hair prickled faintly at the back of his neck as he laid a hand on the butt of his force-gun and commenced a cautious prowl toward the source of the muffled noise.

Presently he caught a flash of white, luminous in the gloom of these ruined walls, and went forward with soundless steps, eyes narrowed in the effort to make out what manner of creature this might be that wept alone in time-forgotten ruins. It was a woman. Or it had the dim outlines of a woman, huddled against an angle of fallen walls and veiled in a fabulous shower of long dark hair. But there was something uncannily odd about her. He could not focus his pale stare upon her outlines. She was scarcely more than a luminous blot of whiteness in the gloom, shimmering with a look of unreality which the sound of her sobs denied.

Before he could make up his mind just what to do, something must have warned the weeping girl that she was no longer alone, for the sound of her tears checked suddenly and she lifted her head, turning to him a face no more distinguishable than her body's outlines. He made no effort to resolve the blurred features into visibility, for out of that luminous mask burned two eyes that caught his with an almost perceptible impact and gripped them in a stare from which he could not have turned if he would.

They were the most amazing eyes he had ever met, colored like moonstone, milkily translucent, so that they looked almost blind. And that magnetic stare held him motionless. In the instant that she gripped him with that fixed, moonstone look he felt oddly as if a tangible bond were taut between them.

Then she spoke, and he wondered if his mind, after all, had begun to give way in the haunted loneliness of dead Illar; for though the words she spoke fell upon his ears in a gibberish of meaningless sounds, yet in his brain a message formed with a clarity that far transcended the halting communication of words. And her milkily colored eyes bored into his with a fierce intensity.

"I'm lost—I'm lost—" wailed the voice in his brain.

A rush of sudden tears brimmed the compelling eyes, veiling their brilliance. And he was free again with that clouding of the moonstone surfaces. Her voice wailed, but the words were meaningless and no knowledge formed in his brain to

match them. Stiffly he stepped back a pace and looked down
at her, a feeling of helpless incredulity rising within him. For
he still could not focus directly upon the shining whiteness
of her, and nothing save those moonstone eyes were clear
to him.

The girl sprang to her feet and rose on tiptoe, gripping his
shoulders with urgent hands. Again the blind intensity of
her eyes took hold of his, with a force almost as tangible as
the clutch of her hands; again that stream of intelligence
poured into his brain, strongly, pleadingly.

"Please, please take me back! I'm so frightened—I can't
find my way—oh, please!"

He blinked down at her, his dazed mind gradually realizing
the basic facts of what was happening. Obviously her milky,
unseeing eyes held a magnetic power that carried her thoughts
to him without the need of a common speech. And they were
the eyes of a powerful mind, the outlets from which a stream
of fierce energy poured into his brain. Yet the words they
conveyed were the words of a terrified and helpless girl. A
strong sense of wariness was rising in him as he considered
the incongruity of speech and power, both of which were
beating upon him more urgently with every breath. The
mind of a forceful and strong-willed woman, carrying the sobs
of a frightened girl. There was no sincerity in it.

"Please, please!" cried her impatience in his brain. "Help
me! Guide me back!"

"Back where?" he heard his own voice asking.

"The Tree!" wailed that queer speech in his brain, while
gibberish was all his ears heard and the moonstone stare transfixed him strongly. "The Tree of Life! Oh, take me back to
the shadow of the Tree!"

A vision of the grille-ornamented well leaped into his
memory. It was the only tree symbol he could think of just
then. But what possible connection could there be between
the well and the lost girl—if she was lost? Another wail in
that unknown tongue, another anguished shake of his
shoulders, brought a sudden resolution into his groping mind.
There could be no harm in leading her back to the well, to

whose grille she must surely be referring. And strong curiosity was growing in his mind. Much more than met the eye was concealed in this queer incident. And a wild guess had flashed through his mind that perhaps she might have come from some subterranean world into which the well descended. It would explain her luminous pallor, if not her blurriness; and, too, her eyes did not seem to function in the light. There was a much more incredible explanation of her presence, but he was not to know it for a few minutes yet.

"Come along," he said, taking the clutching hands gently from his shoulders. "I'll lead you to the well."

She sighed in a deep gust of relief and dropped her compelling eyes from his, murmuring in that strange, gabbling tongue what must have been thanks. He took her by the hand and turned toward the ruined archway of the door.

Against his fingers her flesh was cool and firm. To the touch she was tangible, but even thus near, his eyes refused to focus upon the cloudy opacity of her body, the dark blur of her streaming hair. Nothing but those burning, blinded eyes were strong enough to pierce the veil that parted them.

She stumbled along at his side over the rough floor of the temple, saying nothing more, panting with eagerness to return to her incomprehensible "tree." How much of that eagerness was assumed Smith still could not be quite sure. When they reached the door he halted her for a moment, scanning the sky for danger. Apparently the ships had finished with this quarter of the city, for he could see two or three of them half a mile away, hovering low over Illar's northern section. He could risk it without much peril. He led the girl cautiously out into the sun-hot court.

She could not have known by sight that they neared the well, but when they were within twenty paces of it she flung up her blurred head suddenly and tugged at his hand. It was she who led him that last stretch which parted the two from the well. In the sun the shadow tracery of the grille's symbolic pattern lay vividly outlined on the ground. The girl gave a little gasp of delight. She dropped his hand and ran forward three short steps, and plunged into the very center of that

shadowy pattern on the ground. And what happened then
was too incredible to believe.

The pattern ran over her like a garment, curving to the
curve of her body in the way all shadows do. But as she stood
there striped and laced with the darkness of it, there came
a queer shifting in the lines of black tracery, a subtle, inexplicable movement to one side. And with that motion she
vanished. It was exactly as if that shifting had moved her out
of one world into another. Stupidly Smith stared at the spot
from which she had disappeared.

Then several things happened almost simultaneously. The
zoom of a plane broke suddenly into the quiet, a black shadow
dipped low over the rooftops, and Smith, too late, realized
that he stood defenseless in full view of the searching ships.
There was only one way out, and that was too fantastic to
put faith in, but he had no time to hesitate. With one leap
he plunged full into the midst of the shadow of the tree of life.

Its tracery flowed round him, molding its pattern to his
body. And outside the boundaries everything executed a queer
little sidewise dip and slipped in the most extraordinary
manner, like an optical illusion, into quite another scene.
There was no intervention of blankness. It was as if he looked
through the bars of a grille upon a picture which without
warning slipped sidewise, while between the bars appeared
another scene, a curious, dim landscape, gray as if with the
twilight of early evening. The air had an oddly thickened
look, through which he saw the quiet trees and the flower-
spangled grass of the place with a queer, unreal blending,
like the landscape in a tapestry, all its outlines blurred.

In the midst of this tapestried twilight the burning whiteness of the girl he had followed blazed like a flame. She had
paused a few steps away and stood waiting, apparently quite
sure that he would come after. He grinned a little to himself
as he realized it, knowing that curiosity must almost certainly
have driven him in her wake even if the necessity for shelter
had not compelled his following.

She was clearly visible now, in this thickened dimness—
visible, and very lovely, and a little unreal. She shone with a
burning clarity, the only vivid thing in the whole twilit world.

Eyes upon that blazing whiteness, Smith stepped forward,
scarcely realizing that he had moved.

Slowly he crossed the dark grass toward her. That grass was
soft underfoot, and thick with small, low-blooming flowers of
a shining pallor. Botticelli painted such spangled swards for
the feet of his angels. Upon it the girl's bare feet gleamed
whiter than the blossoms. She wore no garment but the royal
mantle of her hair, sweeping about her in a cloak of shining
darkness that had a queer, unreal tinge of purple in that low
light. It brushed her ankles in its fabulous length. From the
hood of it she watched Smith coming toward her, a smile on
her pale mouth and a light blazing in the deeps of her moonstone eyes. She was not blind now, nor frightened. She stretched
out her hand to him confidently.

"It is my turn now to lead you," she smiled. As before, the
words were gibberish, but the penetrating stare of those strange
white eyes gave them a meaning in the depths of his brain.

Automatically his hand went out to hers. He was a little
dazed, and her eyes were very compelling. Her fingers twined
in his and she set off over the flowery grass, pulling him beside
her. He did not ask where they were going. Lost in the dreamy
spell of the still, gray, enchanted place, he felt no need for
words. He was beginning to see more clearly in the odd, blurring twilight that ran the outlines of things together in that
queer, tapestried manner. And he puzzled in a futile, muddled
way as he went on over what sort of land he had come into.
Overhead was darkness, paling into twilight near the ground,
so that when he looked up he was staring into bottomless
deeps of starless night.

Trees and flowering shrubs and the flower-starred grass
stretched emptily about them in the thick, confusing gloom of
the place. He could see only a little distance through that dim
air. It was as if they walked a strip of tapestried twilight in
some unlighted dream. And the girl, with her lovely, luminous
body and richly colored robe of hair was like a woman in a
tapestry too, unreal and magical.

After a while, when he had become a little adjusted to the
queerness of the whole scene, he began to notice furtive movements in the shrubs and trees they passed. Things flickered too

swiftly for him to catch their outlines, but from the tail of his eye he was aware of motion, and somehow of eyes that watched. That sensation was a familiar one to him, and he kept an uneasy gaze on those shiftings in the shrubbery as they went on. Presently he caught a watcher in full view between bush and tree, and saw that it was a man, a little, furtive, dark-skinned man who dodged hastily back into cover again before Smith's eyes could do more than take in the fact of his existence.

After that he knew what to expect and could make them out more easily: little, darting people with big eyes that shone with a queer, sorrowful darkness from their small, frightened faces as they scuttled through the bushes, dodging always just out of plain sight among the leaves. He could hear the soft rustle of their passage, and once or twice when they passed near a clump of shrubbery he thought he caught the echo of little whispering calls, gentle as the rustle of leaves and somehow full of a strange warning note so clear that he caught it even amid the murmur of their speech. Warning calls, and little furtive hiders in the leaves, and a landscape of tapestried blurring carpeted with Botticelli flower-strewn sward. It was all a dream. He felt quite sure of that.

It was a long while before curiosity awakened in him sufficiently to make him break the stillness. But at last he asked dreamily,

"Where are we going?"

The girl seemed to understand that without the necessity of the bond her hypnotic eyes made, for she turned and caught his eyes in a white stare and answered,

"To Thag. Thag desires you."

"What is Thag?"

In answer to that she launched without preliminary upon a little singsong monolog of explanation whose stereotyped formula made him faintly uneasy with the thought that it must have been made very often to attain the status of a set speech; made to many men, perhaps, whom Thag had desired. And what became of them afterward? he wondered. But the girl was speaking.

"Many ages ago there dwelt in Illar the great King Illar for whom the city was named. He was a magician of mighty power, but not mighty enough to fulfill all his ambitions. So by his arts he called up out of darkness the being known as Thag, and with him struck a bargain. By that bargain Thag was to give of his limitless power, serving Illar all the days of Illar's life, and in return the king was to create a land for Thag's dwelling-place and people it with slaves and furnish a priestess to tend Thag's needs. This is that land. I am that priestess, the latest of a long line of women born to serve Thag. The tree-people are his—his lesser servants.

"I have spoken softly so that the tree-people do not hear, for to them Thag is the center and focus of creation, the end and beginning of all life. But to you I have told the truth."

"But what does Thag want of me?"

"It is not for Thag's servants to question Thag."

"Then what becomes, afterward, of the men Thag desires?" he pursued.

"You must ask Thag that."

She turned her eyes away as she spoke, snapping the mental bond that had flowed between them with a suddenness that left Smith dizzy. He went on at her side more slowly, pulling back a little on the tug of her fingers. By degrees the sense of dreaminess was fading, and alarm began to stir in the deeps of his mind. After all, there was no reason why he need let this blank-eyed priestess lead him up to the very maw of her god. She had lured him into this land by what he knew now to have been a trick; might she not have worse tricks than that in store for him?

She held him, after all, by nothing stronger than the clasp of her fingers, if he could keep his eyes turned from hers. Therein lay her real power, but he could fight it if he chose. And he began to hear more clearly than ever the queer note of warning in the rustling whispers of the tree-folk who still fluttered in and out of sight among the leaves. The twilight place had taken on menace and evil.

Suddenly he made up his mind. He stopped, breaking the clasp of the girl's hand.

"I'm not going," he said.

She swung round in a sweep of richly tinted hair, words jetting from her in a gush of incoherence. But he dared not

meet her eyes, and they conveyed no meaning to him. Resolutely he turned away, ignoring her voice, and set out to
retrace the way they had come. She called after him once, in a
high, clear voice that somehow held a note as warning as that
in the rustling voices of the tree-people, but he kept on dog-
gedly, not looking back. She laughed then, sweetly and scornfully, a laugh that echoed uneasily in his mind long after the
sound of it had died upon the twilit air.

After a while he glanced back over one shoulder, half expecting to see the luminous dazzle of her body still glowing in the
dim glade where he had left her; but the blurred tapestry-
landscape was quite empty.

He went on in the midst of a silence so deep it hurt his ears,
and in a solitude unhaunted even by the shy presences of the
tree-folk. They had vanished with the fire-bright girl, and the
whole twilight land was empty save for himself. He plodded on
across the dark grass, crushing the upturned flower-faces under
his boots and asking himself wearily if he could be mad. There
seemed little other explanation for this hushed and tapestried
solitude that had swallowed him up. In that thunderous quiet,
in that deathly solitude, he went on.

When he had walked for what seemed to him much longer
than it should have taken to reach his starting point, and still
no sign of an exit appeared, he began to wonder if there were
any way out of the gray land of Thag. For the first time he
realized that he had come through no tangible gateway. He
had only stepped out of a shadow, and—now that he thought
of it—there were no shadows here. The grayness swallowed
everything up, leaving the landscape oddly flat, like a badly
drawn picture. He looked about helplessly, quite lost now and
not sure in what direction he should be facing, for there was
nothing here by which to know directions. The trees and
shrubs and the starry grass still stretched about him, uncertainly outlined in that changeless dusk. They seemed to go on
for ever.

But he plodded ahead, unwilling to stop because of a queer
tension in the air, somehow as if all the blurred trees and
shrubs were waiting in breathless anticipation, centering upon
his stumbling figure. But all trace of animate life had vanished

with the disappearance of the priestess' white-glowing figure.
Head down, paying little heed to where he was going, he went
on over the flowery sward.

An odd sense of voids about him startled Smith at last out of
his lethargic plodding. He lifted his head. He stood just at the
edge of a line of trees, dim and indistinct in the unchanging
twilight. Beyond them—he came to himself with a jerk and
stared incredulously. Beyond them the grass ran down to nothingness, merging by imperceptible degrees into a streaked and
arching void—not the sort of emptiness into which a material
body could fall, but a solid *nothing,* curving up toward the
dark zenith as the inside of a sphere curves. No physical thing
could have entered there. It was too utterly void, an inviolable
emptiness which no force could invade.

He stared up along the inward arch of that curving, impassable wall. Here, then, was the edge of the queer land Illar had
wrested out of space itself. This arch must be the curving of
solid space which had been bent awry to enclose the magical
land. There was no escape this way. He could not even bring
himself to approach any nearer to that streaked and arching
blank. He could not have said why, but it woke in him an inner
disquiet so strong that after a moment's staring he turned his
eyes away.

Presently he shrugged and set off along the inside of the line
of trees which parted him from the space-wall. Perhaps there
might be a break somewhere. It was a forlorn hope, but the
best that offered. Wearily he stumbled on over the flowery
grass.

How long he had gone on along that almost imperceptibly
curving line of border he could not have said, but after a
timeless interval of gray solitude he gradually became aware
that a tiny rustling and whispering among the leaves had been
growing louder by degrees for some time. He looked up. In and
out among the trees which bordered that solid wall of nothingness little, indistinguishable figures were flitting. The tree-men
had returned. Queerly grateful for their presence, he went on a
bit more cheerfully, paying no heed to their timid dartings to
and fro, for Smith was wise in the ways of wild life.

Presently, when they saw how little heed he paid them, they

began to grow bolder, their whispers louder. And among those rustling voices he thought he was beginning to catch threads of familiarity. Now and again a word reached his ears that he seemed to recognize, lost amidst the gibberish of their speech. He kept his head down and his hands quiet, plodding along with a cunning stillness that began to bear results.

From the corner of his eye he could see that a little dark tree-man had darted out from cover and paused midway between bush and tree to inspect the queer, tall stranger. Nothing happened to this daring venturer, and soon another risked a pause in the open to stare at the quiet walker among the trees. In a little while a small crowd of the tree-people was moving slowly parallel with his course, staring with all the avid curiosity of wild things at Smith's plodding figure. And among them the rustling whispers grew louder.

Presently the ground dipped down into a little hollow ringed with trees. It was a bit darker here than it had been on the higher level, and as he went down the slope of its side he saw that among the underbrush which filled it were cunningly hidden huts twined together out of the living bushes. Obviously the hollow was a tiny village where the tree-folk dwelt.

He was surer of this when they began to grow bolder as he went down into the dimness of the place. The whispers shrilled a little, and the boldest among his watchers ran almost at his elbow, twittering their queer, broken speech in hushed syllables whose familiarity still bothered him with its haunting echo of words he knew. When he had reached the center of the hollow he became aware that the little folk had spread out in a ring to surround him. Wherever he looked their small, anxious faces and staring eyes confronted him. He grinned to himself and came to a halt, waiting gravely.

None of them seemed quite brave enough to constitute himself spokesman, but among several a hurried whispering broke out in which he caught the words "Thag" and "danger" and "beware." He recognized the meaning of these words without placing in his mind their origins in some tongue he knew. He knit his sun-bleached brows and concentrated harder, striving to wrest from that curious, murmuring whisper some hint of its original root. He had a smattering of more tongues than he could have counted offhand, and it was hard to place these scattered words among any one speech.

But the word "Thag" had a sound like that of the very ancient dryland tongue, which upon Mars is considered at once the oldest and the most uncouth of all the planet's languages. And with that clue to guide him he presently began to catch other syllables which were remotely like syllables from the dryland speech. They were almost unrecognizable, far, far more ancient than the very oldest versions of the tongue he had ever heard repeated, almost primitive in their crudity and simplicity. And for a moment the sheerest awe came over him, as he realized the significance of what he listened to.

The dryland race today is a handful of semi-brutes, degenerate from the ages of past time when they were a mighty people at the apex of an almost forgotten glory. That day is millions of years gone now, too far in the past to have record save in the vaguest folklore. Yet here was a people who spoke the rudiments of that race's tongue as it must have been spoken in the race's dim beginnings, perhaps a million years earlier even than that immemorial time of their triumph. The reeling of millenniums set Smith's mind awhirl with the effort at compassing their span.

There was another connotation in the speaking of that tongue by these timid bush-dwellers, too. It must mean that the forgotten wizard king, Illar, had peopled his sinister, twilight land with the ancestors of today's dryland dwellers. If they shared the same tongue they must share the same lineage. And humanity's remorseless adaptability had done the rest.

It had been no kinder here than in the outside world, where the ancient plainsmen who had roamed Mars' green prairies had dwindled with their dying plains, degenerating at last into a shrunken, leather-skinned bestiality. For here that same race root had declined into these tiny, slinking creatures with their dusky skins and great, staring eyes and their voices that never rose above a whisper. What tragedies must lie behind that gradual degeneration!

All about him the whispers still ran. He was beginning to suspect that through countless ages of hiding and murmuring those voices must have lost the ability to speak aloud. And he wondered with a little inward chill what terror it was which had transformed a free and fearless people into these tiny wild things whispering in the underbrush.

The little anxious voices had shrilled into vehemence now, all of them chattering together in their queer, soft, rustling whispers. Looking back later upon that timeless space he had passed in the hollow, Smith remembered it as some curious nightmare—dimness and tapestried blurring, and a hush like death over the whole twilight land, and the timid voices whispering, whispering, eloquent with terror and warning.

He groped back among his memories and brought forth a phrase or two remembered from long ago, an archaic rendering of the immemorial tongue they spoke. It was the simplest version he could remember of the complex speech now used, but he knew that to them it must sound fantastically strange. Instinctively he whispered as he spoke it, feeling like an actor in a play as he mouthed the ancient idiom,

"I—I cannot understand. Speak—more slowly—"

A torrent of words greeted this rendering of their tongue. Then there was a great deal of hushing and hissing, and presently two or three between them began laboriously to recite an involved speech, one syllable at a time. Always two or more shared the task. Never in his converse with them did he address anyone directly. Ages of terror had bred all directness out of them.

"Thag," they said. "Thag, the terrible—Thag, the omnipotent—Thag, the unescapable. Beware of Thag."

For a moment Smith stood quiet, grinning down at them despite himself. There must not be too much of intelligence left among this branch of the race, either, for surely such a warning was superfluous. Yet they had mastered their agonies of timidity to give it. All virtue could not yet have been bred out of them, then. They still had kindness and a sort of desperate courage rooted deep in fear.

"What is Thag?" he managed to inquire, voicing the archaic syllables uncertainly. And they must have understood the meaning if not the phraseology, for another spate of whispered tumult burst from the clustering tribe. Then, as before, several took up the task of answering.

"Thag—Thag, the end and the beginning, the center of creation. When Thag breathes the world trembles. The earth was made for Thag's dwelling-place. All things are Thag's. Oh, beware! Beware!"

This much he pieced together out of their diffuse whisperings, catching up the fragments of words he knew and fitting them into the pattern.

"What—what is the danger?" he managed to ask.

"Thag—hungers. Thag must be fed. It is we who—feed—him, but there are times when he desires other food than us. It is then he sends his priestess forth to lure—food—in. Oh, beware of Thag!"

"You mean then, that she—the priestess—brought me in for—food?"

A chorus of grave, murmuring affirmatives.

"Then why did she leave me?"

"There is no escape from Thag. Thag is the center of creation. All things are Thag's. When he calls, you must answer. When he hungers, he will have you. Beware of Thag!"

Smith considered that for a moment in silence. In the main he felt confident that he had understood their warning correctly, and he had little reason to doubt that they knew whereof they spoke. Thag might not be the center of the universe, but if they said he could call a victim from anywhere in the land, Smith was not disposed to doubt it. The priestess' willingness to let him leave her unhindered, yes, even her scornful laughter as he looked back, told the same story. Whatever Thag might be, his power in this land could not be doubted. He made up his mind suddenly what he must do, and turned to the breathlessly waiting little folk.

"Which way—lies Thag?" he asked.

A score of dark, thin arms pointed. Smith turned his head speculatively toward the spot they indicated. In this changeless twilight all sense of direction had long since left him, but he marked the line as well as he could by the formation of the trees, then turned to the little people with a ceremonious farewell rising to his lips.

"My thanks for—" he began, to be interrupted by a chorus of whispering cries of protest. They seemed to sense his intention, and their pleadings were frantic. A panic anxiety for him glowed upon every little terrified face turned up to his, and their eyes were wide with protest and terror. Helplessly he looked down.

"I—I must go," he tried stumblingly to say. "My only chance is to take Thag unawares, before he sends for me."

He could not know if they understood. Their chattering went on undiminished, and they even went so far as to lay tiny hands on him, as if they would prevent him by force from seeking out the terror of their lives.

"No, no, no!" they wailed murmurously. "You do not know what it is you seek! You do not know Thag! Stay here! Beware of Thag!"

A little prickling of unease went down Smith's back as he listened. Thag must be very terrible indeed if even half this alarm had foundation. And to be quite frank with himself, he would greatly have preferred to remain here in the hidden quiet of the hollow, with its illusion of shelter, for as long as he was allowed to stay. But he was not of the stuff that yields very easily to its own terrors, and hope burned strongly in him still. So he squared his broad shoulders and turned resolutely in the direction the tree-folk had indicated.

When they saw that he meant to go, their protests sank to a wail of bitter grieving. With that sound moaning behind him he went up out of the hollow, like a man setting forth to the music of his own dirge. A few of the bravest went with him a little way, flitting through the underbrush and darting from tree to tree in a timidity so deeply ingrained that even when no immediate peril threatened they dared not go openly through the twilight.

Their presence was comforting to Smith as he went on. A futile desire to help the little terror-ridden tribe was rising in him, a useless gratitude for their warning and their friendliness, their genuine grieving at his departure and their odd, paradoxical bravery even in the midst of hereditary terror. But he knew that he could do nothing for them, when he was not at all sure he could even save himself. Something of their panic had communicated itself to him, and he advanced with a sinking at the pit of his stomach. Fear of the unknown is so poignant a thing, feeding on its own terror, that he found his hands beginning to shake a little and his throat going dry as he went on.

The rustling and whispering among the bushes dwindled as his followers one by one dropped away, the bravest staying the longest, but even they failing in courage as Smith advanced steadily in that direction from which all their lives they had been taught to turn their faces. Presently he realized that he was alone once more. He went on more quickly, anxious to come face to face with this horror of the twilight and dispel at least the fearfulness of its mystery.

The silence was like death. Not a breeze stirred the leaves, and the only sound was his own breathing, the heavy thud of his own heart. Somehow he felt sure that he was coming nearer to his goal. The hush seemed to confirm it. He loosened the force-gun at his thigh.

In that changeless twilight the ground was sloping down once more into a broader hollow. He descended slowly, every sense alert for danger, not knowing if Thag was beast or human or elemental, visible or invisible. The trees were beginning to thin. He knew that he had almost reached his goal.

He paused at the edge of the last line of trees. A clearing spread out before him at the bottom of the hollow, quiet in the dim, translucent air. He could focus directly upon no outlines anywhere, for the tapestried blurring of the place. But when he saw what stood in the very center of the clearing he stopped dead-still, like one turned to stone, and a shock of utter cold went chilling through him. Yet he could not have said why.

For in the clearing's center stood the Tree of Life. He had met the symbol too often in patterns and designs not to recognize it, but here that fabulous thing was living, growing, actually springing up from a rooted firmness in the spangled grass as any tree might spring. Yet it could not be real. Its thin brown trunk, of no recognizable substance, smooth and gleaming, mounted in the traditional spiral; its twelve fantastically curving branches arched delicately outward from the central stem. It was bare of leaves. No foliage masked the serpentine brown spiral of the trunk. But at the tip of each symbolic branch flowered a blossom of bloody rose so vivid he could scarcely focus his dazzled eyes upon them.

This tree alone of all objects in the dim land was sharply distinct to the eye—terribly distinct, remorselessly clear. No words can describe the amazing menace that dwelt among its branches. Smith's flesh crept as he stared, yet he could not for all his staring make out why peril was so eloquent there. To all appearances here stood only a fabulous symbol miraculously come to life; yet danger breathed out from it so strongly that Smith felt the hair lifting on his neck as he stared.

It was no ordinary danger. A nameless, choking, paralyzed panic was swelling in his throat as he gazed upon the perilous beauty of the Tree. Somehow the arches and curves of its branches seemed to limn a pattern so dreadful that his heart beat faster as he gazed upon it. But he could not guess why, though somehow the answer was hovering just out of reach of his conscious mind. From that first glimpse of it his instincts shuddered like a shying stallion, yet reason still looked in vain for an answer.

Nor was the Tree merely a vegetable growth. It was alive, terribly, ominously alive. He could not have said how he knew that, for it stood motionless in its empty clearing, not a branch trembling, yet in its immobility more awfully vital than any animate thing. The very sight of it woke in Smith an insane urging to flight, to put worlds between himself and this inexplicably dreadful thing.

Crazy impulses stirred in his brain, coming to insane birth at the calling of the Tree's peril—the desperate need to shut out the sight of that thing that was blasphemy, to put out his own sight rather than gaze longer upon the perilous grace of its branches, to slit his own throat that he might not need to dwell in the same world which housed so frightful a sight as the Tree.

All this was a mad battering in his brain. The strength of him was enough to isolate it in a far corner of his consciousness, where it seethed and shrieked half heeded while he turned the cool control which the spaceways life had taught him to the solution of this urgent question. But even so his hand was moist and shaking on his gun-butt, and the breath rasped in his dry throat.

Why—he asked himself in a determined groping after steadiness—should the mere sight of a tree, even so fabulous a one as this, rouse that insane panic in the gazer? What peril could dwell invisibly in a tree so frightful that the living horror of it could drive a man mad with the very fact of its unseen presence? He clenched his teeth hard and stared resolutely at that terrible beauty in the clearing, fighting down the sick panic that rose in his throat as his eyes forced themselves to dwell upon the Tree.

Gradually the revulsion subsided. After a nightmare of striving he mustered the strength to force it down far enough to allow reason's entry once more. Sternly holding down that frantic terror under the surface of consciousness, he stared resolutely at the Tree. And he knew that this was Thag.

It could be nothing else, for surely two such dreadful things could not dwell in one land. It must be Thag, and he could understand now the immemorial terror in which the tree-folk held it, but he did not yet grasp in what way it threatened them physically. The inexplicable dreadfulness of it was a menace to the mind's very existence, but surely a rooted tree, however terrible to look at, could wield little actual danger.

As he reasoned, his eyes were seeking restlessly among the branches, searching for the answer to their dreadfulness. After all, this thing wore the aspect of an old pattern, and in that pattern there was nothing dreadful. The tree of life had made up the design upon that well-top in Illar through whose shadow he had entered here, and nothing in that bronze grille-work had roused terror. Then why—? What living menace dwelt invisibly among these branches to twist them into curves of horror?

A fragment of old verse drifted through his mind as he stared in perplexity:

> *What immortal hand or eye*
> *Could frame thy fearful symmetry?*

And for the first time the true significance of a "fearful symmetry" broke upon him. Truly a more than human agency

must have arched these subtle curves so delicately into dreadfulness, into such an awful beauty that the very sight of it
made those atavistic terrors he was so sternly holding down
leap in a gibbering terror.

A tremor rippled over the Tree. Smith froze rigid, staring
with startled eyes. No breath of wind had stirred through the
clearing, but the Tree was moving with a slow, serpentine
grace, writhing its branches leisurely in a horrible travesty of
voluptuous enjoyment. And upon their tips the blood-red
flowers were spreading like cobra's hoods, swelling and stretching their petals out and glowing with a hue so eye-piercingly
vivid that it transcended the bounds of color and blazed forth
like pure light.

But it was not toward Smith that they stirred. They were
arching out from the central trunk toward the far side of the
clearing. After a moment Smith tore his eyes away from the
indescribably dreadful flexibility of those branches and looked
to see the cause of their writhing.

A blaze of luminous white had appeared among the trees
across the clearing. The priestess had returned. He watched
her pacing slowly toward the Tree, walking with a precise and
delicate grace as liquidly lovely as the motion of the Tree.
Her fabulous hair swung down about her in a swaying robe
that rippled at every step away from the moon-white beauty
of her body. Straight toward the Tree she paced, and all the
blossoms glowed more vividly at her nearness, the branches
stretching toward her, rippling with eagerness.

Priestess though she was, he could not believe that she was
going to come within touch of that Tree the very sight of
which roused such a panic instinct of revulsion in every fiber
of him. But she did not swerve or slow in her advance. Walking delicately over the flowery grass, arrogantly luminous in
the twilight, so that her body was the center and focus of any
landscape she walked in, she neared her horribly eager god.

Now she was under the Tree, and its trunk had writhed
down over her and she was lifting her arms like a girl to her
lover. With a gliding slowness the flame-tipped branches slid
round her. In that incredible embrace she stood immobile for
a long moment, the Tree arching down with all its curling

limbs, the girl straining upward, her head thrown back and the mantle of her hair swinging free of her body as she lifted her face to the quivering blossoms. The branches gathered her closer in their embrace. Now the blossoms arched near, curving down all about her, touching her very gently, twisting their blazing faces toward the focus of her moon-white body. One poised directly above her face, trembled, brushed her mouth lightly. And the Tree's tremor ran unbroken through the body of the girl it clasped.

The incredible dreadfulness of that embrace was suddenly more than Smith could bear. All his terrors, crushed down with so stern a self-control, without warning burst all bounds and rushed over him in a flood of blind revulsion. A whimper choked up in his throat and quite involuntarily he swung round and plunged into the shielding trees, hands to his eyes in a futile effort to blot out the sight of lovely horror behind him whose vividness was burnt upon his very brain.

Heedlessly he blundered through the trees, no thought in his terror-blank mind save the necessity to run, run, run until he could run no more. He had given up all attempt at reason and rationality; he no longer cared why the beauty of the Tree was so dreadful. He only knew that until all space lay between him and its symmetry he must run and run and run.

What brought that frenzied madness to an end he never knew. When sanity returned to him he was lying face down on the flower-spangled sward in a silence so deep that his ears ached with its heaviness. The grass was cool against his cheek. For a moment he fought the back-flow of knowledge into his emptied mind. When it came, the memory of that horror he had fled from, he started up with a wild thing's swiftness and glared around pale-eyed into the unchanging dusk. He was alone. Not even a rustle in the leaves spoke of the tree-folk's presence.

For a moment he stood there alert, wondering what had roused him, wondering what would come next. He was not left long in doubt. The answer was shrilling very, very faintly through that aching quiet, an infinitesimally tiny, unthinkably far-away murmur which yet pierced his ear-drums with the sharpness of tiny needles. Breathless, he strained in listening.

Swiftly the sound grew louder. It deepened upon the silence, sharpened and shrilled until the thin blade of it was vibrating in the center of his innermost brain.

And still it grew, swelling louder and louder through the twilight world in cadences that were rounding into a queer sort of music and taking on such an unbearable sweetness that Smith pressed his hands over his ears in a futile attempt to shut the sound away. He could not. It rang in steadily deepening intensities through every fiber of his being, piercing him with thousands of tiny music-blades that quivered in his very soul with intolerable beauty. And he thought he sensed in the piercing strength of it a vibration of queer, unnamable power far mightier than anything ever generated by man, the dim echo of some cosmic dynamo's hum.

The sound grew sweeter as it strengthened, with a queer, inexplicable sweetness unlike any music he had ever heard before, rounder and fuller and more complete than any melody made up of separate notes. Stronger and stronger he felt the certainty that it was the song of some mighty power, humming and throbbing and deepening through the twilight until the whole dim land was one trembling reservoir of sound that filled his entire consciousness with its throbbing, driving out all other thoughts and realizations, until he was no more than a shell that vibrated in answer to the calling.

For it was a calling. No one could listen to that intolerable sweetness without knowing the necessity to seek its source. Remotely in the back of his mind Smith remembered the tree-folk's warning, "When Thag calls, you must answer." Not consciously did he recall it, for all his consciousness was answering the siren humming in the air, and, scarcely realizing that he moved, he had turned toward the source of that calling, stumbling blindly over the flowery sward with no thought in his music-brimmed mind but the need to answer that lovely, power-vibrant summoning.

Past him as he went on moved other shapes, little and dark-skinned and ecstatic, gripped like himself in the hypnotic melody. The tree-folk had forgotten even their inbred fear at Thag's calling, and walked boldly through the open twilight, lost in the wonder of the song.

Smith went on with the rest, deaf and blind to the land around him, alive to one thing only, that summons from the siren tune. Unrealizingly, he retraced the course of his frenzied flight, past the trees and bushes he had blundered through, down the slope that led to the Tree's hollow, through the thinning of the underbrush to the very edge of the last line of foliage which marked the valley's rim.

By now the calling was so unbearably intense, so intolerably sweet that somehow in its very strength it set free a part of his dazed mind as it passed the limits of audible things and soared into ecstasies which no senses bound. And though it gripped him ever closer in its magic, a sane part of his brain was waking into realization. For the first time alarm came back into his mind, and by slow degrees the world returned about him. He stared stupidly at the grass moving by under his pacing feet. He lifted a dragging head and saw that the trees no longer rose about him, that a twilit clearing stretched away on all sides toward the forest rim which circled it, that the music was singing from some source so near that—that—

The Tree! Terror leaped within him like a wild thing. The Tree, quivering with unbearable clarity in the thick, dim air, writhed above him, blossoms blazing with bloody radiance and every branch vibrant and undulant to the tune of that unholy song. Then he was aware of the lovely, luminous whiteness of the priestess swaying forward under the swaying limbs, her hair rippling back from the loveliness of her as she moved.

Choked and frenzied with unreasoning terror, he mustered every effort that was in him to turn, to run again like a madman out of that dreadful hollow, to hide himself under the weight of all space from the menace of the Tree. And all the while he fought, all the while panic drummed like mad in his brain, his relentless body plodded on straight toward the hideous loveliness of that siren singer towering above him. From the first he had felt subconsciously that it was Thag who called, and now, in the very center of that ocean of vibrant power, he knew. Gripped in the music's magic, he went on.

All over the clearing other hypnotized victims were advancing slowly, with mechanical steps and wide, frantic eyes as the tree-folk came helplessly to their god's calling. He watched a

group of little, dusky sacrifices pace step by step nearer to the
Tree's vibrant branches. The priestess came forward to meet
them with outstretched arms. He saw her take the foremost
gently by the hands. Unbelieving, hypnotized with horrified
incredulity, he watched her lead the rigid little creature forward under the fabulous Tree whose limbs yearned downward
like hungry snakes; the great flowers glowing with avid color.

He saw the branches twist out and lengthen toward the sacrifice, quivering with eagerness. Then with a tiger's leap they
darted, and the victim was swept out of the priestess' guiding
hands up into the branches that darted round like tangled
snakes in a clot that hid him for an instant from view. Smith
heard a high, shuddering wail ripple out from that knot of
struggling branches, a dreadful cry that held such an infinity
of purest horror and understanding that he could not but
believe that Thag's victims in the moment of their doom must
learn the secret of his horror. After that one frightful cry came
silence. In an instant the limbs fell apart again from emptiness.
The little savage had melted like smoke among their writhing,
too quickly to have been devoured, more as if he had been
snatched into another dimension in the instant the hungry
limbs hid him. Flame-tipped, avid, they were dipping now
toward another victim as the priestess paced serenely forward.

And still Smith's rebellious feet were carrying him on, nearer
and nearer the writhing peril that towered over his head. The
music shrilled like pain. Now he was so close that he could see
the hungry flower-mouths in terrible detail as they faced round
toward him. The limbs quivered and poised like cobras,
reached out with a snakish lengthening, down inexorably
toward his shuddering helplessness. The priestess was turning
her calm white face toward his.

Those arcs and changing curves of the branches as they
neared were sketching lines of pure horror whose meaning he
still could not understand, save that they deepened in dreadfulness as he neared. For the last time that urgent wonder burned
up in his mind why—*why* so simple a thing as this fabulous
Tree should be infused with an indwelling terror strong
enough to send his innermost soul frantic with revulsion. For
the last time—because in that trembling instant as he waited

for their touch, as the music brimmed up with unbearable, brain-wrenching intensity, in that one last moment before the flower-mouths seized him—he saw. He understood.

With eyes opened at last by the instant's ultimate horror, he saw the real Thag. Dimly he knew that until now the thing had been so frightful that his eyes had refused to register its existence, his brain to acknowledge the possibility of such dreadfulness. It had literally been too terrible to see, though his instinct knew the presence of infinite horror. But now, in the grip of that mad, hypnotic song, in the instant before unbearable terror enfolded him, his eyes opened to full sight, and he saw.

That Tree was only Thag's outline, sketched three-dimensionally upon the twilight. Its dreadfully curving branches had been no more than Thag's barest contours, yet even they had made his very soul sick with intuitive revulsion. But now, seeing the true horror, his mind was too numb to do more than register its presence: Thag, hovering monstrously between earth and heaven, billowing and surging up there in the translucent twilight, tethered to the ground by the Tree's bending stem and reaching ravenously after the hypnotized fodder that his calling brought helpless into his clutches. One by one he snatched them up, one by one absorbed them into the great, unseeable horror of his being. That, then, was the reason why they vanished so instantaneously, sucked into the concealing folds of a thing too dreadful for normal eyes to see.

The priestess was pacing forward. Above her the branches arched and leaned. Caught in a timeless paralysis of horror, Smith stared upward into the enormous bulk of Thag while the music hummed intolerably in his shrinking brain—Thag, the monstrous thing from darkness, called up by Illar in those long-forgotten times when Mars was a green planet. Foolishly his brain wandered among the ramifications of what had happened so long ago that time itself had forgotten, refusing to recognize the fate that was upon himself. He knew a tingle of respect for the ages-dead wizard who had dared command a being like this to his services—this vast, blind, hovering thing, ravenous for human flesh, indistinguishable even now save in

those terrible outlines that sent panic leaping through him
with every motion of the Tree's fearful symmetry.

All this flashed through his dazed mind in the one blinding
instant of understanding. Then the priestess' luminous whiteness swam up before his hypnotized stare. Her hands were upon
him, gently guiding his mechanical footsteps, very gently leading him forward into—into—

The writhing branches struck downward, straight for his
face. And in one flashing leap the moment's infinite horror
galvanized him out of his paralysis. Why, he could not have
said. It is not given to many men to know the ultimate essen-
tials of all horror, concentrated into one fundamental unit. To
most men it would have had that same paralyzing effect up
to the very instant of destruction. But in Smith there must
have been a bed-rock of subtle violence, an unyielding, inflexible vehemence upon which the structure of his whole life was
reared. Few men have it. And when that ultimate intensity of
terror struck the basic flint of him, reaching down through
mind and soul into the deepest depths of his being, it struck a
spark from that inflexible barbarian buried at the roots of him
which had force enough to shock him out of his stupor.

In the instant of release his hand swept like an unloosed
spring, of its own volition, straight for the butt of his power-
gun. He was dragging it free as the Tree's branches snatched
him from its priestess' hands. The fire-colored blossoms burnt
his flesh as they closed round him, the hot branches gripping
like the touch of ravenous fingers. The whole Tree was hot
and throbbing with a dreadful travesty of fleshly life as it
whipped him aloft into the hovering bulk of incarnate horror
above.

In the instantaneous upward leap of the flower-tipped limbs
Smith fought like a demon to free his gun-hand from the gripping coils. For the first time Thag knew rebellion in his very
clutches, and the ecstasy of that music which had dinned in
Smith's ears so strongly that by now it seemed almost silence
was swooping down a long arc into wrath, and the branches
tightened with hot insistency, lifting the rebellious offering
into Thag's monstrous, indescribable bulk.

But even as they rose, Smith was twisting in their clutch to

maneuver his hand into a position from which he could blast
that undulant tree trunk into nothingness. He knew intuitively
the futility of firing up into Thag's imponderable mass. Thag
was not of the world he knew; the flame blast might well be
harmless to that mighty hoverer in the twilight. But at the
Tree's root, where Thag's essential being merged from the
imponderable to the material, rooting in earthly soil, he should
be vulnerable if he were vulnerable at all. Struggling in the
tight, hot coils, breathing the nameless essence of horror, Smith
fought to free his hand.

The music that had rung so long in his ears was changing
as the branches lifted him higher, losing its melody and merging by swift degrees into a hum of vast and vibrant power that
deepened in intensity as the limbs drew him upward into
Thag's monstrous bulk, the singing force of a thing mightier
than any dynamo ever built. Blinded and dazed by the force
thundering through every atom of his body, he twisted his
hand in one last, convulsive effort, and fired.

He saw the flame leap in a dazzling gush straight for the
trunk below. It struck. He heard the sizzle of annihilated
matter. He saw the trunk quiver convulsively from the very
roots, and the whole fabulous Tree shook once with an ominous tremor. But before that tremor could shiver up the
branches to him the hum of the living dynamo which was
closing round his body shrilled up arcs of pure intensity into a
thundering silence.

Then without a moment's warning the world exploded. So
instantaneously did all this happen that the gun-blast's roar
had not yet echoed into silence before a mightier sound than
the brain could bear exploded outward from the very center of
his own being. Before the awful power of it everything reeled
into a shaken oblivion. He felt himself falling. . . .

A queer, penetrating light shining upon his closed eyes
roused Smith by degrees into wakefulness again. He lifted
heavy lids and stared upward into the unwinking eye of Mars'
racing nearer moon. He lay there blinking dazedly for a while
before enough of memory returned to rouse him. Then he sat
up painfully, for every fiber of him ached, and stared round on
a scene of the wildest destruction. He lay in the midst of a

wide, rough circle which held nothing but powdered stone.
About it, rising raggedly in the moving moonlight, the blocks
of time-forgotten Illar loomed.

But they were no longer piled one upon another in a rough
travesty of the city they once had shaped. Some force mightier
than any of man's explosives seemed to have hurled them with
such violence from their beds that their very atoms had been
disrupted by the force of it, crumbling them into dust. And in
the very center of the havoc lay Smith, unhurt.

He stared in bewilderment about the moonlight ruins. In
the silence it seemed to him that the very air still quivered in
shocked vibrations. And as he stared he realized that no force
save one could have wrought such destruction upon the ancient
stones. Nor was there any explosive known to man which
would have wrought this strange, pulverizing havoc upon the
blocks of Illar. That force had hummed unbearably through
the living dynamo of Thag, a force so powerful that space
itself had bent to enclose it. Suddenly he realized what must
have happened.

Not Illar, but Thag himself had warped the walls of space to
enfold the twilit world, and nothing but Thag's living power
could have held it so bent to segregate the little, terror-ridden
land inviolate.

Then when the Tree's roots parted, Thag's anchorage in the
material world failed and in one great gust of unthinkable
energy the warped space-walls had ceased to bend. Those
arches of solid space had snapped back into their original pattern, hurling the land and all its dwellers into—into— His
mind balked in the effort to picture what must have happened,
into what ultimate dimension those denizens must have
vanished.

Only himself, enfolded deep in Thag's very essence, the
intolerable power of the explosion had not touched. So when
the warped space-curve ceased to be, and Thag's hold upon
reality failed, he must have been dropped back out of the dis-
solving folds upon the spot where the Tree had stood in the
space-circled world, through that vanished world-floor into the
spot he had been snatched from in the instant of the dim land's
dissolution. It must have happened after the terrible force of

the explosion had spent itself, before Thag dared move even
himself through the walls of changing energy into his own far
land again.

Smith sighed and lifted a hand to his throbbing head, rising
slowly to his feet. What time had elapsed he could not guess,
but he must assume that the Patrol still searched for him.
Wearily he set out across the circle of havoc toward the nearest
shelter which Illar offered. The dust rose in ghostly, moonlit
clouds under his feet.

Jirel Meets Magic

OVER Guischard's fallen drawbridge thundered Joiry's warrior lady, sword swinging, voice shouting hoarsely inside her helmet. The scarlet plume of her crest rippled in the wind. Straight into the massed defenders at the gate she plunged, careering through them by the very impetuosity of the charge, the weight of her mighty warhorse opening up a gap for the men at her heels to widen. For a while there was tumult unspeakable there under the archway, the yells of fighters and the clang of mail on mail and the screams of stricken men. Jirel of Joiry was a shouting battle-machine from which Guischard's men reeled in bloody confusion as she whirled and slashed and slew in the narrow confines of the gateway, her great stallion's iron hoofs weapons as potent as her own whistling blade.

In her full armor she was impregnable to the men on foot, and the horse's armor protected him from their vengeful blades, so that alone, almost, she might have won the gateway. By sheer weight and impetuosity she carried the battle through the defenders under the arch. They gave way before the mighty war-horse and his screaming rider. Jirel's swinging sword and the stallion's trampling feet cleared a path for Joiry's men to follow, and at last into Guischard's court poured the steel-clad hordes of Guischard's conquerors.

Jirel's eyes were yellow with blood-lust behind the helmet bars, and her voice echoed savagely from the steel cage that confined it, "Giraud! Bring me Giraud! A gold piece to the man who brings me the wizard Giraud!"

She waited impatiently in the courtyard, reining her excited charger in mincing circles over the flags, unable to dismount

164

alone in her heavy armor and disdainful of the threats of
possible arbalesters in the arrow-slits that looked down upon
her from Guischard's frowning gray walls. A crossbow shaft
was the only thing she had to fear in her impregnable mail.

She waited in mounting impatience, a formidable figure in
her bloody armor, the great sword lying across her saddlebow
and her eager, angry voice echoing hoarsely from the helmet,
"Giraud! Make haste, you varlets! Bring me Giraud!"

There was such bloodthirsty impatience in that hollowly
booming voice that the men who were returning from searching the castle hung back as they crossed the court toward their
lady in reluctant twos and threes, failure eloquent upon their
faces.

"What!" screamed Jirel furiously. "You, Giles! Have you
brought me Giraud? Watkin! Where is that wizard Giraud?
Answer me, I say!"

"We've scoured the castle, my lady," said one of the men
fearfully as the angry voice paused. "The wizard is gone."

"Now God defend me!" groaned Joiry's lady. "God help a
poor woman served by fools! Did you search among the slain?"

"We searched everywhere, Lady Jirel. Giraud has escaped
us."

Jirel called again upon her Maker in a voice that was blasphemy in itself.

"Help me down, then, you hell-spawned knaves," she grated.
"I'll find him myself. He must be here!"

With difficulty they got her off the sidling horse. It took two
men to handle her, and a third to steady the charger. All the
while they struggled with straps and buckles she cursed them
hollowly, emerging limb by limb from the casing of steel and
swearing with a soldier's fluency as the armor came away.
Presently she stood free on the bloody flagstones, a slim,
straight lady, keen as a blade, her red hair a flame to match
the flame of her yellow eyes. Under the armor she wore a tunic
of link-mail from the Holy Land, supple as silk and almost as
light, and a doeskin shirt to protect the milky whiteness of her
skin.

She was a creature of the wildest paradox, this warrior lady
of Joiry, hot as a red coal, chill as steel, satiny of body and iron

of soul. The set of her chin was firm, but her mouth betrayed a tenderness she would have died before admitting. But she was raging now.

"Follow me, then, fools!" she shouted. "I'll find that God-cursed wizard and split his head with this sword if it takes me until the day I die. I swear it. I'll teach him what it costs to ambush Joiry men. By heaven, he'll pay with his life for my ten who fell at Massy Ford last week. The foul spell-brewer! He'll learn what it means to defy Joiry!"

Breathing threats and curses, she strode across the court, her men following reluctantly at her heels and casting nervous glances upward at the gray towers of Guischard. It had always borne a bad name, this ominous castle of the wizard Giraud, a place where queer things happened, which no man entered uninvited and whence no prisoner had ever escaped, though the screams of torture echoed often from its walls. Jirel's men would have followed her straight through the gates of hell, but they stormed Guischard at her heels with terror in their hearts and no hope of conquest.

She alone seemed not to know fear of the dark sorceror. Perhaps it was because she had known things so dreadful that mortal perils held no terror for her—there were whispers at Joiry of their lady, and of things that had happened there which no man dared think on. But when Guischard fell, and the wizard's defenders fled before Jirel's mighty steed and the onrush of Joiry's men, they had plucked up heart, thinking that perhaps the ominous tales of Giraud had been gossip only, since the castle fell as any ordinary lord's castle might fall. But now—there were whispers again, and nervous glances over the shoulder, and men huddled together as they re-entered Guischard at their lady's hurrying heels. A castle from which a wizard might vanish into thin air, with all the exits watched, must be a haunted place, better burned and forgotten. They followed Jirel reluctantly, half ashamed but fearful.

In Jirel's stormy heart there was no room for terror as she plunged into the gloom of the archway that opened upon Guischard's great central hall. Anger that the man might have escaped her was a torch to light the way, and she paused in

the door with eager anticipation, sweeping the corpse-strewn
hall at a glance, searching for some clue to explain how her
quarry had disappeared.

"He can't have escaped," she told herself confidently.
"There's no way out. He *must* be here somewhere." And she
stepped into the hall, turning over the bodies she passed with a
careless foot to make sure that death had not robbed her of
vengeance.

An hour later, as they searched the last tower, she was still
telling herself that the wizard could not have gone without her
knowledge. She had taken special pains about that. There was
a secret passage to the river, but she had had that watched.
And an underwater door opened into the moat, but he could
not have gone that way without meeting her men. Secret paths
and open, she had found them all and posted a guard at each,
and Giraud had not left the castle by any door that led out.
She climbed the stairs of the last tower wearily, her confidence
shaken.

An iron-barred oaken door closed the top of the steps, and
Jirel drew back as her men lifted the heavy cross-pieces and
opened it for her. It had not been barred from within. She
stepped into the little round room inside, hope fading completely as she saw that it too was empty, save for the body of a
page-boy lying on the uncarpeted floor. Blood had made a congealing pool about him, and as Jirel looked she saw something
which roused her flagging hopes. Feet had trodden in that
blood, not the mailed feet of armed men, but the tread of
shapeless cloth shoes such as surely none but Giraud would
have worn when the castle was besieged and falling, and every
man's help needed. Those bloody tracks led straight across the
room toward the wall, and in that wall—a window.

Jirel stared. To her a window was a narrow slit deep in
stone, made for the shooting of arrows, and never covered save
in the coldest weather. But this window was broad and low,
and instead of the usual animal pelt for hangings a curtain of
purple velvet had been drawn back to disclose shutters carved
out of something that might have been ivory had any beast
alive been huge enough to yield such great unbroken sheets of

whiteness. The shutters were unlatched, swinging slightly ajar, and upon them Jirel saw the smear of bloody fingers.

With a little triumphant cry she sprang forward. Here, then, was the secret way Giraud had gone. What lay beyond the window she could not guess. Perhaps an unsuspected passage, or a hidden room. Laughing exultantly, she swung open the ivory shutters.

There was a gasp from the men behind her. She did not hear it. She stood quite still, staring with incredulous eyes. For those ivory gates had opened upon no dark stone hiding-place or secret tunnel. They did not even reveal the afternoon sky outside, nor did they admit the shouts of her men still subduing the last of the defenders in the court below. Instead she was looking out upon a green woodland over which brooded a violet day like no day she had ever seen before. In paralyzed amazement she looked down, seeing not the bloody flags of the courtyard far below, but a mossy carpet at a level with the floor. And on that moss she saw the mark of blood-stained feet. This window might be a magic one, opening into strange lands, but through it had gone the man she swore to kill, and where he fled she must follow.

She lifted her eyes from the tracked moss and stared out again through the dimness under the trees. It was a lovelier land than anything seen even in dreams; so lovely that it made her heart ache with its strange, unearthly enchantment—green woodland hushed and brooding in the hushed violet day. There was a promise of peace there, and forgetfulness and rest. Suddenly the harsh, shouting, noisy world behind her seemed very far away and chill. She moved forward and laid her hand upon the ivory shutters, staring out.

The shuffle of the scared men behind her awakened Jirel from the enchantment that had gripped her. She turned. The dreamy magic of the woodland loosed its hold as she faced the men again, but its memory lingered. She shook her red head a little, meeting their fearful eyes. She nodded toward the open window.

"Giraud has gone out there," she said. "Give me your dagger, Giles. This sword is too heavy to carry far."

"But lady—Lady Jirel—dear lady—you can't go out there—
Saint Guilda save us! Lady Jirel!"

Jirel's crisp voice cut short the babble of protest.

"Your dagger, Giles. I've sworn to slay Giraud, and slay him
I shall, in whatever land he hides. Giles!"

A man-at-arms shuffled forward with averted face, handing
her his dagger. She gave him the sword she carried and thrust
the long-bladed knife into her belt. She turned again to the
window. Green and cool and lovely, the woodland lay waiting.
She thought as she set her knee upon the sill that she must
have explored this violet calm even had her oath not driven
her; for there was an enchantment about the place that drew
her irresistibly. She pulled up her other knee and jumped
lightly. The mossy ground received her without a jar.

For a few moments Jirel stood very still, watching, listening.
Bird songs trilled intermittently about her, and breezes stirred
the leaves. From very far away she thought she caught the
echoes of a song when the wind blew, and there was something
subtly irritating about its simple melody that seemed to seesaw
endlessly up and down on two notes. She was glad when the
wind died and the song no longer shrilled in her ears.

It occurred to her that before she ventured far she must
mark the window she had entered by, and she turned curiously,
wondering how it looked from this side. What she saw sent an
inexplicable little chill down her back. Behind her lay a heap
of moldering ruins, moss-grown, crumbling into decay. Fire
had blackened the stones in ages past. She could see that it
must have been a castle, for the original lines of it were not yet
quite lost. Only one low wall remained standing now, and in
it opened the window through which she had come. There was
something hauntingly familiar about the lines of those moldering stones, and she turned away with a vague unease, not quite
understanding why. A little path wound away under the low-
hanging trees, and she followed it slowly, eyes alert for signs
that Giraud had passed this way. Birds trilled drowsily in the
leaves overhead, queer, unrecognizable songs like the music of
no birds she knew. The violet light was calm and sweet about
her.

She had gone on in the bird-haunted quiet for many minutes

before she caught the first hint of anything at odds with the perfect peace about her. A whiff of wood-smoke drifted to her nostrils on a vagrant breeze. When she rounded the next bend of the path she saw what had caused it. A tree lay across the way in a smother of shaking leaves and branches. She knew that she must skirt it, for the branches were too tangled to penetrate, and she turned out of the path, following the trunk toward its broken base.

She had gone only a few steps before the sound of a curious sobbing came to her ears. It was the gasp of choked breathing, and she had heard sounds like that too often before not to know that she approached death in some form or another. She laid her hand on her knife-hilt and crept forward softly.

The tree trunk had been severed as if by a blast of heat, for the stump was charred black and still smoking. Beyond the stump a queer tableau was being enacted, and she stopped quite still, staring through the leaves.

Upon the moss a naked girl was lying, gasping her life out behind the hands in which her face was buried. There was no mistaking the death-sound in that failing breath, although her body was unmarked. Hair of a strange green-gold pallor streamed over her bare white body, and by the fragility and tenuosity of that body Jirel knew that she could not be wholly human.

Above the dying girl a tall woman stood. And that woman was a magnet for Jirel's fascinated eyes. She was generously curved, sleepy-eyed. Black hair bound her head sleekly, and her skin was like rich, dark, creamy velvet. A violet robe wrapped her carelessly, leaving arms and one curved shoulder bare, and her girdle was a snake of something like purple glass. It might have been carved from some vast jewel, save for its size and unbroken clarity. Her feet were thrust bare into silver sandals. But it was her face that held Jirel's yellow gaze.

The sleepy eyes under heavily drooping lids were purple as gems, and the darkly crimson mouth curled in a smile so hateful that fury rushed up in Jirel's heart as she watched. That lazy purple gaze dwelt aloofly upon the gasping girl on the moss. The woman was saying in a voice as rich and deep as thick-piled velvet,

"—nor will any other of the dryad folk presume to work forbidden magic in my woodlands for a long, long while to come. Your fate shall be a deadly example to them, Irsla. You dared too greatly. None who defy Jarisme live. Hear me, Irsla!"

The sobbing breath had slowed as the woman spoke, as if life were slipping fast from the dryad-girl on the moss; and as she realized it the speaker's arm lifted and a finger of white fire leaped from her outstretched hand, stabbing the white body at her feet. And the girl Irsla started like one shocked back into life.

"Hear me out, dryad! Let your end be a warning to—"

The girl's quickened breath slowed again as the white brilliance left her, and again the woman's hand rose, again the light-blade stabbed. From behind her shielding hands the dryad gasped,

"Oh, mercy, mercy, Jarisme! Let me die!"

"When I have finished. Not before. Life and death are mine to command here, and I am not yet done with you. Your stolen magic—"

She paused, for Irsla had slumped once more upon the moss, breath scarcely stirring her. As Jarisme's light-dealing hand rose for the third time Jirel leapt forward. Partly it was intuitive hatred of the lazy-eyed woman, partly revolt at this cat-and-mouse play with a dying girl for victim. She swung her arm in an arc that cleared the branches from her path, and called out in her clear, strong voice,

"Have done, woman! Let her die in peace."

Slowly Jarisme's purple eyes rose. They met Jirel's hot yellow glare. Almost physical impact was in that first meeting of their eyes, and hatred flashed between them instantly, like the flash of blades—the instinctive hatred of total opposites, born enemies. Each stiffened subtly, as cats do in the instant before combat. But Jirel thought she saw in the purple gaze, behind all its kindling anger, a faint disquiet, a nameless uncertainty.

"Who are you?" asked Jarisme, very softly, very dangerously.

Something in that unsureness behind her angry eyes prompted Jirel to answer boldly,

"Jirel of Joiry. I seek the wizard Giraud, who fled me here. Stop tormenting that wretched girl and tell me where to find him. I can make it worth your while."

Her tone was imperiously mandatory, and behind Jarisme's drooping lips an answering flare of anger lighted, almost drowning out that faint unease.

"You do not know me," she observed, her voice very gentle. "I am the sorceress Jarisme, and high ruler over all this land. Did you think to buy me, then, earth-woman?"

Jirel smiled her sweetest, most poisonous smile.

"You will forgive me," she purred. "At the first glance at you I did not think your price could be high. . . ."

A petty malice had inspired the speech, and Jirel was sorry as it left her lips, for she knew that the scorn which blazed up in Jarisme's eyes was justified. The sorceress made a contemptuous gesture of dismissal.

"I shall waste no more of my time here," she said. "Get back to your little lands, Jirel of Joiry, and tempt me no further."

The purple gaze rested briefly on the motionless dryad at her feet, flicked Jirel's hot eyes with a glance of scorn which yet did not wholly hide that curious uncertainty in its depths. One hand slid behind her, oddly as if she were seeking a doorlatch in empty air. Then like a heat-shimmer the air danced about her, and in an instant she was gone.

Jirel blinked. Her ears had deceived her as well as her eyes, she thought, for as the sorceress vanished a door closed softly somewhere. Yet look though she would, the green glade was empty, the violet air untroubled. No Jarisme anywhere—no door. Jirel shrugged after a moment's bewilderment. She had met magic before.

A sound from the scarcely breathing girl upon the moss distracted her, and she dropped to her knees beside the dying dryad. There was no mark or wound upon her, yet Jirel knew that death could be only a matter of moments. And dimly she recalled that, so legend said, a tree-sprite never survived the death of its tree. Gently she turned the girl over, wondering if she were beyond help.

At the feel of those gentle hands the dryad's lids quivered

and rose. Brook-brown eyes looked up at Jirel, with green swimming in their deeps like leaf-reflections in a woodland pool.

"My thanks to you," faltered the girl in a ghostly murmur. "But get you back to your home now—before Jarisme's anger slays you."

Jirel shook her red head stubbornly.

"I must find Giraud first, and kill him, as I have sworn to do. But I will wait. Is there anything I can do?"

The green-reflecting eyes searched hers for a moment. The dryad must have read resolution there, for she shook her head a little.

"I must die—with my tree. But if you are determined—hear me. I owe you—a debt. There is a talisman—braided in my hair. When I—am dead—take it. It is Jarisme's sign. All her subjects wear them. It will guide you to her—and to Giraud. He is ever beside her. I know. I think it was her anger at you—that made her forget to take it from me, after she had dealt me my death. But why she did not slay you—I do not know. Jarisme is quick —to kill. No matter—listen now. If you must have Giraud—you must take a risk that no one here—has ever taken—before. Break this talisman—at Jarisme's feet. I do not know—what will happen then. Something—very terrible. It releases powers —even she can not control. It may—destroy you too. But—it is— a chance. May you—have—all good—"

The faltering voice failed. Jirel, bending her head, caught only meaningless murmurs that trailed away to nothing. The green-gold head dropped suddenly forward on her sustaining arm. Through the forest all about her went one long, quivering sigh, as if an intangible breeze ruffled the trees. Yet no leaves stirred.

Jirel bent and kissed the dryad's forehead, then laid her very gently back on the moss. And as she did so her hand in the masses of strangely colored hair came upon something sharp and hard. She remembered the talisman. It tingled in her fingers as she drew it out—an odd little jagged crystal sparkling with curious aliveness from the fire burning in its heart.

When she had risen to her feet, leaving the dead dryad lying upon the moss which seemed so perfectly her couch, she saw

that the inner brilliance streaming in its wedge-shaped pattern
through the crystal was pointing a quivering apex forward and
to the right. Irsla had said it would guide her. Experimentally
she twisted her hand to the left. Yes, the shaking light shifted
within the crystal, pointing always toward the right, and
Jarisme.

One last long glance she gave to the dryad on the moss. Then
she set off again down the path, the little magical thing stinging
her hand as she walked. And as she went she wondered. This
strong hatred which had flared so instinctively between her and
the sorceress was hot enough to burn any trace of fear from her
mind, and she remembered that look of uncertainty in the
purple gaze that had shot such hatred at her. Why? Why had
she not been slain as Irsla was slain, for defiance of this queer
land's ruler?

For a while she paced unheedingly along under the trees.
Then abruptly the foliage ceased and a broad meadow lay
before her, green in the clear, violet day. Beyond the meadow
the slim shaft of a tower rose dazzlingly white, and toward it
in steady radiance that magical talisman pointed.

From very far away she thought she still caught the echoes
of that song when the wind blew, an irritating monotony that
made her ears ache. She was glad when the wind died and the
song no longer shrilled in her ears.

Out across the meadow she went. Far ahead she could make
out purple mountains like low clouds on the horizon, and here
and there in the distances clumps of woodland dotted the
meadows. She walked on more rapidly now, for she was sure
that the white tower housed Jarisme, and with her Giraud.
And she must have gone more swiftly than she knew, for with
almost magical speed the shining shaft drew nearer.

She could see the arch of its doorway, bluely violet within.
The top of the shaft was battlemented, and she caught splashes
of color between the teeth of the stone scarps, as if flowers were
massed there and spilling blossoms against the whiteness of the
tower. The singsong music was louder than ever, and much
nearer. Jirel's heart beat a bit heavily as she advanced, wondering what sort of a sorceress this Jarisme might be, what dangers
lay before her in the path of her vow's fulfillment. Now the

white tower rose up over her, and she was crossing the little
space before the door, peering in dubiously. All she could see
was dimness and violet mist.

She laid her hand upon the dagger, took a deep breath and
stepped boldly in under the arch. In the instant her feet left
the solid earth she saw that this violet mist filled the whole
shaft of the tower, that there was no floor. Emptiness engulfed
her, and all reality ceased.

She was falling through clouds of violet blankness, but in no
recognizable direction. It might have been up, down, or sidewise through space. Everything had vanished in the violet
nothing. She knew an endless moment of vertigo and rushing
motion; then the dizzy emptiness vanished in a breath and she
was standing in a gasping surprise upon the roof of Jarisme's
tower.

She knew where she was by the white battlements ringing
her round, banked with strange blossoms in muted colors. In
the center of the circular, marble-paved place a low couch,
cushioned in glowing yellow, stood in the midst of a heap of
furs. Two people sat side by side on the couch. One was
Giraud. Black-robed, dark-visaged, he stared at Jirel with a
flicker of disquiet in his small, dull eyes. He said nothing.

Jirel dismissed him with a glance, scarcely realizing his presence. For Jarisme had lowered from her lips a long, silver flute.
Jirel realized that the queer, maddening music must have come
from that gleaming length, for it no longer echoed in her ears.
Jarisme was holding the instrument now in midair, regarding
Jirel over it with a purple-eyed gaze that was somehow thought-
ful and a little apprehensive, though anger glowed in it, too.

"So," she said richly, in her slow, deep voice. "For the second
time you defy me."

At these words Giraud turned his head sharply and stared at
the sorceress' impassive profile. She did not return his gaze,
but after a moment he looked quickly back at Jirel, and in his
eyes too she saw that flicker of alarm, and with it a sort of
scared respect. It puzzled her, and she did not like being
puzzled. She said a little breathlessly,

"If you like, yes. Give me that skulking potion-brewer beside you and set me down again outside this damned tower of trickery. I came to kill your pet spellmonger here for treachery done me in my own world by this creature who dared not stay to face me."

Her peremptory words hung in the air like the echoes of a gong. For a while no one spoke. Jarisme smiled more subtly than before, an insolent, slow smile that made Jirel's pulses hammer with the desire to smash it down the woman's lush, creamy throat. At last Jarisme said, in a voice as rich and deep as thick-piled velvet,

"Hot words, hot words, soldier-woman! Do you really imagine that your earthly squabbles matter to Jarisme?"

"What matters to Jarisme is of little moment to me," Jirel said contemptuously. "All I want is this skulker here, whom I have sworn to kill."

Jarisme's slow smile was maddening. "You demand it of me —Jarisme?" she asked with soft incredulity. "Only fools offend me, woman, and they but once. None commands me. You will have to learn that."

Jirel smiled thinly. "At what price, then, do you value your pet cur?"

Giraud half rose from the couch at that last insult, his dark face darker with a surge of anger. Jarisme pushed him back with a lazy hand.

"This is between your—friend—and me," she said. "I do not think, soldier"—the appellation was the deadliest of insults in the tone she used—"that any price you could offer would interest me."

"And yet your interest is very easily caught." Jirel flashed a contemptuous glance at Giraud, restive under the woman's restraining hand.

Jarisme's rich pallor flushed a little. Her voice was sharper as she said,

"Do not tempt me too far, earthling."

Jirel's yellow eyes defied her. "I am not afraid."

The sorceress' purple gaze surveyed her slowly. When Jarisme spoke again a tinge of reluctant admiration lightened the slow scorn of her voice.

"No—you are not afraid. And a fool not to be. Fools annoy me, Jirel of Joiry."

She laid the flute down on her knee and lazily lifted a ringless hand. Anger was glowing in her eyes now, blotting out all trace of that little haunting fear. But Giraud caught the rising hand, bending, whispering urgently in her ear. Jirel caught a part of what he said, "—what happens to those who tamper with their own destiny—" And she saw the anger fade from the sorceress' face as apprehension brightened there again. Jarisme looked at Jirel with a long, hard look and shrugged her ample shoulders.

"Yes," she murmured. "Yes, Giraud. It is wisest so." And to Jirel, "Live, then, earthling. Find your way back to your own land if you can, but I warn you, do not trouble me again. I shall not stay my hand if our paths ever cross in the future."

She struck her soft, white palms together sharply. And at the sound the roof-top and the violet sky and the banked flowers at the parapets whirled around Jirel in dizzy confusion. From very far away she heard that clap of peremptory hands still echoing, but it seemed to her that the great, smokily colored blossoms were undergoing an inexplicable transformation. They quivered and spread and thrust upward from the edges of the tower to arch over her head. Her feet were pressing a mossy ground, and the sweet, earthy odors of a garden rose about her. Blinking, she stared around as the world slowly steadied.

She was no longer on the roof-top. As far as she could see through the tangled stems, great flowering plants sprang up in the gloaming of a strange, enchanted forest. She was completely submerged in greenery, and the illusion of under-water filled her eyes, for the violet light that filtered through the leaves was diffused and broken into a submarine dimness. Uncertainly she began to grope her way forward, staring about to see what sort of a miracle had enfolded her.

It was a bower in fairyland. She had come into a tropical garden of great, muted blooms and jungle silences. In the diffused light the flowers nodded sleepily among the leaves, hypnotically lovely, hypnotically soporific with their soft colors and drowsy, never-ending motion. The fragrance was overpowering. She went on slowly, treading moss that gave back no sound. Here under the canopy of leaves was a little separate world of color and silence and perfume. Dreamily she made her way among the flowers.

Their fragrance was so strongly sweet that it went to her head, and she walked in a waking dream. Because of this curious, scented trance in which she went she was never quite sure if she had actually seen that motion among the leaves, and looked closer, and made out a huge, incredible serpent of violet transparency, a giant replica of the snake that girdled Jarisme's waist, but miraculously alive, miraculously supple and gliding, miraculously twisting its soundless way among the blossoms and staring at her with impassive, purple eyes.

While it glided along beside her she had other strange visions too, and could never remember just what they were, or why she caught familiar traces in the tiny, laughing faces that peered at her from among the flowers, or half believed the wild, impossible things they whispered to her, their laughing mouths brushing her ears as they leaned down among the blossoms.

The branches began to thin at last, as she neared the edge of the enchanted place. She walked slowly, half conscious of the great transparent snake like a living jewel writhing along soundlessly at her side, her mind vaguely troubled in its dream by the fading remembrance of what those little, merry voices had told her. When she came to the very edge of the bowery jungle and broke out into clear daylight again she stopped in a daze, staring round in the brightening light as the perfumes slowly cleared from her head.

Sanity and realization returned to her at last. She shook her red head dizzily and looked round, half expecting, despite her returning clarity, to see the great serpent gliding across the grass. But there was nothing. Of course she had dreamed. Of course those little laughing voices had not told her that—that— she clutched after the vanishing tags of remembrance, and caught nothing. Ruefully she laughed and brushed away the clinging memories, looking round to see where she was.

She stood at the crest of a little hill. Below her the flower-fragrant jungle nodded, a little patch of enchanted greenery

clothing the slopes of the hill. Beyond and below green
meadows stretched away to a far-off line of forest which she
thought she recognized as that in which she had first met
Jarisme. But the white tower which had risen in the midst of
the meadows was magically gone. Where it had stood, unbroken greenery lay under the violet clarity of the sky.

As she stared round in bewilderment a faint prickling stung
her palm, and she glanced down, remembering the talisman
clutched in her hand. The quivering light was streaming in a
long wedge toward some point behind her. She turned. She was
in the foothills of those purple mountains she had glimpsed
from the edge of the woods. High and shimmering, they rose
above her. And, hazily in the heat-waves that danced among
their heights, she saw the tower.

Jirel groaned to herself. Those peaks were steep and rocky.
Well, no help for it. She must climb. She growled a soldier's
oath in her throat and turned wearily toward the rising slopes.
They were rough and deeply slashed with ravines. Violet heat
beat up from the reflecting rocks, and tiny, brilliantly colored
things scuttled from her path—orange lizards and coral red
scorpions and little snakes like bright blue jewels.

It seemed to her as she stumbled upward among the broken
stones that the tower was climbing too. Time after time she
gained upon it, and time after time when she lifted her eyes
after a grueling struggle up steep ravines, that mocking flicker
of whiteness shimmered still high and unattainable on some
distant peak. It had the mistiness of unreality, and if her talisman's guide had not pointed steadily upward she would have
thought it an illusion to lead her astray.

But after what seemed hours of struggle, there came the time
when, glancing up, she saw the shaft rising on the topmost
peak of all, white as snow against the clear violet sky. And
after that it shifted no more. She took heart now, for at last
she seemed to be gaining. Every laborious step carried her
nearer that lofty shining upon the mountain's highest peak.

She paused after a while, looking up and wiping the moisture from her forehead where the red curls clung. As she stood
there something among the rocks moved, and out from behind

a boulder a long, slinking feline creature came. It was not like
any beast she had ever seen before. Its shining pelt was fabu-
lously golden, brocaded with queer patterns of darker gold,
and down against its heavy jaws curved two fangs whiter than
ivory. With a grace as gliding as water it paced down the
ravine toward her.

Jirel's heart contracted. Somehow she found the knife-hilt
in her hand, though she had no recollection of having drawn
it. She was staring hard at the lovely and terrible cat, trying to
understand the haunting familiarity about its eyes. They were
purple, like jewels. Slowly recognition dawned. She had met
that purple gaze before, insolent under sleepy lids. Jarisme's
eyes. Yes, and the snake in her dream had watched her with a
purple stare too. Jarisme?

She closed her hand tightly about the crystal, knowing that
she must conceal from the sorceress her one potent weapon,
waiting until the time came to turn it against its maker. She
shifted her knife so that light glinted down the blade. They
stood quite still for a moment, yellow-eyed woman and fabulous, purple-eyed cat, staring at each other with hostility eloquent in every line of each. Jirel clenched her knife tight,
warily eyeing the steel-clawed paws on which the golden beast
went so softly. They could have ripped her to ribbons before
the blade struck home.

She saw a queer expression flicker across the somber purple
gaze that met hers, and the beautiful cat crouched a little, tail
jerking, lip twitched back to expose shining fangs. It was about
to spring. For an interminable moment she waited for that
hurtling golden death to launch itself upon her, tense, rigid,
knife steady in her hand. . . .

It sprang. She dropped to one knee in the split second of its
leaping, instinctively hiding the crystal, but thrusting up her
dagger in defense. The great beast sailed easily over her head.
As it hurtled past, a peal of derisive laughter rang in her ears,
and she heard quite clearly the sound of a slamming door. She
scrambled up and whirled in one motion, knife ready. The
defile was quite empty in the violet day. There was no door
anywhere. Jarisme had vanished.

A little shaken, Jirel sheathed her blade. She was not afraid.
Anger burned out all trace of fear as she remembered the scorn
in that ringing laugh. She took up her course again toward the
tower, white and resolute, not looking back.

The tower was drawing near again. She toiled upward.
Jarisme showed no further sign of her presence, but Jirel felt
eyes upon her, purple eyes, scornful and sleepy. She could see
the tower clearly, just above her at the crest of the highest
peak, up to which a long arc of steps curved steeply. They were
very old, these steps, so worn that many were little more than
irregularities on the stone. Jirel wondered what feet had worn
them so, to what door they had originally led.

She was panting when she reached the top and peered in
under the arch of the door. To her surprise she found herself
staring into a broad, semicircular hallway, whose walls were
lined with innumerable doors. She remembered the violet
nothingness into which she had stepped the last time she
crossed the sill, and wondered as she thrust a tentative foot
over it if the hall were an illusion and she were really about to
plunge once more into that cloudy abyss of falling. But the
floor was firm.

She stepped inside and paused, looking round in some bewilderment and wondering where to turn now. She could
smell peril in the air. Almost she could taste the magic that
hovered like a mist over the whole enchanted place. Little
warning prickles ran down her back as she went forward very
softly and pushed open one of those innumerable doors. Behind it a gallery stretched down miles of haze-shrouded extent.
Arrow-straight it ran, the arches of the ceiling making an endless parade that melted into violet distance. And as she stood
looking down the cloudy vista, something like a puff of smoke
obscured her vision for an instant—smoke that eddied and
billowed and rolled away from the shape of that golden cat
which had vanished in the mountain ravine.

It paced slowly down the hall toward her, graceful and
lovely, muscles rippling under the brocaded golden coat and
purple eyes fixed upon her in a scornful stare. Jirel's hand went
to the knife in her belt, hatred choking up in her throat as she

met the purple eyes. But in the corridor a voice was echoing softly, Jarisme's voice, saying,

"Then it is war between us, Jirel of Joiry. For you have defied my mercy, and you must be punished. Your punishment I have chosen—the simplest, and the subtlest, and the most terrible of all punishments, the worst that could befall a human creature. Can you guess it? No? Then wonder a while, for I am not prepared yet to administer it fully . . . or shall I kill you now? Eh-h-h? . . ."

The curious, long-drawn query melted into a purring snarl, and the great cat's lip lifted, a flare of murderous light flaming up in the purple eyes. It had been pacing nearer all the while that light voice had echoed in the air. Now its roar crescendoed into a crashing thunder that rang from the walls, and the steel springs of its golden body tightened for a leap straight at Jirel's throat. Scarcely a dozen paces away, she saw the brocaded beauty of it crouching, taut and poised, saw the powerful body quiver and tighten—and spring. In instinctive panic she leaped back and slammed the door in its face.

Derisive laughter belled through the air. A cloud of thin smoke eddied through the crack around the door and puffed in her face with all the insolence of a blow. Then the air was clear again. The red mist of murder swam before Jirel's eyes. Blind with anger, breath beating thickly in her throat, she snatched at the door again, ripping the dagger from her belt. Through that furious haze she glared down the corridor. It was empty. She closed the door a second time and leaned against it, trembling with anger, until the mist had cleared from her head and she could control her shaking hand well enough to replace the dagger.

When she had calmed a little she turned to scan the hall, wondering what to do next. And she saw that there was no escape now, even had she wished, for the door she had entered by was gone. All about her now closed the door-studded walls, enigmatic, imprisoning. And the very fact of their presence was an insult, suggesting that Jarisme had feared she would flee if the entrance were left open. Jirel forced herself into calmness again. She was not afraid, but she knew herself in deadly peril.

She was revolving the sorceress' threat as she cast about for some indication to guide her next step. The simplest and subtlest and most terrible of punishments—what could it be? Jirel knew much of the ways of torture—her dungeons were as blood-stained as any of her neighbors'—but she knew too that Jarisme had not meant only the pain of the flesh. There was a subtler menace in her words. It would be a feminine vengeance, and more terrible than anything iron and fire could inflict. She knew that. She knew also that no door she could open now would lead to freedom, but she could not stay quiet, waiting. She glanced along the rows of dark, identical panels. Anything that magic could contrive might lie behind them. In the face of peril more deadly than death she could not resist the temptation to pull open the nearest one and peer within.

A gust of wind blew in her face and rattled the door. Dust was in that wind, and bitter cold. Through an inner grille of iron, locked across the opening, she saw a dazzle of whiteness like sun on snow in the instant before she slammed the door shut on the piercing gust. But the incident had whetted her curiosity. She moved along the wall and opened another.

This time she was looking through another locked grille into a dimness of gray smoke shot through with flame. The smell of burning rose in her nostrils, and she could hear faintly, as from vast distances, the sound of groans and the shivering echo of screams. Shuddering, she closed the door.

When she opened the next one she caught her breath and stared. Before her a thick crystal door separated her from bottomless space. She pressed her face to the cold glass and stared out and down. Nothingness met her gaze. Dark and silence and the blaze of unwinking stars. It was day outside the tower, but she looked into fathomless night. And as she stared, a long streak of light flashed across the blackness and faded. It was not a shooting star. By straining her eyes she could make out something like a thin sliver of silver flashing across the dark, its flaming tail fading behind it in the sky. And the sight made her ill with sudden vertigo. Bottomless void reeled around her, and she fell back into the hallway, slamming the door upon that terrifying glimpse of starry nothingness.

It was several minutes before she could bring herself to try the next door. When she did, swinging it open timorously, a familiar sweetness of flower perfume floated out and she found herself gazing through a grille of iron bars deep into that drowsy jungle of blossoms and scent and silence which she had crossed at the mountain's foot. A wave of remembrance washed over her. For an instant she could hear those tiny, laughing voices again, and she felt the presence of the great snake at her side, and the wild, mirth-ridden secrets of the little gay voices rang in her ears. Then she was awake again, and the memory vanished as dreams do, leaving nothing but tantalizing fragments of forgotten secrets drifting through her mind. She knew as she stared that she could step straight into that flowery fairyland again if the bars would open. But there was no escape from this magical place, though she might look through any number of opening doors into far lands and near.

She was beginning to understand the significance of the hall. It must be from here that Jarisme by her magical knowledge journeyed into other lands and times and worlds through the doors that opened between her domain and those strange, outland places. Perhaps she had sorcerer friends there, and paid them visits and brought back greater knowledge, stepping from world to world, from century to century, through her enchanted doorways. Jirel felt certain that one of these enigmatic openings would give upon that mountain pass where the golden cat with its scornful purple eyes had sprung at her, and vanished, and laughed backward as the door slammed upon it, and upon the woodland glade where the dryad died. But she knew that bars would close these places away even if she could find them.

She went on with her explorations. One door opened upon a steamy fern-forest of gigantic growths, out of whose deeps floated musky, reptilian odors, and the distant sound of beasts bellowing hollowly. And another upon a gray desert stretching flat and lifeless to the horizon, wan under the light of a dim red sun.

But at last she came to one that opened not into alien lands but upon a stairway winding down into solid rock whose walls showed the mark of the tools that had hollowed them. No

sound came up the shaft of the stairs, and a gray light darkened down their silent reaches. Jirel peered in vain for some
hint of what lay below. But at last, because inactivity had
palled upon her and she knew that all ways were hopeless for
escape, she entered the doorway and went slowly down the
steps. It occurred to her that possibly she might find Jarisme
below, engaged in some obscure magic in the lower regions,
and she was eager to come to grips with her enemy.

The light darkened as she descended, until she was groping
her way through obscurity round and round the curving stairs.
When the steps ended at a depth she could not guess, she could
tell that she had emerged into a low-roofed corridor only by
feeling the walls and ceiling that met her exploring hands, for
the thickest dark hid everything. She made her slow way along
the stone hall, which wound and twisted and dipped at unex-
pected angles until she lost all sense of direction. But she
knew she had gone a long way when she began to see the faint
gleam of light ahead.

Presently she began to catch the faraway sound of a familiar
song—Jarisme's monotonous little flute melody on two notes,
and she was sure then that her intuition had been true, that
the sorceress was down here somewhere. She drew her dagger in
the gloom and went on more warily.

An arched opening ended the passage. Through the arch
poured a blaze of dancing white luminance. Jirel paused,
blinking and trying to make out what strange place she was
entering. The room before her was filled with the baffling glitter and shimmer and mirage of reflecting surfaces so bewilder-
ingly that she could not tell which was real and which mirror,
and which dancing light. The brilliance dazzled in her face
and dimmed into twilight and blazed again as the mirrors
shifted. Little currents of dark shivered through the chaos and
brightened into white sparkle once more. That monotonous
music came to her through the quivering lights and reflections,
now strongly, now faintly in the distance.

The whole place was a chaos of blaze and confusion. She
could not know if the room were small or large, a cavern or a
palace hall. Queer reflections danced through the dazzle of it.

She could see her own image looking back at her from a dozen, a score, a hundred moving planes that grotesquely distorted her and then flickered out again, casting a blaze of light in her blinded eyes. Dizzily she blinked into the reeling wilderness of planes.

Then she saw Jarisme in her violet robe watching her from a hundred identical golden couches reflected upon a hundred surfaces. The figure held a flute to its lips, and the music pulsed from it in perfect time with the pulsing of the sorceress' swelling white throat. Jirel stared round in confusion at the myriad Jarismes all piping the interminable monotones. A hundred sensual, dreamy faces turned to her, a hundred white arms dropped as the flute left a hundred red mouths that Jarisme might smile ironic welcome a hundredfold more scornful for its multiplicity.

When the music ceased, all the flashing dazzle suddenly stilled. Jirel blinked as the chaos resolved itself into shining order, the hundred Jarismes merging into one sleepy-eyed woman lounging upon her golden couch in a vast crystal-walled chamber shaped like the semicircular half of a great, round, domed room. Behind the couch a veil of violet mist hung like a curtain shutting off what would have formed the other half of the circular room.

"Enter," said the sorceress with the graciousness of one who knows herself in full command of the situation. "I thought you might find the way here. I am preparing a ceremony which will concern you intimately. Perhaps you would like to watch? This is to be an experiment, and for that reason a greater honor is to be yours than you can ever have known before; for the company I am assembling to watch your punishment is a more distinguished one than you could understand. Come here, inside the circle."

Jirel advanced, dagger still clenched in one hand, the other closed about her bit of broken crystal. She saw now that the couch stood in the center of a ring engraved in the floor with curious, cabalistic symbols. Beyond it the cloudy violet curtain swayed and eddied within itself, a vast, billowing wall of mist. Dubiously she stepped over the circle and stood eyeing Jarisme, her yellow gaze hot with rigidly curbed emotion. Jarisme smiled and lifted the flute to her lips again.

As the irritating two notes began their seesawing tune Jirel saw something amazing happen. She knew then that the flute was a magic one, and the song magical too. The notes took on a form that overstepped the boundaries of the aural and partook in some inexplicable way of all the other senses too. She could feel them, taste them, smell them, see them. In a queer way they were visible, pouring in twos from the flute and dashing outward like little needles of light. The walls reflected them, and those reflections became swifter and brighter and more numerous until the air was full of flying slivers of silvery brilliance, until shimmers began to dance among them and over them, and that bewildering shift of mirrored planes started up once more. Again reflections crossed and dazzled and multiplied in the shining air as the flute poured out its flashing double notes.

Jirel forgot the sorceress beside her, the music that grated on her ears, even her own peril, in watching the pictures that shimmered and vanished in the mirrored surfaces. She saw flashes of scenes she had glimpsed through the doors of Jarisme's hallway. She saw stranger places than that, passing in instant-brief snatches over the silvery planes. She saw jagged black mountains with purple dawns rising behind them and stars in unknown figures across the dark skies; she saw gray seas flat and motionless beneath gray clouds; she saw smooth meadows rolling horizonward under the glare of double suns. All these and many more awoke to the magic of Jarisme's flute, and melted again to give way to others.

Jirel had the strange fancy, as the music went on, that it was audible in those lands whose brief pictures were flickering across the background of its visible notes. It seemed to be piercing immeasurable distances, ringing across the cloudy seas, echoing under the double suns, calling insistently in strange lands and far, unknown places, over deserts and mountains that man's feet had never trod, reaching other worlds and other times and crying its two-toned monotony through the darkness of interstellar space. All of this, to Jirel, was no more than a vague realization that it must be so. It meant

nothing to her, whose world was a flat plane arched by the
heaven-pierced bowl of the sky. Magic, she told herself, and
gave up trying to understand.

Presently the tempo of the fluting changed. The same two
notes still shrilled endlessly up and down, but it was no longer
a clarion call ringing across borderlands into strange worlds.
Now it was slower, statelier. And the notes of visible silver that
had darted crazily against the crystal walls and reflected back
again took on an order that ranked them into one shining
plane. Upon that plane Jirel saw the outlines of a familiar
scene gradually take shape. The great door-lined hall above
mirrored itself in faithful replica before her eyes. The music
went on changelessly.

Then, as she watched, one of those innumerable doors
quivered. She held her breath. Slowly it swung open upon that
gray desert under the red sun which she had seen before she
closed it quickly away behind concealing panels. Again as she
looked, that sense of utter desolation and weariness and despair
came over her, so uncannily dreary was the scene. Now the
door stood wide, its locked grille no longer closing it, and as
the music went on she could see a dazzle like a jagged twist of
lightning begin to shimmer in its aperture. The gleam strengthened. She saw it quiver once, twice, then sweep forward with
blinding speed through the open doorway. And as she tried to
follow it with her eyes another moving door distracted her.

This time the steamy fern-forest was revealed as the panels
swung back. But upon the threshold sprawled something so
frightful that Jirel's free hand flew to her lips and a scream
beat up in her throat. It was black—shapeless and black and
slimy. And it was alive. Like a heap of putrescently shining
jelly it heaved itself over the door-sill and began to flow across
the floor, inching its way along like a vast blind ameba. But
she knew without being told that it was horribly wise, horribly
old. Behind it a black trail of slime smeared the floor.

Jirel shuddered and turned her eyes away. Another door was
swinging open. Through it she saw a place she had not chanced
upon before, a country of bare red rock strewn jaggedly under
a sky so darkly blue that it might have been black, with stars

glimmering in it more clearly than stars of earth. Across this red, broken desert a figure came striding that she knew could be only a figment of magic, so tall it was, so spidery-thin, so grotesquely human despite its bulbous head and vast chest. She could not see it clearly, for about it like a robe it clutched a veil of blinding light. On those incredibly long, thin legs it stepped across the door-sill, drew its dazzling garment closer about it, and strode forward. As it neared, the light was so blinding that she could not look upon it. Her averted eyes caught the motion of a fourth door.

This time she saw that flowery ravine again, dim in its under-water illusion of diffused light. And out from among the flowers writhed a great serpent-creature, not of the transparent crystal she had seen in her dream, but iridescently scaled. Nor was it entirely serpent, for from the thickened neck sprang a head which could not be called wholly unhuman. The thing carried itself as proudly as a cobra, and as it glided across the threshold its single, many-faceted eye caught Jirel's in the reflection. The eye flashed once, dizzyingly, and she reeled back in sick shock, the violence of that glance burning through her veins like fire. When she regained control of herself many other doors were standing open upon scenes both familiar and strange. During her daze other denizens of those strange worlds must have entered at the call of the magic flute.

She was just in time to see an utterly indescribable thing flutter into the hall from a world which so violated her eyes that she got no more than a glimpse of it as she flung up out-raged hands to shut it out. She did not lower that shield until Jarisme's amused voice said in an undertone, "Behold your audience, Jirel of Joiry," and she realized that the music had ceased and a vast silence was pressing against her ears. Then she looked out, and drew a long breath. She was beyond surprise and shock now, and she stared with the dazed incredulity of one who knows herself in a nightmare.

Ranged outside the circle that enclosed the two women sat what was surely the strangest company ever assembled. They were grouped with a queer irregularity which, though mean-ingless to Jirel, yet gave the impression of definite purpose and design. It had a symmetry so strongly marked that even though it fell outside her range of comprehension she could not but feel the rightness of it.

The light-robed dweller in the red barrens sat there, and the great black blob of shapeless jelly heaved gently on the crystal floor. She saw others she had watched enter, and many more. One was a female creature whose robe of peacock iridescence sprang from her shoulders in great drooping wings and folded round her like a bat's leathery cloak. And her neighbor was a fat gray slug of monster size, palpitating endlessly. One of the crowd looked exactly like a tall white lily swaying on a stalk of silver pallor, but from its chalice poured a light so ominously tinted that she shuddered and turned her eyes away.

Jarisme had risen from her couch. Very tall and regal in her violet robe, she rose against the back-drop of mist which veiled the other half of the room. As she lifted her arms, the incredible company turned to her with an eager expectancy. Jirel shuddered. Then Jarisme's flute spoke softly. It was a different sort of music from the clarion that called them together, from the stately melody which welcomed them through the opening doors. But it harped still on the two seesawing notes, with low, rippling sounds so different from the other two that Jirel marveled at the range of the sorceress' ability on the two notes.

For a few moments as the song went on, nothing happened. Then a motion behind Jarisme caught Jirel's eye. The curtain of violet mist was swaying. The music beat at it and it quivered to the tune. It shook within itself, and paled and thinned, and from behind it a light began to glow. Then on a last low monotone it dissipated wholly and Jirel was staring at a vast globe of quivering light which loomed up under the stupendous arch that soared outward to form the second half of the chamber.

As the last clouds faded she saw that the thing was a huge crystal sphere, rising upon the coils of a translucent purple base in the shape of a serpent. And in the heart of the globe burned a still flame, living, animate, instinct with a life so alien that Jirel stared in utter bewilderment. It was a thing she knew to be alive—yet she knew it could *not* be alive. But she recognized even in her daze of incomprehension its relation to the tiny fragment of crystal she clutched in her hand. In that too

the still flame burned. It stung her hand faintly in reminder
that she possessed a weapon which could destroy Jarisme,
though it might destroy its wielder in the process. The thought
gave her a sort of desperate courage.

Jarisme was ignoring her now. She had turned to face the
great globe with lifted arms and shining head thrown back.
And from her lips a piercingly sweet sound fluted, midway between hum and whistle. Jirel had the wild fancy that she could
see that sound arrowing straight into the heart of the vast
sphere bulking so high over them all. And in the heart of that
still, living flame a little glow of red began to quiver.

Through the trembling air shrilled a second sound. From
the corner of her eye Jirel could see that a dark figure had
moved forward into the circle and fallen to its knees at the
sorceress' side. She knew it for Giraud. Like two blades the
notes quivered in the utter hush that lay upon the assembly,
and in the globe that red glow deepened.

One by one, other voices joined the chorus, queer, uncanny
sounds some of them, from throats not shaped for speech. No
two voices blended. The chorus was one of single, unrelated
notes. And as each voice struck the globe, the fire burned more
crimson, until its still pallor had flushed wholly into red. High
above the rest soared Jarisme's knife-keen fluting. She lifted
her arms higher, and the voices rose in answer. She lowered
them, and the blade-like music swooped down an almost visible
arc to a lower key. Jirel felt that she could all but see the notes
spearing straight from each singer into the vast sphere that
dwarfed them all. There was no melody in it, but a sharply
definite pattern as alien and unmistakable as the symmetry of
their grouping in the room. And as Jarisme's arms rose, lifting
the voices higher, the flame burned more deeply red, and paled
again as the voices fell.

Three times that stately, violet-robed figure gestured with
lifted arms, and three times the living flame deepened and
paled. Then Jarisme's voice soared in a high, triumphant cry
and she whirled with spread arms, facing the company. In one
caught breath, all voices ceased. Silence fell upon them like a
blow. Jarisme was no longer priestess, but goddess, as she
fronted them in that dead stillness with exultant face and

blazing eyes. And in one motion they bowed before her as
corn bows under wind. Alien things, shapeless monsters, face-
less, eyeless, unrecognizable creatures from unknowable dimensions, abased themselves to the crystal floor before the splendor
of light in Jarisme's eyes. For a moment of utter silence the
tableau held. Then the sorceress' arms fell.

Ripplingly the company rose. Beyond Jarisme the vast globe
had paled again into that living, quiet flame of golden pallor.
Immense, brooding, alive, it loomed up above them. Into the
strained stillness Jarisme's low voice broke. She was speaking in
Jirel's native tongue, but the air, as she went on, quivered
thickly with something like waves of sound that were pitched
for other organs than human ears. Every word that left her lips
made another wave through the thickened air. The assembly
shimmered before Jirel's eyes in that broken clarity as a
meadow quivers under heat waves.

"Worshippers of the Light," said Jarisme sweetly, "be welcomed from your far dwellings into the presence of the Flame.
We who serve it have called you to the worship, but before you
return, another sort of ceremony is to be held, which we have
felt will interest you all. For we have called it truly the simplest
and subtlest and most terrible of all punishments for a human
creature.

"It is our purpose to attempt a reversal of this woman's physical and mental self in such a way as to cause her body to become rigidly motionless while her mind—her soul—looks eternally backward along the path it has traveled. You who are
human, or have known humanity, will understand what deadly
torture that can be. For no human creature, by the laws that
govern it, can have led a life whose intimate review is anything
but pain. To be frozen into eternal reflections, reviewing all
the futility and pain of life, all the pain that thoughtless or
intentional acts have caused others, all the spreading conse-
quences of every act—that, to a human being, would be the
most dreadful of all torments."

In the silence that fell as her voice ceased, Giraud laid a
hand on Jarisme's arm. Jirel saw terror in his eyes.

"Remember," he uttered, "remember, for those who tamper

with their known destiny a more fearful thing may come
than—"

Jarisme shrugged off the restraining hand impatiently. She
turned to Jirel.

"Know, earthling," she said in a queerly strained voice, "that
in the books of the future it is written that Jarisme the Sorceress must die at the hands of the one human creature who defies
her thrice—and that human creature a woman. Twice I have
been weak, and spared you. Once in the forest, once on the
roof-top, you cast your puny defiance in my face, and I stayed
my hand for fear of what is written. But the third time shall
not come. Though you are my appointed slayer, you shall not
slay. With my own magic I break Fate's sequence, now, and
we shall see!"

In the blaze of her purple eyes Jirel saw that the moment
had come. She braced herself, fingers closing about the fragment of crystal in her hand uncertainly as she hesitated, wondering if the time had come for the breaking of her talisman
at the sorceress' feet. She hesitated too long, though her waiting was only a split second in duration. For Jarisme's magic
was more supremely simple than Jirel could have guessed. The
sorceress turned a blazing purple gaze upon her and sharply
snapped her plump fingers in the earthwoman's face.

At the sound Jirel's whole world turned inside out about
her. It was the sheerest physical agony. Everything vanished
as that terrible shift took place. She felt her own body being
jerked inexplicably around in a reversal like nothing that any
living creature could ever have experienced before. It was a
backward-facing in a direction which could have had no existence until that instant. She felt the newness in the second before sight came to her—a breathless, soundless, new-born *now*
in which she was the first dweller, created simultaneously with
the new plane of being. Then sight broke upon her consciousness.

The thing spread out before her was so stupendous that she
would have screamed if she had possessed an animate body. All
life was open to her gaze. The sight was too immeasurable for
her to grasp it fully—too vast for her human consciousness to

look upon at all save in flashing shutter-glimpses without relation or significance. Motion and immobility existed simultaneously in the thing before her. Endless activity shuttling to and
fro—yet the whole vast panorama was frozen in a timeless calm
through which a mighty pattern ran whose very immensity was
enough to strike terror into her soul. Threaded through it the
backward trail of her own life stretched. As she gazed upon it
such floods of conflicting emotion washed over her that she
could not see anything clearly, but she was fiercely insisting to
her inner consciousness that she would not—*would not*—look
back, dared not, could not—and all the while her sight was
running past days and weeks along the path which led inexorably toward the one scene she could not bear to think of.

Very remotely, as her conscious sight retraced the backward
way, she was aware of overlapping planes of existence in the
stretch of limitless activity before her. Shapes other than human, scenes that had no meaning to her, quivered and shifted
and boiled with changing lives—yet lay motionless in the
mighty pattern. She scarcely heeded them. For her, of all that
panoramic impossibility one scene alone had meaning—the one
scene toward which her sight was racing now, do what she
would to stop it—the one scene that she knew she could never
bear to see again.

Yet when her sight reached that place the pain did not begin
at once. She gazed almost calmly upon that little interval of
darkness and flaring light, the glare of torches shining upon a
girl's bent red head and on a man's long body sprawled motionless upon flagstones. In the deepest stillness she stared. She
felt no urge to look farther, on beyond the scene into the past.
This was the climax, the center of all her life—this torch-lit
moment on the flagstones. Vividly she was back again in the
past, felt the hardness of the cold flags against her knees, and
the numbness of her heart as she stared down into a dead
man's face. Timelessly she dwelt upon that long-ago heart-
break, and within her something swelled unbearably.

That something was a mounting emotion too great to have
name, too complexly blending agony and grief and hatred and
love—and rebellion; so strong that all the rest of the stupendous thing before her was blotted out in the gathering storm

of what seethed in her innermost consciousness. She was aware
of nothing but that overwhelming emotion. And it was boiling
into one great unbearable explosion of violence in which rage
took precedence over all. Rage at life for permitting such pain
to be. Rage at Jarisme for forcing her into memory. Such rage
that everything shook before it, and melted and ran together
in a heat of rebellion, and—something snapped. The panorama
reeled and shivered and collapsed into the dark of semi-
oblivion.

Through the clouds of her half-consciousness the agony of
change stabbed at her. Half understanding, she welcomed it,
though the piercing anguish of that reversal was so strong it
dragged her out of her daze again and wrung her anew in the
grinding pain of that change which defied all natural laws. In
heedless impatience she waited for the torture to pass. Exultation was welling up in her, for she knew that her own violence
had melted the spell by which Jarisme held her. She knew what
she must do when she stood free again, and conscious power
flowed intoxicatingly through her.

She opened her eyes. She was standing rigidly before the
great fire-quickened globe. The amazing company was grouped
around her intently, and Jarisme, facing her, had taken one
angry, incredulous step forward as she saw her own spell break.
Upon that tableau Jirel's hot yellow eyes opened, and she
laughed in grim exultation and swung up her arm. Violet light
glinted upon crystal.

In the instant Jarisme saw what she intended, convulsive
terror wiped all other expression from her face. A cry of mingled inarticulatenesses thundered up from the transfixed
crowd. Giraud started forward from among them, frantic
hands clawing out toward her.

"No, no!" shrieked Jarisme. "Wait!"

It was too late. The crystal dashed itself from Jirel's down-
swinging arm, the light in it blazing. With a splintering crash
it struck the floor at the sorceress' sandaled feet and flew into
shining fragments.

For an instant nothing happened. Jirel held her breath,
waiting. Giraud had flung himself flat on the shining floor,
reaching out for her in a last desperate effort. His hands had

flown out to seize her, and found only her ankles. He clung to
them now with a paralyzed grip, his face hidden between his
arms. Jarisme cowered motionless, arms clasped about her
head as if she were trying to hide. The motley throng of watchers was rigid in fatalistic quiet. In tense silence they waited.

Then in the great globe above them the pale flame flickered.
Jarisme's gaspingly caught breath sounded loud in the utter
quiet. Again the flame shook. And again. Then abruptly it
went out. Darkness stunned them for a moment; then a low
muttering roar rumbled up out of the stillness, louder and
deeper and stronger until it pressed unbearably upon Jirel's
ears and her head was one great aching surge of sound. Above
that roar a sharply crackling noise broke, and the crystal walls
of the room trembled, reeled dizzily—split open in long jagged
rents through which the violet day poured in thin fingers of
light. Overhead the shattering sound of falling walls roared
loud. Jarisme's magic tower was crumbling all around them.
Through the long, shivering cracks in the walls the pale violet
day poured more strongly, serene in the chaos.

In that clear light Jirel saw a motion among the throng.
Jarisme had risen to her full height. She saw the sleek black
head go up in an odd, defiant, desperate poise, and above the
soul-shaking tumult she heard the sorceress' voice scream,

"Urda! Urda-sla!"

In the midst of the roar of the falling walls for the briefest
instant a deathly silence dropped. And out of that silence, like
an answer to the sorceress' cry, came a Noise, an indescribable,
intolerable loudness like the crack of cyclopean thunder. And
suddenly in the sky above them, visible through the crumbling
crystal walls, a long black wedge opened. It was like a strip of
darkest midnight splitting the violet day, a midnight through
which stars shone unbearably near, unbearably bright.

Jirel stared up in dumb surprise at that streak of starry night
cleaving the daylit sky. Jarisme stood rigid, arms outstretched,
defiantly fronting the thunderous dark whose apex was drawing nearer and nearer, driving downward like a vast celestial
spear. She did not flinch as it reached toward the tower. Jirel
saw the darkness sweep forward like a racing shadow. Then it

was upon them, and the earth shuddered under her feet, and from very far away she heard Jarisme scream.

When consciousness returned to her, she sat up painfully and stared around. She lay upon green grass, bruised and aching, but unharmed. The violet day was serene and unbroken once more. The purple peaks had vanished. No longer was she high among mountains. Instead, the green meadow where she had first seen Jarisme's tower stretched about her. In its dissolution it must have returned to its original site, flashing back along the magical ways it had traveled as the sorceress' magic was broken. For the tower too was gone. A little distance away she saw a heap of marble blocks outlining a rough circle, where that white shaft had risen. But the stones were weathered and cracked like the old, old stones of an ancient ruin.

She had been staring at this for many minutes, trying to focus her bewildered mind upon its significance, before the sound of groaning which had been going on for some time impressed itself on her brain. She turned. A little way off, Giraud lay in a tangle of torn black robes. Of Jarisme and the rest she saw no sign. Painfully she got to her feet and staggered to the wizard, turning him over with a disdainful toe. He opened his eyes and stared at her with a cloudy gaze into which recognition and realization slowly crept.

"Are you hurt?" she demanded.

He pulled himself to a sitting position and flexed his limbs experimentally. Finally he shook his head, more in answer to his own investigation than to her query, and got slowly to his feet. Jirel's eyes sought the weapon at his hip.

"I am going to kill you now," she said calmly. "Draw your sword, wizard."

The little dull eyes flashed up to her face. He stared. Whatever he saw in the yellow gaze must have satisfied him that she meant what she said, but he did not draw, nor did he fall back. A tight little smile drew his mouth askew, and he lifted his black-robed arms. Jirel saw them rise, and her gaze followed the gesture automatically. Up they went, up. And then in the queerest fashion she lost all control of her own eyes, so that they followed some invisible upward line which drew her on

and on skyward until she was rigidly staring at a fixed point of
invisibility at the spot where the lines of Giraud's arms would
have crossed, were they extended to a measureless distance.
Somehow she actually saw that point, and could not look away.
Gripped in the magic of those lifted arms, she stood rigid, not
even realizing what had happened, unable even to think in the
moveless magic of Giraud.

His little mocking chuckle reached her from immeasurably
far away.

"Kill me?" he was laughing thickly. "Kill me, Giraud? Why,
it was you who saved me, Joiry! Why else should I have clung
to your ankles so tightly? For I knew that when the Light died,
the only one who could hope to live would be the one who
slew it—nor was that a certainty, either. But I took the risk,
and well I did, or I would be with Jarisme now in the outer
dark whence she called up her no-god of the void to save her
from oblivion. I warned her what would happen if she tam-
pered with Fate. And I would rather—yes, much rather—be
here, in this pleasant violet land which I shall rule alone now.
Thanks to you, Joiry! Kill me, eh? I think not!"

That thick, mocking chuckle reached her remotely, penetrated her magic-stilled mind. It echoed round and round
there, for a long while, before she realized what it meant. But
at last she remembered, and her mind woke a little from its
inertia, and such anger swept over her that its heat was an
actual pain. Giraud, the runaway sorcerer, laughing at Joiry!
Holding Jirel of Joiry in his spell! Mocking her! Blindly she
wrenched at the bonds of magic, blindly urged her body forward. She could see nothing but that non-existent point where
the lifted arms would have crossed, in measureless distances,
but she felt the dagger-hilt in her hand, and she lunged forward through invisibility, and did not even know when the
blade sank home.

Sight returned to her then in a stunning flood. She rubbed
dazed eyes and shook herself and stared round the green
meadow in the violet day uncomprehendingly, for her mind
was not yet fully awake. Not until she looked down did she
remember.

Giraud lay there. The black robes were furled like wings

over his quiet body, but red in a thick flood was spreading on the grass, and from the tangled garments her dagger-hilt stood up. Jirel stared down at him, emotionless, her whole body still almost asleep from the power of the dead man's magic. She could not even feel triumph. She pulled the blade free automatically and wiped it on his robes. Then she sat down beside the body and rested her head in her hands, forcing herself to awaken.

After a long while she looked up again, the old hot light rising in her eyes, life flushing back into her face once more. Shaking off the last shreds of the spell, she got to her feet, sheathing the dagger. About her the violet-misted meadows were very still. No living creature moved anywhere in sight. The trees were motionless in the unstirring air. And beyond the ruins of the marble tower she saw the opening in the woods out of which her path had come, very long ago.

Jirel squared her shoulders and turned her back upon her vow fulfilled, and without a backward glance set off across the grass toward the tree-hid ruins which held the gate to home.

Scarlet Dream

NORTHWEST SMITH bought the shawl in the Lakkmanda
Markets of Mars. It was one of his chiefest joys to wander
through the stalls and stands of that greatest of market-places
whose wares are drawn from all the planets of the solar system,
and beyond. So many songs have been sung and so many tales
written of that fascinating chaos called the Lakkmanda Markets that there is little need to detail it here.

He shouldered his way through the colorful cosmopolitan
throng, the speech of a thousand races beating in his ears, the
mingled odors of perfume and sweat and spice and food and
the thousand nameless smells of the place assailing his nostrils.
Venders cried their wares in the tongues of a score of worlds.

As he strolled through the thick of the crowd, savoring the
confusion and the odors and the sights from lands beyond
counting, his eye was caught by a flash of that peculiar gera-
nium scarlet that seems to lift itself bodily from its background
and smite the eye with all but physical violence. It came from
a shawl thrown carelessly across a carved chest, typically Martian drylander work by the exquisite detail of that carving, so
oddly at variance with the characteristics of the harsh dryland
race. He recognized the Venusian origin of the brass tray on
the shawl, and knew the heap of carved ivory beasts that the
tray held as the work of one of the least-known races on Jupiter's largest moon, but from all his wide experience he could
draw no remembrance of any such woven work as that of the
shawl. Idly curious, he paused at the booth and asked of its
attendant,

"How much for the scarf?"

The man—he was a canal Martian—glanced over his shoulder and said carelessly, "Oh, that. You can have it for half a *cris*—gives me a headache to look at the thing."

Smith grinned and said, "I'll give you five dollars."

"Ten."

"Six and a half, and that's my last offer."

"Oh, take the thing." The Martian smiled and lifted the tray of ivory beasts from the chest.

Smith drew out the shawl. It clung to his hands like a live thing, softer and lighter than Martian "lamb's-wool." He felt sure it was woven from the hair of some beast rather than from vegetable fiber, for the electric clinging of it sparkled with life. And the crazy pattern dazzled him with its utter strangeness. Unlike any pattern he had seen in all the years of his far wanderings, the wild, leaping scarlet threaded its nameless design in one continuous, tangled line through the twilight blue of the background. That dim blue was clouded exquisitely with violet and green—sleepy evening colors against which the staring scarlet flamed like something more sinister and alive than color. He felt that he could almost put his hand between the color and the cloth, so vividly did it start up from its background.

"Where in the universe did this come from?" he demanded of the attendant.

The man shrugged.

"Who knows? It came in with a bale of scrap cloth from New York. I was a little curious about it myself, and called the market-master there to trace it. He says it was sold for scrap by a down-and-out Venusian who claimed he'd found it in a derelict ship floating around one of the asteroids. He didn't know what nationality the ship had been—a very early model, he said, probably one of the first space-ships, made before the identification symbols were adopted. I've wondered why he sold the thing for scrap. He could have got double the price, anyhow, if he'd made any effort."

"Funny." Smith stared down at the dizzy pattern writhing through the cloth in his hands. "Well, it's warm and light enough. If it doesn't drive me crazy trying to follow the pattern, I'll sleep warm at night."

He crumpled it in one hand, the whole six-foot square of it folding easily into his palm, and stuffed the silky bundle into his pocket—and thereupon forgot it until after his return to his quarters that evening.

He had taken one of the cubicle steel rooms in the great steel lodging-houses the Martian government offers for a very nominal rent to transients. The original purpose was to house those motley hordes of spacemen that swarm every port city of the civilized planets, offering them accommodations cheap and satisfactory enough so that they will not seek the black byways of the town and there fall in with the denizens of the Martian underworld whose lawlessness is a byword among space sailors.

The great steel building that housed Smith and countless others was not entirely free from the influences of Martian by-ways, and if the police had actually searched the place with any degree of thoroughness a large percentage of its dwellers might have been transferred to the Emperor's prisons—Smith almost certainly among them, for his activities were rarely within the law and though he could not recall at the moment any particularly flagrant sins committed in Lakkdarol, a charge could certainly have been found against him by the most half-hearted searcher. However, the likelihood of a police raid was very remote, and Smith, as he went in under the steel portals of the great door, rubbed shoulders with smugglers and pirates and fugitives and sinners of all the sins that keep the spaceways thronged.

In his little cubicle he switched on the light and saw a dozen blurred replicas of himself, reflected dimly in the steel walls, spring into being with the sudden glow. In that curious company he moved forward to a chair and pulled out the crumpled shawl. Shaking it in the mirror-walled room produced a sudden wild writhing of scarlet patterns over walls and floor and ceiling, and for an instant the room whirled in an inexplicable kaleidoscope and he had the impression that the four-dimensional walls had opened suddenly to undreamed-of vastnesses where living scarlet in wild, unruly patterns shivered through the void.

Then in a moment the walls closed in again and the dim reflections quieted and became only the images of a tall, brown man with pale eyes, holding a curious shawl in his hands. There was a strange, sensuous pleasure in the clinging of the silky wool to his fingers, the lightness of it, the warmth. He spread it out on the table and traced the screaming scarlet pattern with his finger, trying to follow that one writhing line through the intricacies of its path, and the more he stared the more irritatingly clear it became to him that there must be a purpose in that whirl of color, that if he stared long enough, surely he must trace it out. . . .

When he slept that night he spread the bright shawl across his bed, and the brilliance of it colored his dreams fantastically. . . .

That threading scarlet was a labyrinthine path down which he stumbled blindly, and at every turn he looked back and saw himself in myriad replicas, always wandering lost and alone through the pattern of the path. Sometimes it shook itself under his feet, and whenever he thought he saw the end it would writhe into fresh intricacies. . . .

The sky was a great shawl threaded with scarlet lightning that shivered and squirmed as he watched, then wound itself into the familiar, dizzy pattern that became one mighty Word in a nameless writing, whose meaning he shuddered on the verge of understanding, and woke in icy terror just before the significance of it broke upon his brain. . . .

He slept again, and saw the shawl hanging in a blue dusk the color of its background, stared and stared until the square of it melted imperceptibly into the dimness and the scarlet was a pattern incised lividly upon a gate . . . a gate of strange outline in a high wall, half seen through that curious, cloudy twilight blurred with exquisite patches of green and violet, so that it seemed no mortal twilight, but some strange and lovely evening in a land where the air was suffused with colored mists, and no winds blew. He felt himself moving forward, without effort, and the gate opened before him. . . .

He was mounting a long flight of steps. In one of the metamorphoses of dreams it did not surprise him that the gate had vanished, or that he had no remembrance of having climbed the long flight stretching away behind him. The lovely colored twilight still veiled the air, so that he could see but dimly the steps rising before him and melting into the mist.

And now, suddenly, he was aware of a stirring in the dimness, and a girl came flying down the stairs in headlong, stumbling terror. He could see the shadow of it on her face, and her long, bright-colored hair streamed out behind her, and from head to foot she was dabbled with blood. In her blind flight she must not have seen him, for she came plunging downward three steps at a time and blundered full into him as he stood undecided, watching. The impact all but unbalanced him, but his arms closed instinctively about her and for a moment she hung in his embrace, utterly spent, gasping against his broad leather breast and too breathless even to wonder who had stopped her. The smell of fresh blood rose to his nostrils from her dreadfully spattered garments.

Finally she lifted her head and raised a flushed, creamy-brown face to him, gulping in air through lips the color of holly berries. Her dabbled hair, so fantastically golden that it might have been almost orange, shivered about her as she clung to him with lifted, lovely face. In that dizzy moment he saw that her eyes were sherry-brown with tints of red, and the fantastic, colored beauty of her face had a wild tinge of something utterly at odds with anything he had ever known before. It might have been the look in her eyes. . . .

"Oh!" she gasped. "It—it has her! Let me go! . . . Let me—"

Smith shook her gently.

"What has her?" he demanded. "Who? Listen to me! You're covered with blood, do you know it? Are you hurt?"

She shook her head wildly.

"No—no—let me go! I must—not my blood—hers. . . ."

She sobbed on the last word, and suddenly collapsed in his arms, weeping with a violent intensity that shook her from head to foot. Smith gazed helplessly about over the orange head, then gathered the shaking girl in his arms and went on up the steps through the violet gloaming.

He must have climbed for all of five minutes before the twilight thinned a little and he saw that the stairs ended at the head of a long hallway, high-arched like a cathedral aisle. A

row of low doors ran down one side of the hall, and he turned
aside at random into the nearest. It gave upon a gallery whose
arches opened into blue space. A low bench ran along the wall
under the gallery windows, and he crossed toward it, gently
setting down the sobbing girl and supporting her against his
shoulder.

"My sister," she wept. "It has her—oh, my sister!"

"Don't cry, don't cry," Smith heard his own voice saying,
surprisingly. "It's all a dream, you know. Don't cry—there
never was any sister—you don't exist at all—don't cry so."

She jerked her head up at that, startled out of her sobs for
a moment, and stared at him with sherry-brown eyes drowned
in tears. Her lashes clung together in wet, starry points. She
stared with searching eyes, taking in the leather-brownness of
him, his spaceman's suit, his scarred dark face and eyes paler
than steel. And then a look of infinite pity softened the strangeness of her face, and she said gently,

"Oh . . . you come from—from—you still believe that you
dream!"

"I _know_ I'm dreaming," persisted Smith childishly. "I'm lying asleep in Lakkdarol and dreaming of you, and all this, and
when I wake—"

She shook her head sadly.

"You will never wake. You have come into a more deadly
dream than you could ever guess. There is no waking from this
land."

"What do you mean? Why not?" A little absurd panic was
starting up in his mind at the sorrow and the pity in her voice,
the sureness of her words. Yet this was one of those rare dreams
wherein he knew quite definitely that he dreamed. He could
not be mistaken. . . .

"There are many dream countries," she said, "many nebulous, unreal half-lands where the souls of sleepers wander,
places that have an actual, tenuous existence, if one knows the
way. . . . But here—it has happened before, you see—one may
not blunder without passing a door that opens one way only.
And he who has the key to open it may come through, but he
can never find the way into his own waking land again. Tell
me—what key opened the door to you?"

"The shawl," Smith murmured. "The shawl . . . of course. That damnable red pattern, dizzy—"

He passed a hand across his eyes, for the memory of it, writhing, alive, searingly scarlet, burned behind his eyelids.

"What was it?" she demanded, breathlessly, he thought, as if a half-hopeless eagerness forced the question from her lips. "Can you remember?"

"A red pattern," he said slowly, "a thread of bright scarlet woven into a blue shawl—nightmare pattern—painted on the gate I came by . . . but it's only a dream, of course. In a few minutes I'll wake. . . ."

She clutched his knee excitedly.

"Can you remember?" she demanded. "The pattern—the red pattern? The Word?"

"Word?" he wondered stupidly. "Word—in the sky? No—no, I don't want to remember—crazy pattern, you know. Can't forget it—but no, I couldn't tell you what it was, or trace it for you. Never was anything like it—thank God. It was on that shawl. . . ."

"Woven on a shawl," she murmured to herself. "Yes, of course. But how you ever came by it, in your world—when it— when *it*—oh!"

Memory of whatever tragedy had sent her flying down the stairs swept back in a flood, and her face crumpled into tears again. "My sister!"

"Tell me what happened." Smith woke from his daze at the sound of her sob. "Can't I help? Please let me try—tell me about it."

"My sister," she said faintly. "It caught her in the hall— caught her before my eyes—spattered me with her blood. Oh! . . ."

"It?" puzzled Smith. "What? Is there danger?" and his hand moved instinctively toward his gun.

She caught the gesture and smiled a little scornfully through her tears.

"It," she said. "The—the Thing. No gun can harm it, no man can fight it— It came, and that was all."

"But what is it? What does it look like? Is it near?"

"It's everywhere. One never knows—until the mist begins to

thicken and the pulse of red shows through—and then it's too late. We do not fight it, or think of it overmuch—life would be unbearable. For it hungers and must be fed, and we who feed it strive to live as happily as we may before the Thing comes for us. But one can never know."

"Where did it come from? What is it?"

"No one knows—it has always been here—always will be . . . too nebulous to die or be killed—a Thing out of some alien place we couldn't understand, I suppose—somewhere so long ago, or in some such unthinkable dimension that we will never have any knowledge of its origin. But as I say, we try not to think."

"If it eats flesh," said Smith stubbornly, "it must be vulnerable—and I have my gun."

"Try if you like," she shrugged. "Others have tried—and it still comes. It dwells here, we believe, if it dwells anywhere. We are—taken—more often in these halls than elsewhere. When you are weary of life you might bring your gun and wait under this roof. You may not have long to wait."

"I'm not ready to try the experiment just yet," Smith grinned. "If the Thing lives here, why do you come?"

She shrugged again, apathetically. "If we do not, it will come after us when it hungers. And we come here for—for our food." She shot him a curious glance from under lowered lids. "You wouldn't understand. But as you say, it's a dangerous place. We'd best go now—you will come with me, won't you? I shall be lonely, now." And her eyes brimmed again.

"Of course. I'm sorry, my dear. I'll do what I can for you—until I wake." He grinned at the fantastic sound of this.

"You will not wake," she said quietly. "Better not to hope, I think. You are trapped here with the rest of us and here you must stay until you die."

He rose and held out his hand.

"Let's go, then," he said. "Maybe you're right, but—well, come on."

She took his hand and jumped up. The orange hair, too fantastically colored for anything outside a dream, swung about her brilliantly. He saw now that she wore a single white garment, brief and belted, over the creamy brownness of her body. It was torn now, and hideously stained. She made a picture of strange and vivid loveliness, all white and gold and bloody, in the misted twilight of the gallery.

"Where are we going?" she asked Smith. "Out there?" And he nodded toward the blueness beyond the windows.

She drew her shoulders together in a little shudder of distaste.

"Oh, no," she said.

"What is it?"

"Listen." She took him by the arms and lifted a serious face to his. "If you must stay here—and you must, for there is only one way out save death, and that is a worse way even than dying—you must learn to ask no questions about the—the Temple. This is the Temple. Here it dwells. Here we—feed.

"There are halls we know, and we keep to them. It is wiser. You saved my life when you stopped me on those stairs—no one has ever gone down into that mist and darkness, and returned. I should have known, seeing you climb them, that you were not of us . . . for whatever lies beyond, wherever that stairway leads—it is better not to know. It is better not to look out the windows of this place. We have learned that, too. For from the outside the Temple looks strange enough, but from the inside, looking out, one is liable to see things it is better not to see. . . . What that blue space is, on which this gallery opens, I do not know—I have no wish to know. There are windows here opening on stranger things than this—but we turn our eyes away when we pass them. You will learn. . . ."

She took his hand, smiling a little.

"Come with me, now."

And in silence they left the gallery opening on space and went down the hall where the blue mist floated so beautifully with its clouds of violet and green confusing the eye, and a great stillness all about.

The hallway led straight, as nearly as he could see, for the floating clouds veiled it, toward the great portals of the Temple. In the form of a mighty triple arch it opened out of the clouded twilight upon a shining day like no day he had ever seen on any planet. The light came from no visible source, and there was a lucid quality about it, nebulous but unmistakable, as if one were looking through the depths of a crystal, or through clear water that trembled a little now and then. It was diffused through the translucent day from a sky as shining and unfamiliar as everything else in this amazing dreamland.

They stood under the great arch of the Temple, looking out over the shining land beyond. Afterward he could never quite remember what had made it so unutterably strange, so indefinably dreadful. There were trees, feathery masses of green and bronze above the bronze-green grass; the bright air shimmered, and through the leaves he caught the glimmer of water not far away. At first glance it seemed a perfectly normal scene—yet tiny details caught his eye that sent ripples of coldness down his back. The grass, for instance. . . .

When they stepped down upon it and began to cross the meadow toward the trees beyond which water gleamed, he saw that the blades were short and soft as fur, and they seemed to cling to his companion's bare feet as she walked. As he looked out over the meadow he saw that long waves of it, from every direction, were rippling toward them as if the wind blew from all sides at once toward the common center that was themselves. Yet no wind blew.

"It—it's alive," he stammered, startled. "The grass!"

"Yes, of course," she said indifferently.

And then he realized that though the feathery fronds of the trees waved now and then, gracefully together, there was no wind. And they did not sway in one direction only, but by twos and threes in many ways, dipping and rising with a secret, contained life of their own.

When they reached the belt of woodland he looked up curiously and heard the whisper and rustle of leaves above him, bending down as if in curiosity as the two passed beneath. They never bent far enough to touch them, but a sinister air of watchfulness, of aliveness, brooded over the whole uncannily alive landscape, and the ripples of the grass followed them wherever they went.

The lake, like that twilight in the Temple, was a sleepy blue clouded with violet and green, not like real water, for the colored blurs did not diffuse or change as it rippled.

On the shore, a little above the water line, stood a tiny, shrine-like building of some creamy stone, its walls no more than a series of arches open to the blue, translucent day. The girl led him to the doorway and gestured within negligently.

"I live here," she said.

Smith stared. It was quite empty save for two low couches with a blue coverlet thrown across each. Very classic it looked, with its whiteness and austerity, the arches opening on a vista of woodland and grass beyond.

"Doesn't it ever get cold?" he asked. "Where do you eat? Where are your books and food and clothes?"

"I have some spare tunics under my couch," she said. "That's all. No books, no other clothing, no food. We feed at the Temple. And it is never any colder or warmer than this."

"But what do you do?"

"Do? Oh, swim in the lake, sleep and rest and wander through the woods. Time passes very quickly."

"Idyllic," murmured Smith, "but rather tiresome, I should think."

"When one knows," she said, "that the next moment may be one's last, life is savored to the full. One stretches the hours out as long as possible. No, for us it is not tiresome."

"But have you no cities? Where are the other people?"

"It is best not to collect in crowds. Somehow they seem to draw—it. We live in twos and threes—sometimes alone. We have no cities. We do nothing—what purpose in beginning anything when we know we shall not live to end it? Why even think too long of one thing? Come down to the lake."

She took his hand and led him across the clinging grass to the sandy brink of the water, and they sank in silence on the narrow beach. Smith looked out over the lake where vague colors misted the blue, trying not to think of the fantastic things that were happening to him. Indeed, it was hard to do much thinking, here, in the midst of the blueness and the silence, the very air dreamy about them . . . the cloudy water lapping the shore with tiny, soft sounds like the breathing of a sleeper. The place was heavy with the stillness and the

dreamy colors, and Smith was never sure, afterward, whether
in his dream he did not sleep for a while; for presently he
heard a stir at his side and the girl reseated herself, clad in a
fresh tunic, all the blood washed away. He could not remember her having left, but it did not trouble him.

The light had for some time been sinking and blurring, and
imperceptibly a cloudy blue twilight closed about them, seeming somehow to rise from the blurring lake, for it partook of
that same dreamy blueness clouded with vague colors. Smith
thought that he would be content never to rise again from that
cool sand, to sit here for ever in the blurring twilight and the
silence of his dream. How long he did sit there he never knew.
The blue peace enfolded him utterly, until he was steeped in
its misty evening colors and permeated through and through
with the tranced quiet.

The darkness had deepened until he could no longer see any
more than the nearest wavelets lapping the sand. Beyond, and
all about, the dream-world melted into the violet-misted blueness of the twilight. He was not aware that he had turned his
head, but presently he found himself looking down on the girl
beside him. She was lying on the pale sand, her hair a fan of
darkness to frame the pallor of her face. In the twilight her
mouth was dark too, and from the darkness under her lashes
he slowly became aware that she was watching him unwinkingly.

For a long while he sat there, gazing down, meeting the half-
hooded eyes in silence. And presently, with the effortless de-
tachment of one who moves in a dream, he bent down to meet
her lifting arms. The sand was cool and sweet, and her mouth
tasted faintly of blood.

2

There was no sunrise in that land. Lucid day brightened
slowly over the breathing landscape, and grass and trees stirred
with wakening awareness, rather horribly in the beauty of the
morning. When Smith woke, he saw the girl coming up from
the lake, shaking blue water from her orange hair. Blue drop-
lets clung to the creaminess of her skin, and she was laughing
and flushed from head to foot in the glowing dawn.

Smith sat up on his couch and pushed back the blue coverlet.

"I'm hungry," he said. "When and what do we eat?"

The laughter vanished from her face in a breath. She gave
her hair a troubled shake and said doubtfully,

"Hungry?"

"Yes, starved! Didn't you say you get your food at the Temple? Let's go up there."

She sent him a sidelong, enigmatic glance from under her
lashes as she turned aside.

"Very well," she said.

"Anything wrong?" He reached out as she passed and pulled
her to his knee, kissing the troubled mouth lightly. And again
he tasted blood.

"Oh, no." She ruffled his hair and rose. "I'll be ready in a
moment, and then we'll go."

And so again they passed the belt of woods where the trees
bent down to watch, and crossed the rippling grassland. From
all directions long waves of it came blowing toward them as
before, and the fur-like blades clung to their feet. Smith tried
not to notice. Everywhere, he was seeing this morning, an
undercurrent of nameless unpleasantness ran beneath the surface of this lovely land.

As they crosed the live grass a memory suddenly returned
to him, and he said, "What did you mean, yesterday, when you
said that there was a way—out—other than death?"

She did not meet his eyes as she answered, in that troubled
voice, "Worse than dying, I said. A way out we do not speak
of here."

"But if there's any way at all, I must know of it," he persisted. "Tell me."

She swept the orange hair like a veil between them, bending
her head and saying indistinctly, "A way out you could not
take. A way too costly. And—and I do not wish you to go,
now. . . ."

"I must know," said Smith relentlessly.

She paused then, and stood looking up at him, her sherry-
colored eyes disturbed.

"By the way you came," she said at last. "By virtue of the Word. But that gate is impassable."

"Why?"

"It is death to pronounce the Word. Literally. I do not know it now, could not speak it if I would. But in the Temple there is one room where the Word is graven in scarlet on the wall, and its power is so great that the echoes of it ring for ever round and round that room. If one stands before the graven symbol and lets the force of it beat upon his brain he will hear, and know—and shriek the awful syllables aloud—and so die. It is a word from some tongue so alien to all our being that the spoken sound of it, echoing in the throat of a living man, is disrupting enough to rip the very fibers of the human body apart—to blast its atoms asunder, to destroy body and mind as utterly as if they had never been. And because the sound is so disruptive it somehow blasts open for an instant the door between your world and mine. But the danger is dreadful, for it may open the door to other worlds too, and let things through more terrible than we can dream of. Some say it was thus that the Thing gained access to our land eons ago. And if you are not standing exactly where the door opens, on the one spot in the room that is protected, as the center of a whirlwind is quiet, and if you do not pass instantly out of the sound of the Word, it will blast you asunder as it does the one who has pronounced it for you. So you see how impos—" Here she broke off with a little scream and glanced down in half-laughing annoyance, then took two or three little running steps and turned.

"The grass," she explained ruefully, pointing to her feet. The brown bareness of them was dotted with scores of tiny blood-spots. "If one stands too long in one place, barefoot, it will pierce the skin and drink—stupid of me to forget. But come."

Smith went on at her side, looking round with new eyes upon the lovely, pellucid land, too beautiful and frightening for anything outside a dream. All about them the hungry grass came hurrying in long, converging waves as they advanced.

Were the trees, then, flesh-eating too? Cannibal trees and vampire grass—he shuddered a little and looked ahead.

The Temple stood tall before them, a building of some
nameless material as mistily blue as far-off mountains on the
Earth. The mistiness did not condense or clarify as they approached, and the outlines of the place were mysteriously hard
to fix in mind—he could never understand, afterward, just
why. When he tried too hard to concentrate on one particular
corner or tower or window it blurred before his eyes as if the
focus were at fault—as if the whole strange, veiled building
stood just on the borderland of another dimension.

From the immense triple arch of the doorway, as they approached—a triple arch like nothing he had ever seen before,
so irritatingly hard to focus upon that he could not be sure
just wherein its difference lay—a pale blue mist issued smokily.
And when they stepped within they walked into that twilight
dimness he was coming to know so well.

The great hall lay straight and veiled before them, but after
a few steps the girl drew him aside and under another archway, into a long gallery through whose drifting haze he could
see rows of men and women kneeling against the wall with
bowed heads, as if in prayer. She led him down the line to the
end, and he saw then that they knelt before small spigots
curving up from the wall at regular intervals. She dropped to
her knees before one and, motioning him to follow, bent her
head and laid her lips to the up-curved spout. Dubiously he
followed her example.

Instantly with the touch of his mouth on the nameless substance of the spigot something hot and, strangely, at once salty
and sweet flowed into his mouth. There was an acridity about
it that gave a curious tang, and the more he drank the more
avid he became. Hauntingly delicious it was, and warmth
flowed through him more strongly with every draft. Yet somewhere deep within him memory stirred unpleasantly . . .
somewhere, somehow, he had known this hot, acrid, salty taste
before, and—suddenly suspicions struck him like a bludgeon,
and he jerked his lips from the spout as if it burnt. A tiny
thread of scarlet trickled from the wall. He passed the back of

one hand across his lips and brought it away red. He knew that odor, then.

The girl knelt beside him with closed eyes, rapt avidity in every line of her. When he seized her shoulder she twitched away and opened protesting eyes, but did not lift her lips from the spigot. Smith gestured violently, and with one last long draft she rose and turned a half-angry face to his, but laid a finger on her reddened lips.

He followed her in silence past the kneeling lines again. When they reached the hall outside he swung upon her and gripped her shoulders angrily.

"What was that?" he demanded.

Her eyes slid away. She shrugged.

"What were you expecting? We feed as we must, here. You'll learn to drink without a qualm—if it does not come for you too soon."

A moment longer he stared angrily down into her evasive, strangely lovely face. Then he turned without a word and strode down the hallway through the drifting mists toward the door. He heard her bare feet pattering along behind hurriedly, but he did not look back. Not until he had come out into the glowing day and half crossed the grasslands did he relent enough to glance around. She paced at his heels with bowed head, the orange hair swinging about her face and unhappiness eloquent in every motion. The submission of her touched him suddenly, and he paused for her to catch up, smiling down half reluctantly on the bent orange head.

She lifted a tragic face to his, and there were tears in the sherry eyes. So he had no choice but to laugh and lift her up against his leather-clad breast and kiss the drooping mouth into smiles again. But he understood, now, the faintly acrid bitterness of her kisses.

"Still," he said, when they had reached the little white shrine among the trees, "there must be some other food than— that. Does no grain grow? Isn't there any wild life in the woods? Haven't the trees fruit?"

She gave him another sidelong look from under dropped lashes, warily.

"No," she said. "Nothing but the grass grows here. No living thing dwells in this land but man—and it. And as for the fruit of the trees—give thanks that they bloom but once in a lifetime."

"Why?"

"Better not to—speak of it," she said.

The phrase, the constant evasion, was beginning to wear on Smith's nerves. He said nothing of it then, but he turned from her and went down to the beach, dropping to the sand and striving to recapture last night's languor and peace. His hunger was curiously satisfied, even from the few swallows he had taken, and gradually the drowsy content of the day before began to flow over him in deepening waves. After all, it was a lovely land. . . .

That day drew dreamily to a close, and darkness rose in a mist from the misty lake, and he came to find in kisses that tasted of blood a certain tang that but pointed their sweetness. And in the morning he woke to the slowly brightening day, swam with the girl in the blue, tingling waters of the lake—and reluctantly went up through the woods and across the ravenous grass to the Temple, driven by a hunger greater than his repugnance. He went up with a slight nausea rising within him, and yet strangely eager. . . .

Once more the Temple rose veiled and indefinite under the glowing sky, and once more he plunged into the eternal twilight of its corridors, turned aside as one who knows the way, knelt of his own accord in the line of drinkers along the wall. . . .

With the first draft that nausea rose within him almost overwhelmingly, but when the warmth of the drink had spread through him the nausea died and nothing was left but hunger and eagerness, and he drank blindly until the girl's hand on his shoulder roused him.

A sort of intoxication had wakened within him with the burning of that hot, salt drink in his veins, and he went back across the hurrying grass in a half-daze. Through most of the pellucid day it lasted, and the slow dark was rising from the lake before clearness returned to him.

3

And so life resolved itself into a very simple thing. The days glowed by and the blurred darknesses came and went. Life held little any more but the bright clarity of the day and the dimness of the dark, morning journeys to drink at the Temple fountain and the bitter kisses of the girl with the orange hair. Time had ceased for him. Slow day followed slow day, and the same round of living circled over and over, and the only change—perhaps he did not see it then—was the deepening look in the girl's eyes when they rested upon him, her growing silences.

One evening just as the first faint dimness was clouding the air, and the lake smoked hazily, he happened to glance off across its surface and thought he saw through the rising mists the outline of very far mountains, and he asked curiously.

"What lies beyond the lake? Aren't those mountains over there?"

The girl turned her head quickly and her sherry-brown eyes darkened with something like dread.

"I don't know," she said. "We believe it best not to wonder what lies—beyond."

And suddenly Smith's irritation with the old evasions woke and he said violently,

"Damn your beliefs! I'm sick of that answer to every question I ask! Don't you ever wonder about anything? Are you all so thoroughly cowed by this dread of something unseen that every spark of your spirit is dead?"

She turned the sorrowful, sherry gaze upon him.

"We learn by experience," she said. "Those who wonder—those who investigate—die. We live in a land alive with danger, incomprehensible, intangible, terrible. Life is bearable only if we do not look too closely—only if we accept conditions and make the most of them. You must not ask questions if you would live.

"As for the mountains beyond, and all the unknown country that lies over the horizons—they are as unreachable as a mirage. For in a land where no food grows, where we must visit the Temple daily or strave, how could an explorer provision himself for a journey? No, we are bound here by unbreakable bonds, and we must live here until we die."

Smith shrugged. The languor of the evening was coming upon him, and the brief flare of irritation had died as swiftly as it rose.

Yet from that outburst dated the beginning of his discontent. Somehow, despite the lovely languor of the place, despite the sweet bitterness of the Temple fountains and the sweeter bitterness of the kisses that were his for the asking, he could not drive from his mind the vision of those far mountains veiled in rising haze. Unrest had wakened within him, and like some sleeper arising from a lotus-dream his mind turned more and more frequently to the desire for action, adventure, some other use for his danger-hardened body than the exigencies of sleep and food and love.

On all sides stretched the moving, restless woods, farther than the eye could reach. The grasslands rippled, and over the dim horizon the far mountains beckoned him. Even the mystery of the Temple and its endless twilight began to torment his waking moments. He dallied with the idea of exploring those hallways which the dwellers in this lotus-land avoided, of gazing from the strange windows that opened upon inexplicable blue. Surely life, even here, must hold some more fervent meaning than that he followed now. What lay beyond the wood and grasslands? What mysterious country did those mountains wall?

He began to harry his companion with questions that woke more and more often the look of dread behind her eyes, but he gained little satisfaction. She belonged to a people without history, without ambition, their lives bent wholly toward wringing from each moment its full sweetness in anticipation of the terror to come. Evasion was the keynote of their existence, perhaps with reason. Perhaps all the adventurous spirits among them had followed their curiosity into danger and death, and the only ones left were the submissive souls who led their bucolically voluptuous lives in this Elysium so shadowed with horror.

In this colored lotus-land, memories of the world he had left grew upon him more and more vividly: he remembered the hurrying crowds of the planets' capitals, the lights, the noise, the laughter. He saw space-ships cleaving the night sky with flame, flashing from world to world through the star-flecked darkness. He remembered sudden brawls in saloons and space-sailor dives when the air was alive with shouts and tumult, and heat-guns slashed their blue-hot blades of flame and the smell of burnt flesh hung heavy. Life marched in pageant past his remembering eyes, violent, vivid, shoulder to shoulder with death. And nostalgia wrenched at him for the lovely, terrible, brawling worlds he had left behind.

Daily the unrest grew upon him. The girl made pathetic little attempts to find some sort of entertainment that would occupy his ranging mind. She led him on timid excursions into the living woods, even conquered her horror of the Temple enough to follow him on timorous tiptoe as he explored a little way down the corridors which did not arouse in her too anguished a terror. But she must have known from the first that it was hopeless.

One day as they lay on the sand watching the lake ripple bluely under a crystal sky, Smith's eyes, dwelling on the faint shadow of the mountains, half unseeingly, suddenly narrowed into a hardness as bright and pale as steel. Muscle ridged his abruptly set jaw and he sat upright with a jerk, pushing away the girl who had been leaning on his shoulder.

"I'm through," he said harshly, and rose.

"What—what is it?" The girl stumbled to her feet.

"I'm going away—anywhere. To those mountains, I think. I'm leaving now!"

"But—you wish to die, then?"

"Better the real thing than a living death like this," he said. "At least I'll have a little more excitement first."

"But, what of your food? There's nothing to keep you alive, even if you escape the greater dangers. Why, you'll dare not even lie down on the grass at night—it would eat you alive! You have no chance at all to live if you leave this grove—and me."

"If I must die, I shall," he said. "I've been thinking it over, and I've made up my mind. I could explore the Temple and

so come on *it* and die. But do *something* I must, and it seems
to me my best chance is in trying to reach some country where
food grows before I starve. It's worth trying. I can't go on
like this."

She looked at him miserably, tears brimming her sherry eyes.
He opened his mouth to speak, but before he could say a
word her eyes strayed beyond his shoulder and suddenly she
smiled, a dreadful, frozen little smile.

"You will not go," she said. "Death has come for us now."

She said it so calmly, so unafraid that he did not understand
until she pointed beyond him. He turned.

The air between them and the shrine was curiously agitated.
As he watched, it began to resolve itself into a nebulous blue
mist that thickened and darkened . . . blurry tinges of violet
and green began to blow through it vaguely, and then by imperceptible degrees a flush of rose appeared in the mist—
deepened, thickened, contracted into burning scarlet that
seared his eyes, pulsed alively—and he knew that it had come.

An aura of menace seemed to radiate from it, strengthening
as the mist strengthened, reaching out in hunger toward his
mind. He felt it as tangibly as he saw it—cloudy danger reaching out avidly for them both.

The girl was not afraid. Somehow he knew this, though he
dared not turn, dared not wrench his eyes from that hynotically
pulsing scarlet. . . . She whispered very softly from behind
him,

"So I die with you, I am content." And the sound of her
voice freed him from the snare of the crimson pulse.

He barked a wolfish laugh, abruptly—welcoming even this
diversion from the eternal idyl he had been living—and the
gun leaping to his hand spurted a long blue flame so instantly
that the girl behind him caught her breath. The steel-blue
dazzle illumined the gathering mist lividly, passed through it
without obstruction and charred the ground beyond. Smith
set his teeth and swung a figure-eight pattern of flame through
and through the mist, lacing it with blue heat. And when that
finger of fire crossed the scarlet pulse the impact jarred the
whole nebulous cloud violently, so that its outlines wavered

and shrank, and the pulse of crimson sizzled under the heat—shriveled—began to fade in desperate haste.

Smith swept the ray back and forth along the redness, tracing its pattern with destruction, but it faded too swiftly for him. In little more than an instant it had paled and disembodied and vanished save for a fading flush of rose, and the blue-hot blade of his flame sizzled harmlessly through the disappearing mist to sear the ground beyond. He switched off the heat, then, and stood breathing a little unevenly as the death-cloud thinned and paled and vanished before his eyes, until no trace of it was left and the air glowed lucid and transparent once more.

The unmistakable odor of burning flesh caught at his nostrils, and he wondered for a moment if the Thing had indeed materialized a nucleus of matter, and then he saw that the smell came from the seared grass his flame had struck. The tiny, furry blades were all writhing away from the burnt spot, straining at their roots as if a wind blew them back, and from the blackened area a thick smoke rose, reeking with the odor of burnt meat. Smith, remembering their vampire habits, turned away, half nauseated.

The girl had sunk to the sand behind him, trembling violently now that the danger was gone.

"Is—it dead?" she breathed, when she could master her quivering mouth.

"I don't know. No way of telling. Probably not."

"What will—will you do now?"

He slid the heat-gun back into its holster and settled the belt purposefully.

"What I started out to do."

The girl scrambled up in desperate haste.

"Wait!" she gasped, "wait!" and clutched at his arm to steady herself. And he waited until the trembling had passed. Then she went on, "Come up to the Temple once more before you go."

"All right. Not a bad idea. It may be a long time before my next—meal."

And so again they crossed the fur-soft grass that bore down upon them in long ripples from every part of the meadow.

The Temple rose dim and unreal before them, and as they entered blue twilight folded them dreamily about. Smith turned by habit toward the gallery of the drinkers, but the girl laid upon his arm a hand that shook a little, and murmured,

"Come this way."

He followed in growing surprise down the hallway through the drifting mists and away from the gallery he knew so well. It seemed to him that the mist thickened as they advanced, and in the uncertain light he could never be sure that the walls did not waver as nebulously as the blurring air. He felt a curious impulse to step through their intangible barriers and out of the hall into—what?

Presently steps rose under his feet, almost imperceptibly, and after a while the pressure on his arm drew him aside. They went in under a low, heavy arch of stone and entered the strangest room he had ever seen. It appeared to be seven-sided, as nearly as he could judge through the drifting mist, and curious, converging lines were graven deep in the floor.

It seemed to him that forces outside his comprehension were beating violently against the seven walls, circling like hurricanes through the dimness until the whole room was a maelstrom of invisible tumult.

When he lifted his eyes to the wall, he knew where he was. Blazoned on the dim stone, burning through the twilight like some other-dimensional fire, the scarlet pattern writhed across the wall.

The sight of it, somehow, set up a commotion in his brain, and it was with whirling head and stumbling feet that he answered to the pressure on his arm. Dimly he realized that he stood at the very center of those strange, converging lines, feeling forces beyond reason coursing through him along paths outside any knowledge he possessed.

Then for one moment arms clasped his neck and a warm, fragrant body pressed against him, and a voice sobbed in his ear,

"If you must leave me, then go back through the Door, beloved—life without you—more dreadful even than a death like this. . . ." A kiss that stung of blood clung to his lips for an instant; then the clasp loosened and he stood alone.

Through the twilight he saw her dimly outlined against the Word. And he thought, as she stood there, that it was as if the invisible currents beat bodily against her, so that she swayed and wavered before him, her outlines blurring and forming again as the forces from which he was so mystically protected buffeted her mercilessly.

And he saw knowledge dawning terribly upon her face, as the meaning of the Word seeped slowly into her mind. The sweet brown face twisted hideously, the blood-red lips writhed apart to shriek a Word—in a moment of clarity he actually saw her tongue twisting incredibly to form the syllables of the unspeakable thing never meant for human lips to frame. Her mouth opened into an impossible shape . . . she gasped in the blurry mist and shrieked aloud. . . .

4

Smith was walking along a twisting path so scarlet that he could not bear to look down, a path that wound and unwound and shook itself under his feet so that he stumbled at every step. He was groping through a blinding mist clouded with violet and green, and in his ears a dreadful whisper rang—the first syllable of an unutterable Word. . . . Whenever he neared the end of the path it shook itself under him and doubled back, and weariness like a drug was sinking into his brain, and the sleepy twilight colors of the mist lulled him, and—

"He's waking up!" said an exultant voice in his ear.

Smith lifted heavy eyelids upon a room without walls—a room wherein multiple figures extending into infinity moved to and fro in countless hosts. . . .

"Smith! N. W.! Wake up!" urged that familiar voice from somewhere near.

He blinked. The myriad diminishing figures resolved themselves into the reflections of two men in a steel-walled room, bending over him. The friendly, anxious face of his partner, Yarol the Venusian, leaned above the bed.

"By Pharol, N. W.," said the well-remembered, ribald voice, "you've been asleep for a week! We thought you'd never come out of it—must have been an awful brand of whisky!"

Smith managed a feeble grin—amazing how weak he felt—
and turned an inquiring gaze upon the other figure.

"I'm a doctor," said that individual, meeting the questing
stare. "Your friend called me in three days ago and I've been
working on you ever since. It must have been all of five or
six days since you fell into this coma—have you any idea what
caused it?"

Smith's pale eyes roved the room. He did not find what he
sought, and though his weak murmur answered the doctor's
question, the man was never to know it.

"Shawl?"

"I threw the damned thing away," confessed Yarol. "Stood
it for three days and then gave up. That red pattern gave me
the worst headache I've had since we found that case of black
wine on the asteroid. Remember?"

"Where—?"

"Gave it to a space-rat checking out for Venus. Sorry. Did
you really want it? I'll buy you another."

Smith did not answer. The weakness was rushing up about
him in gray waves. He closed his eyes, hearing the echoes of
that first dreadful syllable whispering through his head . . .
whisper from a dream. . . . Yarol heard him murmur softly,

"And—I never even knew—her name. . . ."